Bonded Betrayal

A NOVEL BY

Nanette M. Buchanan

Type of Work: Fiction
First Edition: 2012
ISBN-978-0-9793883-5-4

I Pen Books

www.NanetteMBuchanan.com

Acknowledgements

This journey has been challenging yet rewarding. I can't begin to think of how the lessons I've learned has given me a clearer vision to continue on. Writing brings me peace. I hope that reading my work does the same for you.

To my family;

I write as you patiently wait. I read as you patiently listen. I complain, rewrite and read as you smile, sigh and comment. I thank you all. Katia, this is your baby......I hope I did you proud.

To my readers;

I share this work as I have others, for you to enjoy and share. Thank you for your well wishes, comments and support.

It is my pleasure to once again share what I Pen.

There's a cliché that states one should not date their best friend. Whatever the reasons, the fear of losing a friendship or not finding true love; most use this cliché as a golden rule.

Memories

Brianne reached into the mailbox and without fumbling the various sized envelopes she retrieved; she stuck her key in the front door lock. The task had become second nature, as routine as kicking off her shoes and pushing the button on the phone to hear the messages for the day. She smiled to herself as she read the envelopes addressed to her and her roommate Kalliah Carter.

Kalliah would be pleased to know that the McKinley High School's ten-year class reunion invitations had arrived. She sorted the mail leaving Kalliah's invitation on the top of junk mail with their expected phone bill. Brianne hesitated as she thought about opening the bill, but changed her mind. She left it on the sideboard that sat in the hall with the other bills that they shared. She pushed the button on the phone again only to hear the beep indicating there were no calls.

Brianne and Kalliah shared the home that Brianne purchased shortly after landing her job as a Crisis Counselor in the Virginia Schools system. The two had been inseparable since the death of Brianne's parents during their sophomore year in high school. Kalliah found work shortly after she completed the University of Virginia at Phillips Marketing Group and remained in Virginia. They didn't seem to miss their hometown in Washington, D.C., although Kalliah traveled there periodically to visit family and a few friends.

Brianne carried her personal mail with her to the kitchen where she continued her after-work routine. There was no message left on the refrigerator which meant Kalliah would be home early enough to cook. The roommates rotated kitchen duty, which included cooking. Leaving a message would mean the other would have to cook for the evening.

It had been five years, and the two formed a bond that made others envious. They shared everything except their men. They had the same taste in décor and clothing, a strong belief in God and cleanliness. Family and friends was a cherished breed, but they had no problem dumping them if they caused drama. These values added to the respect and love they held for each other.

The home was small but comfortable. There were four bedrooms; one was used as an office, two baths, a kitchen, living room and small dining area. Brianne didn't imagine herself with a husband or family, so she was ecstatic when her best friend agreed to move in to share the space. Her love for gardening kept the grass and flowerbeds that surrounded the house beautiful year round. The yard was small with a tire that hung from a large walnut tree. Its branches and leaves gave plenty of shade. It was where Brianne did her meditating when her job became a mental burden.

Brianne got the remainder of her fruit salad from the refrigerator and went into her bedroom to change clothes. She was a big girl, one that the men teased and few offered a serious relationship. She had her dates but most turned out to be short-lived possibilities. The men always promised more while she settled for less. Brianne blamed it on her weight. She went on diets off and on for years but over eating, eating for pleasure, and eating the wrong foods always won the battle before the results of her diets would prove she could lose the weight. Her round face and smooth skin spoke to most men as well as her flawless hairstyles, beautiful smile and a heartwarming personality. She saw none of those qualities as beauty. She kept to herself, when not at work and socializing with a few males she labeled as "just friends". If she needed an escort they would always make themselves available.

Kalliah would compliment her often about her attire as she left for work, teasingly telling her that it was a "Catch that man day". Brianne didn't bait her hook deliberately. She had never been good at being forward with men.

As the thought of the high school reunion crossed her mind, so did her weight. There would be comparisons made between her and the other female classmates. She threw the invitation on the dresser as she shook her head "no." She indulged herself in eating more fruit as she took off her clothes and unhooked her bra with a sigh of relief. Her back and feet gave her trouble daily, longing for her end of the day relaxation. She found her lounge wear under her robe hanging on the closet door. Brianne was pleased at the thought of stretching across her bed.

The previews of Oprah's show promised it would be worth watching. She pushed the button on the remote hoping her recorder didn't do its own thing and forget to record the soaps and Oprah for the day. She went to her closet searching through outfits, preparing for work the next day. One of the hangers jarred a box on the shelf causing papers, old pictures and books to fall at her feet.

"Damn."

She and Kalliah had been looking through their yearbook and pictures laughing about the possible lives their classmates were living now. A picture of her, Kalliah and Cherese floated to the floor. Cherese Taylor, who was the only other female she still dealt with regularly from high school, called to say the information for the reunion was posted on the internet. They would have to update their personal information for the reunion committee to mail their invitations. Cherese begged them to come earlier than the date of the reunion or stay later so they could spend a few days shopping and visiting old friends. Kalliah updated the information and told Cherese she would convince Brianne to change her mind.

The container that held both books and papers laid flipped over on the floor. Brianne picked up the papers putting them back in the container and threw the yearbook on the bed. She thought about Kalliah's words, "We need a vacation." She talked for most of the night telling Brianne that she deserved a break from drama and kids at the school. As her feet gave a silent yell, she answered the call by ignoring the papers and sitting on her bed. She positioned her back to meet the headboard for support as she ate from her bowl of fruit. She promised herself she would not fall asleep as she did each afternoon.

Brianne reached across the bed and grabbed the McKinley High School "Years in Review" yearbook. The first few pages of the yearbook didn't stir any pleasant memories. The pictures taken around the school, the faculty, and the underclassmen were all a part of her four years of disaster. McKinley High was one of the last places Brianne Gibson wanted to revisit.

****

Cherese dialed her husband's cell number again. When the call-tone "Shawty is a Ten" played after her third attempt to reach him, she knew he wouldn't be home in time for dinner. There was no need to call again and no need to prepare the meal she had planned for them. She put the lettuce and tomatoes back in the refrigerator. She didn't want a salad anyway.

The thought of a smaller meal frustrated her. She had no choice but to accept eating alone. It was no longer a question, whether or not he was cheating, it didn't matter, he wasn't home. Kyle told her she was being petty about the late hours or the time he spent with his friends. Cherese told her unmarried friends that Kyle was stepping out on her, and she knew it. Kalliah agreed with Kyle's excuses, but her friend wasn't married or eating dinner alone three nights a week.

Cherese could feel her emotions taking over. She didn't want to spend another night crying. Her therapist told her the medication would help her bouts with anxiety but the pills were dwindling fast, and the pharmacy would surely question her request for an early refill. She knew there was no more than four pills left in the bottle.

Grey Goose would take the edge off, and she could save the pills for a more serious attack. She poured more than two shots into a glass and mixed it with orange juice. Stirring it with her finger, she went to the family room to relax. The program on the television was a blur behind her tears. The phone rang, and unlike other nights when she jumped anxiously hoping Kyle was on the other end, Cherese let it ring until she heard Kalliah's voice.

"Hey, Reese, girl we received the invitations and the confirmation of our payments. I'm so excited. I'm glad we booked the suite early. It sounds like the weekend will be full of fun. Call me when you get in."

Cherese snatched the phone from its cradle. "Hello, Kalliah?"

"Girl, I was about to hang up. You okay, you sound like you just woke up?"

"I'll be alright. So you got the invites and the rest of the packet?" Charese questioned trying to sound perky.

"The packet came a week ago. We sent the money after we filled out the form online. I guess the invitations are our tickets for the banquet."

"I don't remember what the page said."

"Reese, you okay?"

"I'll be alright. How's Brianne?"

"I'm still working on her. She didn't even seem to be excited about the packet or the invitations. It's been over ten years, and I guess she's still hurting."

"I can understand it. Some of us still hurt."

"What does that mean?"

"Nothing, have you heard from anyone else?"

"No, I didn't expect to. Besides you live right there, no one has contacted you?"

"Not from our little group of friends. I saw Miles and Stephon, but they didn't mention the reunion, neither did I. They did say your boy asked about you though."

"My boy who?"

"Dante', like you didn't know. "

"Cherese where's Kyle?"

She could hear her friend's short breaths between each sob. Kalliah knew the answer to her question.

"Kalliah, call me later."

Cherese hung up the phone and drank from her now half-filled glass. She wiped the tears from her eyes as she reached for her yearbook sitting on the glass end table. A roar of audience laughter filled the room from the sitcom on the television. Cherese pushed the off button on the remote bringing total silence to the air. She turned the pages of the book to where she had placed the envelope addressed Kyle and Cherese Taylor. Her senior picture smiled at her reminding her of the better days.

****

Kalliah wanted to dial Cherese's number again, but she knew there would be no answer. Cherese and Kyle were at it again. Their off and on love started while they all were freshmen in high school. Kyle attended Dunbar High and other than being a rival on the basketball court, he was unknown to most of their classmates.

Kalliah called Cherese after reading the invitation. Brianne was asleep across her bed, and dinner was cooking. Kalliah wished she could have continued the conversation with Cherese. She wanted to hear more about Miles and Stephon. Her calls and conversations with Dante' were less frequent. She truly missed his friendship. Brianne brought the yearbook out of her bedroom smiling as she turned her nose to the air.

"Girl you cooking up a storm; I swear it woke a sistah up. How was your day?"

"You know the usual, how 'bout yours?"

"Same mess different day; I'm glad it's close to the weekend."

"Not close enough. Close is me knowing tomorrow I don't have to get up. We still got tomorrow left. I spoke with Cherese. She said she saw Miles and Stephon. I guess they'll be at the reunion."

Brianne set the dishes on the kitchen island preparing to eat. She didn't look up or comment. Kalliah reached for the yearbook and turned the pages not looking for anything particular.

"I wonder what they all look like now. I mean Miles, Stephon and you know others we haven't seen in years."

"You never see them when you go home?"

"No. I see Dante' every now and then but not Miles or Stephon. I never really stay long enough to see anyone. I go to my parents, and my aunt's home. I visit my grandmother, and then Cherese's if I have time."

"I didn't think about it that way. You're right. A weekend is not enough. Even the four-day weekend is too short. How is your grandmother and Aunt Lucille?"

"Hoping you'll come with me my next visit. C'mon Brianne, it will be fun. We don't have to stay with relatives. I promise if you don't want to go to the reunion, I won't try to force you. I just think you could use a couple of weeks to relax and enjoy the company of old friends."

"I usually use those weeks to catch up on my cases."

"Be honest, you don't catch up and your work doesn't slow down. Take a break with me. Lawd knows I need one."

Kalliah cut off the pots on the stove and removed the meat from the broiler. "Pass me your plate."

The two ate dinner and did the dishes with no further discussion about the reunion. Kalliah wiped the countertop and carried the yearbook to the couch. She got comfortable while waiting for the weekly episode of "House" to come on. Brianne sat at the dining room table with pages of a case file spread in front of her.

Kalliah opened the yearbook to the page where she and Dante' posed together as the "most likely to succeed" male and female. Neither of them had a clue where they were headed after high school. Kalliah touched Dante's picture slowly with her finger rubbing his face, as though she could feel the warmth of his skin. She let her thoughts take her back to when they talked every day. Everyone thought they were more than just friends. They were, in Kalliah's dreams. Dante' had been with her on cold mornings, warm spring days and hot sticky summer nights. She thought about his lips touching hers rather than the peck on the cheek "hello" or the ones on her forehead that said, "See you later."

Kalliah thought about her first sexual experience and how she cried later that night feeling, she betrayed Dante' by letting J.C. get that far. She wanted to talk about it for months afterward, but she could tell Dante' knew. He never said it, but she could tell by his reaction whenever J.C. came around.

The McKinley High's freshman year came and went fast, so did J.C. After the Christmas holiday their freshman year, J.C. decided Kalliah would not be his girlfriend when school reopened. Kalliah cried on Dante's shoulder. He talked softly giving her comfort. He spent the holiday with her and even bought her the first gift of real jewelry she would receive from someone other than family. Kalliah held the necklace between her fingers as she flipped through the next few pages. She still wore it around her neck after ten years.

Kalliah didn't need to lose another friend. The next three years were trying enough without dating "Mr. Popular." She didn't fit the image of the girls Dante' dated and now ten years later she wished she had. She wished she could turn back the pages of time.

Returning to the Past

Miles parked his car in front of the Martin Luther King Towers and waited for Stephon to come out of the front door of the apartment building. He would take his friend to work and hope that at the end of the day Stephon's car was repaired. Carpooling to work seemed simple until Stephon told him his daily list of errands. Miles was tempted to pull off when he noticed Stephon running toward the car attempting to avoid being soaked by the pouring rain.

"Mornin' man. Sorry 'bout that. I didn't see your car pull up with all this rain."

"You would have seen it when I pulled off, shit man you cutting it close."

Stephon couldn't argue the point. The traffic going toward Pennsylvania Avenue would have everything backed up. The only way to avoid it was to get an early start. Miles worked near Stephon, but the traffic would make five minutes out of the way seem like fifteen.

"Did you get your package and invitation yet?" Miles questioned waiting as Stephon buckled his seat belt.

"Naw, I paid for it online. I thought it would have come by now."

"Dante' got his yesterday, and my mother called saying I had mail. I used her address."

"Your girl still won't let you live with her huh?"

"Man, I don't even care, Miles man you know how these chicks can be. It ain't that serious. One minute they on you and the next…"

Miles didn't let Stephon get started with how the women were mistreating him. Since high school Stephon had been in and out of prison for selling drugs. The job he held now was court mandated. If he didn't show up each day, he would be put back in prison. It had been a year since his last bid of eighteen months, but Miles didn't think he was done with living in the fast lane.

"You can't expect a woman to wait for you to get your life together. The last time you came home, what, you stayed with her two nights and then went to that other girl's house. What's up with her, what's her name?"

"Who, I know you didn't think I was gonna stay with Wanda. That chick is whacked. I really don't live with Gina, I'm just squatting. I still have my place."

"That's what I mean. You need to sit down. Your ass is too old for the shit you pull. You got a decent gig now, don't blow it."

Miles blew his horn as all but the car in front of him moved in the congested traffic. "When will your car be ready?"

"Friday, they called yesterday. The part will be there today."

"It's gonna take them three days to fix the bumper?"

"Miles, man you forgot the paint job? My man fucked the front end up remember. I'm lucky I still have a car."

"Remind me not to let your man drive my ride."

Stephon shook his head as Miles laughed at his own comment. "Is Kalliah and Brianne coming to the reunion?"

"Cherese didn't say and I don't think Dante' knows. You still think about school days?"

"Yeah sometimes, it's one of my few accomplishments in life. Other than completing high school and being a father to my boys, I didn't stick to anyone or anything."

Miles listened as the words Stephon spoke now held a different meaning. He had made the statement before, but Miles thought he was just talking. A lot of their classmates wondered how Stephon graduated as one of the top in his class but turned out to be the neighborhood drug dealer. He never was addicted or a user, but he loved the money it provided. When he went to serve time, he found out, he would be a father of twins. Although he didn't have an on-going relationship with their mother, he loved his three-year old sons.

Stephon thanked Miles and told him he would be waiting at four. Miles pulled off looking at the clock. He had five minutes to drive four blocks, look for a parking spot and get to his nine o'clock briefing.

"Friday, damn." Miles thought about the days until then. He offered to help Stephon only because the streets held a temptation for him. Stephon was still addicted to the street life. Since McKinley High, Miles was addicted to his friendship with Dante', Stephon and Cherese.

His family moved to D.C. just as he, and his sister were in their crucial years of education. Miles would be a freshman while his sister was to begin her senior year. The transition was hard for both of them, but his sister's beauty made it easy for immediate acceptance by her peers. Miles brought a reputation with him. He had been a promising addition for the football team, and the spring season competitors would see his skills in track and field. The girls wooed him, and the boys hated his arrogance. Dante' and Stephon welcomed him with open arms.

Miles was a natural on the field and in the books. His senior year he became President of the Student Body relinquishing the title of Most Athletic to Stephon. He never won any awards for romance, although the girls flocked around him.

Dante' and Stephon often wondered why Miles, the athletic hunk, didn't have the prettiest girl in the school on his arm. Miles didn't want the prettiest and the one he wanted had no interest in him. Romance was not his forte. The years hadn't changed his experience.

He often thought about the four years he spent at McKinley High. His friends would be the only reason he would attend the reunion. Maybe, if she showed, he could finally connect with his special someone.

****

Dante' checked the date of the reunion again and marked it in his day planner. He put the information in his cell phone and texted a copy to his home office. It had been quite some time since all of his friends were together for a weekend of fun. He didn't want work to spoil it with calls or appointments. He made a mental note to call Miles. After making the drive from Maryland, he hoped his friend would put him up for the weekend. Although he would be welcomed by his mother, he didn't want to upset her routine. He was sure Stephon had contacted Miles after he called him checking on the mailed invitation. Stephon couldn't tell him if their female counterparts had received their packages or responded. Cherese hadn't spoken to them, but he knew they all would be excited about the upcoming event. Dante' didn't want to leave it up to fate. He picked up his phone, pushed the button for the intercom and spoke in the receiver.

"Ms. Walters, please hold my calls. I'll be on a long-distance call on the other line." He switched lines and dialed the number waiting for a voice on the other end.

"Phillips Marketing Group, may I help you?"

"Ms. Carter, please. This is Mr. Jefferson."

"Please hold Mr. Jefferson."

The music played softly in Dante's ear as he scanned through a folder on his desk.

"Good morning, this is Ms. Carter, may I help you."

"So professional, hey, old friend."

"Dante', what a surprise, how are you?"

"I'm fine and you. What's up in the corporate world?"

"Nothing you don't know about. I heard you were traveling all over the states these days."

"Lonely travel I might add. You should come with me; I could always use the company."

"Dante' stop. It's so good to hear from you. Are you going to the reunion? It seems like it will be fun."

"Yeah, I got the package and the invite. I have to call Miles and check in. I'll be staying with him and Stephon, I guess."

"Why would you have to guess? I thought you stayed there whenever you went home."

"My family is squawking about that, but as usual that's where I'll be. What about you? Are you hooking up with Cherese and what about Brianne, is she gonna to come?"

"I don't know about staying with Cherese. I think Kyle is on the loose again. I was thinking of a suite for the three of us. I'm still working on Brianne. The suite would be better for her too. I'll see my parents and family while I'm in town after the reunion. I decided to take a mini vacation. The reunion will kick it off."

"Hmmm." Dante' turned his day planner to the week of the reunion and smiled seeing the dates were empty.

"Hmmm what?"

"Hmmm vacation time. Is there room for two friends to have dinner or lunch without others?"

"Lunch between friends is always a possibility. I would love to. I can't set a date or time though, you know, until I know what Cherese has planned. She suggested we stay longer."

"We? Oh, you and Brianne are taking time off together?"

"Brianne will probably spend most of her time in the suite, but Cherese and I have talked about visiting friends and family. You know woman stuff."

Dante' put the pen down and closed the book. He sat back in his seat thinking about how he could arrange spending time with Kalliah.

"How's your love life?"

"Still blunt, huh? Its okay I guess. There's no line outside my office if that's what you mean."

"No, are you still with what's her name?"

"I'm glad you don't remember. Maybe you won't think about her more than you do me. Is that why you don't call?"

Kalliah used his personal life as an excuse for keeping her distance. Knowing Dante' was involved with someone made it easy. During their last conversation, he confessed that his girlfriend wanted the relationship to get serious. Kalliah could hear in his voice, he had doubts.

"No you have a hectic schedule and so do I, plus it's hard with us living in other states...."

"Stop it girl, stop." Kalliah could tell he was laughing. "How long will you be in Washington?"

"Two weeks maybe three. I haven't decided." Kalliah smiled thinking of the possibility of being with Dante'.

"Okay, so you and Morris aren't together?"

"His name is Maurice." Kalliah laughed before he replied. "Whatever."

"No, we're together it's hard to explain."

"You're bored."

Dante' said it. Kalliah had been looking for a word to define the problem for months. He was right, she was bored. The light on another line blinked.

"Dante', I have to take this call. I'll talk to you later in the week. If I don't reach you, I will assume we'll talk at the welcome gathering next Friday."

Dante' penciled in the week after the reunion as a vacation with question marks on the days of the week that followed. He would bring his laptop and work from Miles' home if there were any conflicts.

"Well I will definitely wait for your call. Tell Brianne hello for me."

"I will sweetie. Thanks for thinking about me."

"I can't forget you."

****

Stephon looked at the clock. Lunch was in fifteen minutes, and he couldn't wait. The Mailroom had been busy from the time he punched in. It wasn't like the other jobs probation had referred him to. The other employees weren't aware of his background, and everyone treated him fairly. There was nonstop business at the headquarters of Tucker's and Sons LLC. He was determined to move up in the company. He used his lunch hour to talk to a few of the guys who were now working in other departments. They all started in the Mailroom.

Stephon took the elevator to the third floor where the employee's cafeteria was located. Tuna fish salad and chips would be the best pick for the day. He got his tray, filled his cup with soda, and found a seat near the window. Richard Smalls, the Director of Financing nodded his head as he approached Stephon's table. Stephon smiled in return. Richard stopped as though he forgot something and faced Stephon.

"Do you mind if I join you?"

"No, please, have a seat."

"Thank you. I've been meaning to come and speak to you. You work in the Mailroom, right?"

Stephon looked up from his tray. The older man was well dressed. His mixed gray hair gave him the corporate business look. He adjusted himself and took out a pen and small pad.

"Yes, I've been there for more than a year now."

"I've taken the opportunity to check your employment record. I must say—

"Mr. Smalls, I no longer have a desire to live the type of life my records reveal. I mean with me being incarcerated. I really like working here."

Stephon recognized the tone of the conversation. His last employers allowed him to work three months before they claimed they received complaints regarding his background. When it came time for insurance or benefits to start, they laid him off. He discussed the problem with probation but they insisted each employer was aware of his background when he was hired. He had been working at Tucker and Son's LLC for more than a year and no one had questioned his records.

"I see. I wasn't going to mention your criminal record. I noticed you had other employment working in book and record keeping."

"I was a business major in college."

"Mr. Drake we have an opening in the Finance Department. I think with the training we'll provide, you will work well there."

"Thank you; when can I start?"

"There's one problem, a few people are being watched in the department. You'll have some detectives talking to you about it. We need you to help us find out who they are."

"Why me?"

"Mr. Drake these employees are moving funds, or stealing them. The detectives believe the money is being used to traffic drugs. We need an inside person who knows both sides of the game."

"I don't know…."

"We'll teach you the finance side. Your training will be above the norm because we will also show you what has been going on. You'll know who they are and the detectives will tell you their plan for setting the bait to stop them."

"I don't know. I'll have to talk with my lawyer or probation officer. I can't afford to get caught in anything involving drugs. They'll lock me up again."

"They won't. They can't. The detectives will be contacting you. We need a way to communicate with you outside of our offices. Mr. Drake this could benefit you. I'm sure they'll be willing to clear your record. We are willing to promote you first by moving you to the Finance Department, and then give you a permanent position on the executive staff in Financing, once this is over. You see, you will be saving us quite a bit of money. They've been swindling funds for more than three years."

Stephon put the last of his sandwich in his mouth. Mr. Smalls swallowed his soda waiting for Stephon's response.

"I'll need to talk with the detectives first. I want to know what they'll do as far as my record is concerned. I can give you a number for you both to reach me."

"Yes, you do that. Write it down here for me and I'll forward the information. The lead detective's name is Scott Miller. I'm not sure who will be working with him. Is it okay if they call you this evening?"

"Yes, by all means. That's the number to my cell."

The older gentleman rose from his seat picking up his tray as Stephon handed him the pad and pen. "Thank you Mr. Drake, you won't be disappointed with the arrangements, I'm sure. I will be speaking with Mr. Tucker in Finance, to let him know we are working on an agreement."

Stephon stood and followed Mr. Smalls to dispose of their garbage. The men shook hands and promised to talk later. Stephon looked at his watch, he had twenty minutes left for lunch he decided to call Miles and get his opinion.

Miles worked for the courts. His connections gave Stephon one of the best attorneys in Washington, D.C. He wanted Miles to know what he knew before making any decisions. He went to the employee's lounge and made his call.

"Hey dude."

"Your car is fixed?"

"Is that all that's on your mind?"

"Man, what's up?"

"Listen, Mr. Smalls approached me about a position in Finance."

"That's what you wanted right? When does it start?"

"There's a catch. I'll have to work with some detectives to catch employees who have been using the money here for, let's say criminal activity."

"You're joking. Man, how does that work?"

"He said they checked my files. I have what they need on both sides. They can train me for the position with no questions asked and find out about the trafficking I guess with me making deals on the inside."

"You guess? You don't know what you'll be doing?"

"I've got to get all the information from the detective. All I know is my record can be cleared after this, and I'll have an executive position in the Finance Department."

"Damn, you might want to check that out with your lawyer. You don't want them firing you after it's all over."

"I wanted your opinion, what do you think?"

"Well if you don't take it, they may let you go. It seems like you're in a catch twenty two."

"I didn't even think about that."

"Talk to the lawyer before you agree to anything. You might want something in writing. Your clean slate may be costing you. Don't talk to anyone there about it. You don't know who they're watching."

"You're right. You're right. Alright, thanks man. I'll see you at four."

"Hey Dante' called. He'll be up for the reunion and staying a week or more."

"A week or more? Dante's vacationing in Washington?"

"No, you know better than that. I think Kalliah's coming to town."

"Wow. Some things never change, what about Angelina?"

"She's not coming with him. He asked could he stay with me."

"What's up with that, I thought it was getting serious between them."

"Not if Kalliah is still in the picture."

"What, I'm confused. When did he start seeing Kalliah?"

"C'mon man, you and I both know Dante' has always had a thing for Kalliah. I don't think he's ready to commit to Angelina."

"Okay, okay, so this reunion should be interesting."

"See you at four."

Getting Reacquainted

Kyle couldn't remember the time of the welcome reception on the invitation Cherese showed him. He was sure it would conflict with his plans for Friday night. Cherese received two calls from Kalliah confirming their lunch date at twelve. If he played his cards right, he could pack an overnight bag and leave before she got back to the house. His wife's friends would keep her occupied for the weekend, leaving him free to roam.

The marriage was more of an obligation than love. What would it look like if he walked out on her? Cherese was still considered disabled. She was in therapy as well as seeing a psychiatrist. Everyone would blame him, well, not everyone, but he couldn't leave her in her current state. Cherese accused him often of no longer loving her. After the lost of the baby, she let herself go. The doctor said it was depression.

Kyle couldn't see himself looking after her the rest of his life. He reminded her constantly that the doctors gave her a good physical diagnosis. The bruises had healed well, and no one could tell where the stitches repaired her mouth. The fall had been the worst of all she had but Kyle couldn't let her keep questioning him. He was the man of the house, and she learned her lesson the hard way. He knew she understood it after he explained that was why God didn't let her carry the full term. Mentally, she would never be the same.

He put his shorts in the bag and zipped it as he turned to leave. Cherese was standing at the bedroom door. The look in her eyes told him they were headed for another episode.

"I thought you were with your girls. They didn't come in for the reunion?"

Cherese entered the bedroom and went to the closet never acknowledging her husband's statement.

"Did you hear me talking or what? You mad at me or something?"

"No, Kyle. Yes, they're in town. I'll catch up with them later."

"So what you doing here now?"

"I live here, don't I?"

"What the fuck does that mean?"

Cherese pulled her suitcase from the top of the closet and put it on the bed. Kyle turned from the door watching her begin to pack under garments and night gowns from her dresser.

"Where you think you going?"

"I'm staying at the suite with my girls, as you say. I didn't think you would mind since you're never here. They'll be in town for a few days, and the company of friends may do me some good."

"Oh, so you need company now?"

"I don't know what I need. I know what I don't need. What I don't deserve!"

"What's that Cherese? Who's to blame now? Me? Is it, me again?"

"No Kyle, it's us. It's the fact that there is, no us. I don't want to pretend this time. You do you or do her. I'm going to try to enjoy myself this weekend, and the time that they're in town."

"So you just pack your shit and leave?"

"Yours is packed!"

Kyle forgot about the overnight bag in his hand. He threw it on the floor in Cherese's direction. The bag hit her on the back of her legs causing her to stumble in her place. She turned to face her husband with the look of fear in her eyes. Kyle walked toward her and grabbed her face tightly in his hands causing her to drop the bra she held.

"Listen, don't get too smart. I pay the bills. I provide for you, and you'll stay where I pay for you to stay. Take your shit, put it in your drawer and don't make me go off on you."

Kyle pushed her hard causing her to bump the chestnut dresser drawers. Tears flowed from her eyes as she watched him pick up his bag. Cherese stood frozen. She prayed he was leaving. Kyle approached the top of the stairs and yelled back to his wife.

"Oh yeah bitch. The welcome reception starts at seven, be ready, 'cause I will. Who the fuck are you? What you think; I'm not going with you to this damn reunion? I'm your husband, your man, and you will treat me that way. Shit if I got to play this fucking game with your sick ass, then so do you. Love me 'cause you damn sure can't leave me, and I refuse to take care of your ass if I can't watch you."

Kyle's voice faded. She heard him slam the front door. She sat on her bed crying. The door opened again and Cherese quickly got up and went into the bathroom listening as she turned the lock hoping he wouldn't try the door.

"Oh, by the way, your friends won't be here long enough to save your ass. You've only got this weekend. It's on again next week. I won't forget you tried this. It wouldn't be right for you to wear shades the entire weekend."

Kyle's threat hurt as much as his blows. Cherese looked in the medicine cabinet grateful she had more than the four pills.

****

Brianne stepped out of the shower feeling refreshed. She and Kalliah arrived in Washington just in time to shower and change for the welcome party. The kick off celebration for the reunion was being held at the State Plaza Hotel in the downtown district. Brianne always loved the surrounding scenery and after hearing there would be live entertainment, she was determined to enjoy herself.

She thought about visiting a few of her family members while in town and decided she would put that on her agenda for Monday. She didn't even call her aunt to tell her she was coming to the reunion. Just the thought of what she would say made her uncomfortable about being in the only place she could consider home.

Brianne's parents died in a three alarm fire in their home during her freshman year at McKinley High. They bequeathed all their money and assets to their only child. Brianne moved in with her father's older sister. Her aunt Laura was willing to take her into her home until she discovered there was no money left to her.

It took some adjusting for Brianne to live in her Aunt's home. She quickly realized she had become the caretaker for the family with all the chores and responsibility of her cousins. The three boys did what they wanted, and Brianne did as she was told. Laura Gibson had never been married and didn't see the need to marry anyone after the boys reached their teen years. They attended Dunbar High, and Brianne wished she had transferred there shortly after her parents died. Her Aunt saw no need for Brianne to be uprooted from the school or the education her mother wanted for her. Being ridiculed at school and looked at as a burden in her Aunt's home led to Brianne's bitterness. She began to challenge everyone and everything.

Brianne's thoughts of her past quickly changed to the reunion ahead. She looked at the outfits she laid across the bed. Neither of them would hide the fact that she gained eighty pounds over the ten years, since graduating from high school. Kalliah never said anything derogatory about her weight but Brianne knew there would be whispers. The thoughts of **"Boy, she got big; is that Brianne Gibson? That's the girl who…"** repeated in her mind. Brianne couldn't do it. She sat on the bed and cried.

****

Kalliah didn't hear Brianne stirring in the other bedroom at the far end of the suite. The ride to D.C. had been strenuous. She felt guilty about asking Brianne to come and enjoy the company of old friends and relatives. Kalliah walked to the living room and listened to her friend's soft sobs. She walked to the bedroom door and found Brianne pretending to read a novel.

"Girl, what are you reading over there that has you crying so?"

"It's nothing much. One of the students had it as an inspirational book. She's been coming to my office for a month or more now and well...."

"Brianne, if you really can't handle seeing people you don't have to go. I wish you would tell me what has you so wound up about just visiting D.C. I wouldn't ask you if I knew what or who you were avoiding. You know that right? I'm really sorry that I upset you."

Kalliah left Brianne sitting on her bed hoping she hadn't done the wrong thing by inviting her on her only vacation of the year. Brianne didn't bother to answer as she wiped her eyes with the tissue she'd been using since they got on Route 95 North. She stepped into the shower leaving Kalliah unsure what her plans were.

Cherese hadn't called either; she hoped Kyle didn't get mad about her wanting to stay with them in the hotel. A few of the other classmates would be checking in between the welcome reception and breakfast. Cherese wanted to eat breakfast with them in the morning. She walked toward Brianne's door and then changed her mind deciding to call Cherese first.

The phone rang twice before Cherese picked up the line whispering, "Hello?"

"Cherese, are you alright?"

"Yeah, shit girl. No. I don't know what to do. Kyle will be back in time to come with me to the reception. I was certain that bitch would have him tied up for the night. I fucked everything up....Kalliah. I should have waited until his ass left."

"What did you do?"

"I pulled out my suitcase to pack it, and he flipped. You know that same shit about who he is and what I should appreciate."

"Where is he now?"

"I don't know but he'll be back to flaunt his ass around with me like the fucking loving husband. I am so sick of his shit. I really am this time. I just—"

"You just what?"

"I just don't know how to get away from him without him hurting me or somebody else."

"You walk out. Don't look back and file papers on that ass if you have to."

"Sounds good; the reality is you ain't the one getting beat down whenever he feels like it."

"Alright, alright; do it your way. So what's up? Are you coming to the reception or what? Maybe his ass won't show back up."

"I could only hope not. I don't know what hell it would cause if I didn't go. He would probably figure I was staging some romantic encounter and changed my plans after he said he was coming. My whole weekend is ruined."

"Don't claim that shit. I'll call you when we're leaving, if he hasn't come back by then, call him and say we called. He'll change his mind if he's with his chick, maybe she won't let him leave."

"Yeah that makes me feel so much better."

"Cherese have you been drinking?"

Cherese looked at the medicine bottle and the empty glass.

"No, not yet, I was lying down though. I'll get up now, call me when y'all ready."

Kalliah hung up the phone and went to Brianne's closed door. She knocked once remembering her purse and shoes were in the bedroom. Brianne came out the door dressed, but Kalliah could tell she lacked the interest.

"Brianne I don't want you to come if you're doing it just to appease me, that's all I'm gonna say. Cherese is having a problem with Kyle. I guess it's the same-old shit. I'll call her when we get close to her house, she may need a ride."

"If they're having problems, why wouldn't she need the ride?"

"The problem is he'll be coming."

Brianne said a silent prayer as they walked out the door.

****

Dante' packed his car to leave early on Friday morning. The argument with his fiancé lasted most of the night, and he refused to start his morning as the night ended. His bags were packed for an anticipated stay of two weeks. The vacation as far as Angelina knew would be pure leisure. Dante' never said the reunion weekend would be extended. As he pulled up the garage door, he remembered he left his laptop on the kitchen counter. Angelina was waiting for his entrance.

"So I'll be able to reach you at Miles' house?"

"You'll be able to reach me on my cell."

"At Miles' house?"

"Angel, call my cell. Why would you call his number?"

"Why can't I? 'Cause you know you won't be there. What's this really about Dante'? You didn't even bother to ask if I wanted to go?"

"I asked you when I got the information, I asked you before I paid for my ticket, what do you mean I didn't ask you?"

"You didn't ask when you decided to stay for two weeks after the reunion. Does your mother know you'll be hanging around for two weeks?"

"No, I told you it was a last minute thing. Miles and Stephon still have loose ends to tie up, so they may have to work a couple of the days. Angel you just got back from Puerto Rico with your girlfriends, I didn't ride you about it."

"It was planned for months. Besides I wasn't going to see my ex or anyone that was close to being an ex."

"What does that mean?"

"You know what it means, your mother told me about you and Kalliah."

"There's nothing to tell and she has nothing to do with my decision to stay longer. She lives in Virginia. I guess she'll be leaving after the reunion."

"You guess. You know. I know you know. That's bull Dante'. You just proposed and now you want to reacquaint yourself with an old love? What kinda bull is that?"

Dante' shook his head and reached for his laptop.

"Answer me? What's up with that?"

"I proposed didn't I? I mean you didn't ask me. I asked you."

"So you're changing your mind until you find out where you fit into her life?"

"Angel, I'll call you."

"Yeah, I'll be waiting!"

She walked away rattling in Spanish. Dante' understood only a few of the words, but he knew none of them were affectionate. He watched her honey-colored body as she sashayed across his large kitchen floor. They didn't live together, but her decorative touch was present throughout the house. Angel would be house sitting until he returned. Now he was sure she would be snooping around for clues of an affair.

They were engaged a week before her vacation, and that was a month ago. Miles told him he was rushing to a dead end. Angel and Dante' had been in their strained relationship for five years. Miles knew about Angel's past, her indiscretions and warned Dante' that she was not "wifey" material. Dante' proposed hoping for a change. Now he wasn't sure about his decision.

There was none of the traffic that Dante' expected. He was glad the roads were near empty after leaving an hour later than he planned. He arrived at Miles's home, just as he was shaving. Miles answered the door with a face full of shaving cream.

"What's up man? I wasn't expecting you this early. What time did you get up this morning?"

"I was thinking about that Friday morning traffic. I didn't want to get caught up in it. You going to work or what?"

"No but that damn Stephon has to. I'm his chauffeur until this afternoon."

"His car still down huh."

"Yeah, they got it done, but he can't take off from his job. I'll drive him, and we'll pick it up later. Listen, come on in and get comfortable. I'll be a minute and then we'll go get that fool." Miles headed for the bathroom leaving his friend to bring in his bags.

Dante' carried his garment bag and other items into the guest room where he usually stayed when visiting. It was close to seven thirty. His mother would be getting dressed for work. He would wait a couple of hours before calling her; otherwise she would offer to spend the day with him. Dante' was sure Angel called her when he left.

The two friends rode to pick up Stephon laughing and joking about the expectations of the welcome reception.

"Did Cherese speak to Stephon again about what their plans were?"

"What plans?"

"Nothing, I thought maybe she told Stephon what they were doing, you know after the reunion."

"News to me, all I know is that after the weekend, Kalliah and Brianne will be going back to Virginia, and Cherese has that nigga at home to deal with."

"Tell me they're not still going through that."

"Kyle is the same. That girl has been through some shit and you know what? She's still there. She won't leave his ass."

"Maybe he's got something we don't know about." Dante' smiled at his own sarcastic remark.

"Maybe but shit, get your thing off and move on. Why take all that other shit. I believe he's gotten to the point of hitting her too."

"No, that ain't good. I thought you were talking about him dealing with the other chicks. He's abusive?"

"A real nigga. His ignorant ass won't even recognize the woman he's got."

"So why doesn't she leave?"

"I don't know, she calls; we talk, but there's a limit on what or how much she tells me. I know after she lost the baby things changed. She's been in and out of therapy, medication, man the whole nine. But the real problem is Kyle. If she left that punk ass alone she'd get better. She's lost a lot of weight, and you can see it in her face when she's not hiding behind the makeup."

"Have you talked to Kyle? I mean man to man?"

"Nah, I didn't want to fight that damn traffic." Miles answered changing the topic as Stephon got in the car.

"So what's up fellas? Y'all got a whole day of leisure before the reception tonight. Where you headed?"

Miles didn't answer waiting for Dante' to tell them what he expected to do the balance of the day. Dante' let the questions he had about Cherese and Kyle fade as did the conversation.

"Man I won't be planning anything for the next two weeks. Hopefully, I'll be too busy to miss scheduling shit. That's what I get paid to do and as of today, I'm on vacation. So how do you like this job you got?"

"They got me. I wouldn't have even looked at this place for a job. I'm in the Mailroom, but things are in the works for another position at the office."

"Alright, so you'll stay away from that street stuff. That's good."

"Yeah, I'm not getting any younger. Besides my boys need to see their father in another light."

"How are they; you still with their mother?"

"They're good. No, she moved to California."

"Your kids are in California?"

"No, she left them on her mother and father. That's why I got to get it together man. Right now they're small and cute but two boys growing up in the hood. Her parents aren't ready to handle that again. I'm gonna file for custody, but I have to have my act together. I told them that and we've been working it out ever since. I have them on the weekends most of the time and holidays. It's going well."

"So, Tracy doesn't come home at all?" Dante' couldn't understand her actions.

"No she hasn't in three years. She had them, stayed a few months and left. She's getting married, so she says, but she doesn't want them to be a part of her life."

"Damn chick was whacked when you met her."

"Miles, it ain't like you never had a whacked-out chick."

"Not one that I didn't wear a condom with; besides my love life ain't that busy."

"I forgot, Mr. Waiting For the Right One. Anyway, I help raise them as much as I can until I can get custody. Her parents agree with my plans, and it's all good."

"Damn, I wouldn't think Tracy would leave her kids like that. Just like the shit with Cherese—"

"What shit with Cherese?"

Miles interrupted before Dante' could repeat their conversation.

"Yo man, go to work. This is your stop, see you at four. Hey you want us to pick up your car. It would save us some running later. We can drop it back here and meet up later."

Stephon was thinking about Dante's last words pausing before he answered. "Yeah that'll work. Here's the receipt call me." Stephon pulled out his wallet fishing between the billfolds for the yellow receipt. "I can meet you here at lunch and get the keys from you, and I'll park it. Just pull up here."

Miles got out of the car and reached across the roof as Stephon handed him the paper. "Bet, see you then. Call those guys and let them know we'll be there. What time did they say it would be ready?"

"Anytime after ten."

"Alright, I'll see you around twelve."

Dante' waited for Miles to get back in the car before asking him why he cut the conversation short when they were talking about Cherese. "What's going on?"

"We're gonna pick up his ride after ten. Have you had breakfast? We can eat and then pick it up."

"Man, you're good at dodging shit. What's up with Stephon and Cherese?"

"Stephon and Cherese?

"Yeah, you didn't want him to know about Cherese."

"I think he still thinks of her as a brother would, you know that ole' I'll defend you shit. Stephon doesn't need that he'd kill Kyle and…."

"And…?"

"And nothing, he doesn't know what's going on. No one does but the girls, me and now you. Cherese didn't want anyone to know."

"I forgot they dealt with each other in school. Kyle threatened to kick his ass too didn't he?"

"Yeah but that ain't Kyle's worry now though."

"Oh, Cherese has somebody?"

"Nah, but that chick he's dealing with may be the last. I don't think she knows Cherese is back home."

"Back home?"

"Yeah, she was in the hospital and under doctor's care for a good while."

"And that nigga was out seeing other women?"

"Uh huh. What's up with you and Angel?"

"She's okay. I don't know man these two weeks may tell me something different."

"So Kalliah talking like she's down for being with you these two weeks?"

"No nothing like that. We've been friends over the years and we both are in relationships. I just needed time to think about this marriage thing."

"You shoulda thought about that before you gave Angel the ring. You fucking with a Spanish girl man, that could bring problems."

"I ain't worried about it. I know there would be more problems if I married her knowing I really didn't think she was the one."

"You don't think she's the one?"

"Man, some days we're in heavenly bliss, and others, we go to hell and back. I can't live like that."

"Dante' when did you start feeling like this?"

"After I got the invitation to the reunion."

Old Friends

Kalliah parked her car opposite Cherese's. She spotted Cherese getting out of the vehicle. Brianne gave Kalliah a questioning look.

"Girl I don't want more drama. She looks like she's okay though right?"

"Humph, I thought she said she was waiting for him to get dressed. I don't think he would have let her leave the house alone."

Cherese's outfit showed she shopped at the "One of a Kind" boutique. The top to the salmon pantsuit had sheer sleeves and a low front. It fit her well. Her makeup was flawless, but her appearance told it all was a cover. Kalliah sighed knowing what Brianne said was true.

"Well, we'll see. I won't question her now but look at her Bree, she looks sick or tired maybe both. I don't want to be looking at her in a hospital again."

"Shit or a grave."

"What, you think it's gone that far?"

"I think it and you know it. But I stopped trying to pull shit out of her. We're all friends if she chooses to pretend she's hiding it all, let her. That may be her only way to cope."

"Bree coping ain't living." The two unbuckled their seat belts to get out of the car.

"Yeah but when it's all you got, you settle for it."

Cherese tipped quickly in her heels to greet her friends.

"Look at ya'll. Hey, Bree I am so glad you changed your mind." Cherese hugged and kissed each of them being careful not to mess up the hairdos or makeup. "Yall look like new money shit, damn I'm really glad you're gonna be around awhile. We've got so much to catch up on. Not here, I mean you know between us."

Kalliah and Brianne listened as they walked into the hall. The smiles on their faces remained as they were greeted by the reception committee. After receiving their name tags, signing their names to the guestbook, and getting their souvenirs, they proceeded to their table. They got excited seeing old friends and faces, but nothing matched their shouts of joy seeing Dante', Stephon and Miles. The six were seated at the same table, thanks to Cherese. The tables sat ten, and the other four seats were available for their expected guests.

"This is really nice. They've done a lot of work to get this together." Cherese continued her compliments as she waved at people she recognized across the room.

Brianne looked around as though she was searching the area for someone specific. Stephon recognized her nervousness. "Bree you okay?"

"Yeah, Yeah, Cherese, Kyle's not coming?"

Everyone stopped their small talk and looked at Cherese. She took her seat as though Brianne hadn't asked her anything never looking around the room. Dante' answered to ease the momentary tension. "I guess he'll be here later."

"No he won't. Let's not spoil the evening with talk about drama and problems. Dante' you sure look good brotha, you been in the gym?" Cherese responded forcing herself to smile.

"No, Miles is the gym man. I just try to eat right."

"Thought you said we weren't talking about drama and problems?" Brianne laughed, "A gym is drama for me."

"You look fine the way you are."

Brianne gave Stephon a sharp look, and everyone at the table laughed. He often teased Brianne in high school but defended her from others that would make remarks to her about her size.

"I'm glad to see things haven't changed between us; don't make me ignore you the rest of the night."

Stephon winked. Brianne and Stephon were what they considered the misfits of the group. Neither of them felt like they would reach any designated level of success. Brianne was always conscious about her weight and the secrets of her past that haunted her. Stephon would always carry a criminal record. Through it all, they understood each other's pain and disappointments.

"How have you been Stephon, really?"

Stephon and Brianne engaged themselves in a one on one conversation as did Dante' and Cherese. Miles and Kalliah chose to leave the table and mingle with other classmates. The welcome reception was scheduled to last until eleven. The open bar and buffet were complimented by a classmate that had become a popular DJ. He played music from their years in school as well as updated requests. Although the official party was scheduled for Saturday night, the alumni class began partying shortly after they arrived. Miles and Kalliah stopped and got a drink at the bar while watching the dance floor spotting friends and waving hello.

"So how is Cherese really doing? She calls me regularly, but you're her best friend. I mean I'm worried about her."

"Miles, I am too. Have you noticed how worn she looks? I try not to be judgmental, you know. I don't want her to shut me out, but I'm really scared that fool will hurt her."

"Kalliah, he has hurt her. I think she's numb and doesn't know it. That's the scary part. You know what she reminds me of sometimes when we talk? It's like a part of her is trapped… you know, crying out. However, there's also a stronger part of her saying it's waiting for just one chance."

"A chance for what?"

"You know how you women are, revenge. I'm scared she's gonna be pushed into doing something to him and lose herself again. I thought we lost her after the miscarriage."

"Miles what was your take on that? I mean I watched your reaction to what the doctors said and how she explained it all went down, but did you believe that thing about her slipping and falling?"

"No, I accepted it just like you, just because Cherese wanted it that way."

"What happened between you and Cherese?"

"What are you talking about?"

"Kyle blamed you. What was that about?"

"Him looking for someone to blame. Did you know we almost fought that night?"

"Over what?"

"The lie about the fall, Kalliah, I believe just like you; he pushed her."

There was a tap on the mic and the music faded to the sound of the class reunion coordinator's voice. "Good evening all, for those of you that don't remember me, my name is Francine Washington. I'm now Francine Carlson, thanks to my loving husband of five years."

The audience responded with polite claps. "I would like to thank you all for coming out. We are certainly looking forward to the weekend activities. For those of you who haven't signed the guest book please do. It says guest but it's for us to create an up to date email list. That's why it doesn't ask for your phone number. Please ladies indicate your maiden names. We will be trying to do more events than just this ten year traditional reunion so it's important to keep a current contact list. Tonight's reception will be over at eleven. Breakfast for those of you who will be joining us will be at the Sheraton at nine thirty in the morning. If you didn't sign up for breakfast but want to join, or you've changed your mind please see Annette at the souvenir table. Everyone should have a souvenir and oh before I forget is Cherese Taylor here?"

Cherese raised her hand, and the clapping began. "Yes, we all remember our cheerleading captain." Annette brought a folded note to the table and handed it to Cherese.

"Thanks Annette." Francine continued. "I will have the activities for you here at the table as well. Everyone this is our weekend, enjoy."

Kalliah and Miles came back to the table with their drinks refreshed. Dante' and Stephon left Brianne and Cherese to reading the note that apparently had them temporarily paralyzed.

"What's wrong?" Kalliah snatched the note from Cherese's hand.

"I told you to wait. I'll be right here in the parking lot when your ass comes out. What the fuck were you thinking?"

Miles took the note from Kalliah and left the table. Kalliah watched him walk over to Dante' and Stephon. Stephon came back to the table with two beers and took his seat as Dante' and Miles went toward the front door.

"Don't worry they're coming right back."

Kalliah saw the look on Cherese's face. Brianne reached across the table for her hand. Cherese touched her friend acknowledging her support. Brianne knew it was an embarrassing moment for her.

"Stephon would you get me a drink?" Brianne asked hoping to get him away from the table.

"You sure?"

"Yes."

The three ladies sat silent holding hands as though in prayer. "I've got to get better with this."

"Cherese, you don't have to take his shit."

Brianne released her friend's hands. "Somebody's gonna get hurt. Why do you stay with him?"

Cherese glared at Brianne. "He's my husband!"

"Does he know that? Does he treat you like a wife?"

"I'm not gonna argue with you. Neither of you have been married, you wouldn't understand. Marriage is about taking the bitter with the sweet. After all the vows say for better or worse."

Kalliah couldn't believe what she was hearing.

"Cherese, are you listening to yourself? You said earlier that you were tired of his shit."

"She doesn't know what she's tired of, are you still taking that damn medicine?"

"Brianne you sure are being cynical tonight, what have I done to you?"

"It's what you're doing to yourself and just to keep that ass hole."

"You never did like Kyle. I don't think it's fair for you to criticize our marriage."

"Whatever Cherese, I knew I couldn't make you see the darker side of that nigga."

"Brianne, what the fuck are you talking about?"

Stephon placed the drinks on the table. He brought each of them the same drinks they ordered earlier. Kalliah knew it would be her last drink of the night.

****

Dante' and Miles walked back from the parking lot. There was no sign of Kyle. Miles shook his head in deep thought. "God is good."

"What?"

"It's true, God protects fools."

"Hmmn. Why would he do that?"

"God or Kyle?"

Both Dante' and Miles laughed. "Man, this is a mess. What is she supposed to do now? Go home and act like she didn't get the threat?"

"That's how they've been living. Maybe Kalliah and Brianne can convince her to handle this differently."

Miles held the door for Dante' as they reentered the hall. The music was playing as though they had more than forty minutes left to dance and enjoy each other's company. As the two walked pass the bar, they both froze in their steps. Kyle was coming out of the men's room. Miles went to approach him but Dante' held his arm making him wait until Kyle almost bumped against them standing in his path.

"Oh, hey. How's the McKinley High boys doing tonight?"

"Maybe we should be asking you. You sound as though you've tied a few on." Miles wanted him to admit the obvious.

"A few, a celebration is a celebration."

"What are you celebrating?"

"Isn't this a reunion? I mean you're all here, together, getting reacquainted. Are you saying it's not the place for a good time?"

"Kyle, what the fuck…..?"

Dante' stepped between Miles and Kyle. The tone was changing, and he knew the timing wasn't right. Stephon was watching from the table as were other classmates. There wouldn't be a fair fight.

"I'm gonna deal with your ass Kyle. That's a promise."

"Same promise you made before. I'm always around. You know where, and you've got the number. Call me when you're ready, unless my wife begs you not to again."

"Yeah, fortunately for you, she loves your black ass."

"No, unfortunate for you and you know what Miles? You can't have her. I'll kill you first."

Dante' pushed Miles toward their table before he could throw the punch he was ready to deliver. They kept walking as Miles adjusted his clothes.

"C'mon man he's just talking shit. You've been that close to Cherese?"

"Doesn't matter, he needs an ass whooping."

Dante' stopped walking. "Miles, it does. Are you and Cherese dealing?"

"Man, listen, we'll talk but not here or now."

Dante' followed Miles. Cherese was finishing her drink as she continued her explanation for blind love, an excuse for her loving Kyle. Stephon was the only one pretending to listen. Brianne engaged herself in a conversation with members seated at the next table, and Kalliah was watching Kyle as he looked on from the bar. Miles sat next to Cherese interrupting her drunken giggle bringing her attention to the upcoming problem.

"Cherese, are you going home tonight?"

"Of course I am; what does that mean?"

Kalliah turned to join their conversation. "You can stay with us. We have a suite. Maybe you and Kyle could talk after things cool down."

"He's more talk than action. I guess he was trying to scare me." Charese replied sipping from her glass.

"Well he scared me. Are you sure things aren't a little over board with this fighting to make up shit."

Cherese didn't answer. Kalliah didn't want to give her the talk she really had for her. The night had been fun until Kyle arrived, she didn't see the need to make Cherese feel that they had abandoned her. Miles looked for help from Dante' and Stephon, who didn't want to add any comments to the bad air. Kyle approached the table and pulled out the chair on the opposite side of Cherese.

"Well, since no one wanted to invite me to the table, I guess you all thought I knew this seat was for me. Hello Stephon, Kalliah and Brianne."

Stephon and Kalliah mumbled their greetings. Brianne stopped talking to her other classmates when she noticed Kyle joined the table. She glanced at her watch glad it was close to eleven. She immediately excused herself from the conversation she was holding.

"Excuse me, Kalliah its pretty much over for the night. I'm going to say good night to a few of our friends, and I'll meet you in the lobby."

"No, wait for me, you're right. Good night guys are you all coming to the breakfast?"

Dante' spoke for himself, Miles and Stephon. "We'll be there."

Miles and Stephon smiled in agreement. Kalliah saw the opportunity to see what Kyle's intentions were.

"Cherese, will you and Kyle be coming to breakfast or are you still meeting us at the hotel tonight?"

"I don't know I have my car, and Kyle has his. We'll figure it out, and I'll give you a call."

Cherese hoped Kyle didn't pick up on their signal.

"Well okay call me; I'm sure we'll be up for a while."

Dante' watched Kalliah as she waved to others as she made her way to the lobby where Brianne promised to be waiting. Kyle stood guiding Cherese to her feet.

"Well gentleman, I can't say it's been a pleasure, and as usual, you've made me feel unwelcomed. No need for me and my wife to be in your company. We'll see you tomorrow night at the dance, right Cherese?"

Cherese stood willing to answer the question but felt the pressure as Kyle squeezed her wrist. She simply nodded her head not looking at the men. Miles noticed Kyle's grip and reached across the table offering to shake Kyle's hand.

"You may not think so, but it was good to see you both. I hope tomorrow's gathering will give us more time to talk. I think that's why you still feel unwelcomed. Listen man, we're beyond that shit from high school and just to prove it, why don't you come and hang out with us during the day tomorrow? Cherese can spend time with the girls, and we had plans on playing a little golf about midday. We really didn't have anything set in stone so it's just a day with the fellas, beers, drinks, just chillin'."

Kyle thought about the offer. It was a way to spend time with his sweet piece he had been making time for. Cherese wouldn't know the difference, and neither would they. It couldn't have been planned better. Miles handed Kyle his business card and told him to call for the address and tee time. Kyle shook their hands again and as Miles hoped, he didn't grab Cherese again.

Revelations

Dante' opened the passenger door of the car hoping to see Kalliah and Brianne pulling out of their parking spot. The parking lot exit was blocked with cars trying to leave by the only exit that wasn't marked with orange cones.

"Get in, I think I see them over there. I'll catch them outside the lot. Call her on your cell."

Miles backed into the line of cars behind him ignoring the horns that blared in response. Stephon watched the traffic through the rear window. "Come on out you got it."

"Kalliah, this is Dante', listen Cherese should be calling you. I convinced Kyle to spend the afternoon with us tomorrow so you and Brianne can get with her. Maybe we can prevent what we all know may happen."

"She's calling me tonight?"

"I don't know but look out for the call. Maybe you should call her."

"I don't know Dante'. Brianne doesn't want to be a part of it at all. She doesn't want Cherese to think the reason she's not talking to her is because she doesn't like Kyle."

"Why doesn't Brianne like Kyle?"

"Something from back in the day I'm sure. Can you call me back? I don't have my Bluetooth plugged in. Give me a few minutes."

"Sure."

"So what did she say?" Miles turned down the radio, so he and Stephon could hear.

"She doesn't know about Brianne talking to Cherese about Kyle. I didn't know Brianne didn't like Kyle."

"Yeah that goes back to the senior prom."

"Damn, what did I miss?"

"You damn near missed the prom."

"You're right man. Stephon didn't you come late?"

"Yeah, I should have stayed home."

Miles turned right and blew his horn. Kalliah spotted them and gave him the same signal. Dante' dialed her number again.

"Damn, man, give us a minute."

"What Stephon, what?"

"You making plans for the rest of the evening?"

"I don't think so, why?"

"I was gonna say we all could go to their suite and talk this thing over. If Brianne doesn't want to talk to Cherese, I'll keep her company while you and Miles talk to Cherese with Kalliah."

"I'll ask her if that's cool with them."

****

Cherese drove to her home with the music blasting. She didn't hear her cell phone ringing. She parked in her driveway knowing it would only be a matter of minutes before Kyle arrived. She grabbed her purse and rushed to get in the house.

It was more than an hour later when Cherese concluded that Kyle wouldn't be coming home. She took the wine and the glass she had been sipping from upstairs to the bathroom. A hot bubble bath would soothe her nerves. She convinced herself that if she relaxed, she could sleep throughout the night. The ringing of the phone startled her while she was disrobing, putting her nerves immediately on edge again.

"Hello."

"Listen, I'll be home late."

Cherese looked at the clock. She didn't think she was hearing her husband correctly. They left the hall at almost eleven, what did he consider late? She dared not ask him.

"Cherese are you listening?"

"Hmm."

"Hmm? Never mind, I'll see you in the morning. You sound like you're sleeping. Oh, by the way, your friends invited me for golf in the morning, so I guess you and Kalliah can have the day to yourselves. We'll hook up for the fancy evening."

"Thanks, I know you wanted to spend the day together before the dance." She responded sarcastically.

"Whatever. Did you take your medicine? You don't sound right."

"Have a good night Kyle."

Cherese hung up the phone. She didn't know what came over her, but she welcomed the rush being in control gave her. Kalliah was right she needed a way out of the marriage. Just as she headed to the tub her cell phone rang.

"Hello."

"Cherese, girl you okay?"

"Yeah, why?"

"I was just concerned and so was everyone else."

"Where's Miles?"

"He's here do you want to talk with him."

"Kalliah, we need to talk."

"Well he's here."

"No, you and I, alone. Kyle didn't come home."

"So why didn't you just come here."

"I just found out. I thought he was coming here, and apparently he wanted me to think that. He claims he's going to be with Miles tomorrow playing golf. I need to talk to Miles. I'll be there in the morning in time for breakfast. Maybe this is just my fate Kalliah; no child, no husband, and alone."

"Listen we'll talk tomorrow, here's Miles."

Cherese lit the aroma candles and poured another glass of wine. The buzz she had vanished while talking with Kyle, and she needed it to rest. She went to the medicine cabinet to take her prescribed nightly dose. Swallowing the pills she noticed how puffy her eyes looked. She didn't know how Miles could offer her any alternatives to her marriage knowing she was still sick.

"Hey Cherese?"

"Yes, I'm here."

"Are you okay?"

"Yes, I just want to know that you're not going to give Kyle any reason to suspect anything are you?"

"No, I just don't want him thinking he needs to push up on you. He won't know we've talked."

"Thanks."

"You're okay though?"

"Yeah, I'll see you guys in the morning."

"Cherese—"

"I know. I'll be careful."

****

Brianne stood out on the balcony looking onto the streets below. She didn't want her attitude to ruin the rest of the evening for anyone else. Seeing Kyle brought back memories she tried to forget. After years of therapy, she thought she had a grasp on her feelings of guilt. The night filled with old faces and conversations of past events set the stage for Kyle's grand entrance. Brianne almost lost what took years for her to regain, her self-esteem. It left the moment she saw him. Stephon stepped on the balcony careful not to startle her.

"Hey lady."

"Hey, did Cherese get here."

"She's not coming tonight. That's why I came out here. I really don't want to try to salvage the Taylor marriage. I see only one way out of it."

"Stephon, I don't want to be rude but..."

"I'm sorry. I shoulda asked was I interfering?"

"No, you're not. No, you're right; you are interfering if you're gonna talk about Kyle and Cherese."

"I thought you and Cherese were cool."

"We are; I don't want to deal with her and her husband."

"Understood, believe me, I understand totally. But Brianne just for my own peace of mind, did Kyle do something to you in high school."

Brianne turned around quickly and faced Stephon.

"Why did you ask that? Did someone tell you something tonight?" she asked, apparently shaken by his question,

"No, no, I just remember that you and Kyle didn't get along when we were in school."

"You noticed that?"

"Well it was after the prom. Your boyfriend was one of Kyle's friends right?"

"He wasn't what I would call a boyfriend, but we went to the prom together. Stephon did someone tell you something?"

"No, I just noticed that you and Kyle have been distant since then."

"So why did you pay so much attention to it?"

"Well, let's just say I had my reasons."

"Reasons?"

"Listen, it was a long time ago. I shouldn't have brought it up. That was years ago and it doesn't matter now."

"Maybe it does. It depends on what you know and why you won't tell."

"Brianne, my reason for noticing is only because you're fixed on not talking to Kyle. I just remembered you were friends in high school and after the prom; there was a big difference, that's all."

"Okay you're right. I don't like Kyle, and I don't care to be around him; let alone talk to him."

"Oh, okay, let's change the subject."

"Let's, how's your twins?"

"Getting big; I'm trying to get my world together for them. I'm filing for sole custody."

"Yeah I heard about their mother. She's getting married right?"

"That she is what about you? How's your career?"

Their conversation softened, and they sat together on the balcony getting reacquainted. Dante' looked at his watch and wondered if Angel was still up. It was a little after one and the thought of breaking her sleep calling her with not much to say, would have to wait. Kalliah came to sit by her friend.

"What's up?" Kalliah's question brought a smile to Dante's face.

"Nothin', I really hoped Cherese would have come here tonight then I could have dealt with Kyle a little better."

"What are you guys going to say?"

"I don't know. Talk about the women in our lives and hope he brings up his relationship."

"Then if he does, I mean, I don't think he'll openly admit that he's abusive."

"He will; he's arrogant."

"That's true; I wonder when we get into relationships why we wait until we can't stand it anymore before we plan to leave."

"We think we're in love."

"Yeah, that's the hard part, separating what is real love from the fantasy."

"Kalliah, do you love him?"

"Him who?"

"What's his name?"

"Are you trying to be funny?"

"No, do you love him?"

"Do you love Angelina?"

"I don't know."

Kalliah leaned back to look into Dante's face. "What does that mean?"

"It means I don't know. I'm not sure. We've got issues."

"All relationships have issues."

"I don't think all of them have issues like ours."

"Okay, who has the issue? I mean is it hers, yours or something you've created together."

"For the most part, I think it went both ways; you know like all relationships. But now it's my issue totally. I think I love someone else."

"You cheating?"

"No, that's just it, I don't want to cheat. I'm not that kind of guy. But if I love someone else, what do I tell her without her thinking, I'm cheating?"

"Wow. Uh, I'm not sure."

"What's up with you and Morris?"

"Maurice and I need a break. Issues, but I would say more his than mine. He's not attentive enough for me."

"Attentive?"

"Yes, we don't do things together like we did in the beginning, and he takes too much for granted. I haven't returned his calls in weeks, and every time he calls and I answer he acts as though everything is okay."

"Attentive. How could he not...?"

"Finish your thought."

"No, I'm just not understanding... you not getting the love and affection you deserve."

"I get that. Sex is not the problem."

"No you don't, that's not what I meant. Not physically baby, mentally, and emotionally. Damn. What do these guys think? Kyle buys Cherese, and he thinks that's enough and your boy gets his shit off and thinks that's all you want."

"And Mr. Dante' Jefferson is the perfect mate?"

"I hope I will be for someone. We all don't match with those we choose."

"Again, you're talking from experience? When did you become an expert in love and romance?"

"I won't accept that praise, but I've had a lot of time to think about my mistakes. One is to assume that's those things are all you need to have a perfect relationship. The other is to ignore your true feelings."

"And you told Angelina about these feelings?"

Miles came over to Kalliah and handed her the cell phone.

"Cherese will be here in the morning." He nodded to Dante. "You and Stephon about ready?"

"Yeah man. Get your boy; he's talking to Brianne on the balcony. What's up with him?"

Kalliah smiled as Miles only gave a smirk as the answer.

"What?"

"We think Stephon has always had a thing for Brianne."

"You're kiddin'."

"Nope, so now you know. But he won't admit it, not even to himself."

Miles walked to the balcony to say goodnight to Brianne. The three of them returned to Dante' and Kalliah standing at the door.

"Well tomorrow ladies." Miles opened the door and headed toward the elevator. Stephon said his "goodbyes" and followed leaving the door ajar for Dante'.

Kalliah spoke before closing the door. "Dante' call me in the morning."

Dante' leaned to whisper in Kalliah's ear. "Don't go to sleep, I really need to talk to you."

The Way We Were

Kalliah and Brianne talked until they both fell asleep. Dante's comments sparked a trip down memory lane and they both enjoyed reminiscing. As in high school, he had promised to call her, which made her an inquisitive teen until he would fulfill his promise. Brianne teased her about them rekindling their hidden love affair over the weekend. The sun peeped in from the balcony where the vertical blinds were still drawn back.

Brianne opened her eyes from the couch and smiled looking at Kalliah's position in the large recliner. Brianne thought about their hotel expense. "We paid one hundred and nineteen dollars for last night, and I didn't touch the bed. It won't catch me like that tonight."

Brianne's stirring about caused Kalliah to open her eyes slowly not welcoming any reason to wake up. She looked at her watch on her arm, which confirmed they both needed to get dressed if they were going to the class breakfast.

"Ooh damn, that chair didn't feel like that last night."

"Girl I just told myself for the money we're spending, I won't be on that couch again."

They both laughed gathering their belongings heading for the bedrooms. The conversation continued from a distance.

"Cherese is meeting us at the Sheraton?" Brianne yelled preparing to shower.

"I guess so, she didn't say."

"Kyle agreed to go with Dante' and Miles?"

"Bree you and I know that joker probably won't show up."

"That's what I'm saying, Cherese probably won't make it to the breakfast either."

"No, I think she'll be there. Kyle didn't come home and he probably won't be there when she leaves this morning. I know I would be leaving before his ass got there. I don't know how she does it, you know, him coming in from wherever. What is that shit about?"

"It's about intimidation. She probably went along with the little things thinking it made him look like a man. Now that shit has gone too far, and it ain't cute."

Brianne laid out two outfits to make her choice for the day's apparel. She was determined to be comfortable after a rough night on the couch.

"Bree, why won't you talk to her about it? You deal with those crisis situations, and some of them are Domestic Violence. I think you can get the point across to her."

"Kalliah, don't let Cherese fool you. I don't know what her plans are, but she has a plan. I'm worried about her."

"So if she has a plan, why are you worried? As a matter of a fact Miles said the same thing. He's worried about her being pushed to seeking revenge."

"I don't feel sorry for Kyle if that's what you think my worry is. I just hope she doesn't get caught killing his ass or someone else."

Kalliah turned on the shower. Brianne knew her words would make her think. Revenge was the best answer. Brianne wasn't willing to convince Cherese that Kyle didn't deserve whatever she had planned.

****

Dante' and Miles sat drinking coffee at the kitchen table while waiting for Stephon. He called saying he was on his way, but Miles was sure he stopped to see his boys.

"So what's up with you and Cherese man? You didn't want to talk about it around Stephon, but I know something's going on."

"Dante' we've been getting closer since she's been subjected to this abuse from Kyle. I guess you could say real close. I never told anyone because I didn't want the problems that would come with people assuming we were more than friends."

"So is it more than that?"

"For me, man yeah. I might as well say so. I've been sitting in the wings hoping that nigga would fuck up. I've had my relationships, but I always had an eye for Cherese. I missed the opportunity when she wanted to leave him and come live here."

"When was that?"

"Just before the miscarriage, I told her it wasn't right, and she needed to work things out if she could. I didn't know he was beating her down though until I got the call from the hospital."

"So she didn't fall."

"She fell, after he pushed her down the stairs. She had head injuries, bruises on her thighs, ribs and back, not to mention she lost her child."

"Was the child his?"

"Yeah man, that girl wasn't steppin' out on him. The baby was his. I don't think he wanted the child anyway. I don't understand it. The money is hers."

"What money?"

"The money that bought the home, the cars, his clothes, shit, until she got sick, she put him on the map."

"And he's cheatin' on her?"

"Always has been. If he's not running with the next piece that flashes, he's running the next drug deal. Anyway, she was in the hospital for some time; too long for the good brotha to be a devoted husband. A lot of her therapy was done at home as well as in the office. She began calling and crying about him wanting to leave her handicapped. I would go over for lunch and work with her. The mental therapy is ongoing. She blames herself for the miscarriage. She was doing better man, and then this joker decides he wants to be the devoted husband again. The cycle is starting over and it's back to the beatings."

"Damn. Cherese can't see it."

"Yeah, she wants to leave, but you know women."

"So she either wants to make it work or she wants revenge."

"Pretty much, I've been talking to air. I told her once she leaves, and she's sure it's over, I'm there for her. Cherese won't leave it alone, and it's eating at her. She's taking her meds and drinking, stressed, and not thinking straight. Man I got to get her out of that house."

"But Miles if she won't leave, what can you do?"

"I'm gonna tell her I love her. I'm gonna tell her she can stay at my place in Atlanta until this nigga is done."

"What? What you mean done?"

Dante' looked at his friend. The tears were rolling from his eyes. Miles used his napkin to clean his face.

"You heard that joker threaten me last night. I made a call. As soon as she leaves it will be done. We're both better off without him. I can't let him threaten me, and I'm supposed to be her protection."

"Miles, what if this shit backfires?"

"It won't. Believe me, it won't."

Miles got up from the table and went up the stairs without waiting for a response. Dante' took a deep breath his issues with Angelina weren't as bad as he thought.

****

Dante' took the opportunity to call Angelina while waiting. Miles was upstairs longer than he expected and Stephon still hadn't arrived. After the answering machine picked up at his home, he decided to try her cell phone again. She had not answered any of his calls, since he left Maryland. It was moments like these that caused him to feel she was still involved with someone else. Angelina was beautiful. Her Spanish heritage was obvious, and her beauty was complimented with her long hair and a sexy accent.

Dante's arousal by Angelina is what took his thoughts away from his undying love for Kalliah. Shortly after high school he and Kalliah agreed they would cherish their friendship. Neither wanted to chance it for what may have been a lustful moment. Dante' agreed only because that's what Kalliah wanted. Lately, he knew it wasn't lust. He truly loved her.

Angelina kept close to him after his last threat to leave her alone for good. After being arrested for assaulting the man he found her with in his car, it took her months to regain his trust. Now one year later, Dante's thoughts of their on again off again romance made him question why he proposed. Angelina's vacation with her friends was a test of trust, and his trip to Washington was his test of resistance. He couldn't hide the feelings he had for Kalliah. He had to make sure he wouldn't regret marrying someone else.

Dante' closed his phone without leaving a message. She would see the number and call him back. He didn't want to dwell on the possible excuses she would give. He needed a clear head to deal with Kyle.

****

Cherese answered her phone. She recognized Miles' number and was grateful she didn't have to whisper. Kyle didn't come home, and she had gotten up ready to join her friends for breakfast.

"Good mornin'"

"Hi Miles, you guys leaving for the breakfast now?" Cherese waited for Miles to answer. When he didn't she knew what he was thinking. "He didn't come home. It's all good."

"Did you tell him your plans?" Miles asked although he knew the answer.

"Miles that would stir trouble; I'm not sure I'm ready for that. If he finds out, I'll never be able to leave."

Miles listened to the same excuse she gave time and time again. He didn't understand Cherese's resistance to walk away from what was clearly abuse. He offered her his home in Atlanta, Georgia and she refused. Miles assured her Kyle wouldn't have access to her whereabouts and she could rest and get herself together without any worries. Miles made the offer originally being concerned for a friend. He made the offer now because he loved her.

"Alright, when you're ready it's there for you. Do me a favor though, if you can, start making a move, one way or the other?"

"What does that mean?"

"Even if you don't go to my place, you need to go somewhere. How about spending some time away from the house with Brianne and Kalliah? That wouldn't look strange, I mean with them being in town and all. Kyle wouldn't care where you were if he thought you were with them."

"Listen, I've got to get out of here before he comes. I'll see you at the breakfast." Cherese answered rushing him off the phone.

Miles hung up realizing his words would fall on deaf ears.

Dante' called again, leaving two messages on Angelina's cell phone. His phone rang interrupting his thoughts. The possibility of her cheating was becoming an abrupt reality. The ring tone told him she was finally returning his call.

"Good morning." Angel's voice sang in his ear.

"Where are you?"

"Wow, good morning to you too. I'm at my house." Angel answered trying not to snap. She was still upset about his intention to stay longer than his original plans.

"I thought you said you would be staying at my place."

"Dante', what difference does it make, and I didn't quite say that, you suggested it. I said I would check on your house and the mail."

Dante' was sure that Angelina's answer was a confirmation to his suspicions. She would use the time apart to be with someone. He thought after the engagement, he could trust her. Even if what she said was true, he didn't want to second guess her every move. Dante' had no answer and his desire to talk was fading quickly.

"How was the welcome reception?"

"Everything went well. We're waiting for Stephon to go to breakfast. We'll play a few rounds this afternoon."

"You took your clubs?"

"Yes, I'm on vacation."

"You take your clubs on business trips too. I'm glad you'll be relaxing though, you've been real tense lately. Did all your classmates show up?"

Dante' knew the question was leading up to her asking about Kalliah.

"So what are your plans for the weekend?" He asked changing the subject.

"Dante' answer the question please. Don't ignore me like that."

"Yes, everyone is here I guess. It seemed to be full. I don't remember everyone, so I would imagine there are some that didn't show."

"How's Cherese? Is she still with her husband?"

"Angel, you know I hate when you pretend. What, you gonna ask about everyone and get to Kalliah and talk shit? Stop, listen, I'll call you later."

The phone clicked. The dial tone followed. Dante' started to call back, but he knew she would say she didn't know what happened. He didn't understand why she asked questions that would upset her if he answered them. He wouldn't be calling her again until he knew what he wanted to do about their relationship.

****

The breakfast at the Sheraton was filled with memories and updates. Loud conversations and laughter between the alumni buzzed from table to table. Those who hadn't been in touch with each other for years exchanged pictures of families, weddings, and business cards. At ten o'clock members of the reunion committee reminded everyone the time of the dance. They extended the group well wishes until they were to meet again.

"Don't forget to bring any high school memorabilia. It will be great to see who has the most items after ten years. We have a lot planned for the evening. Those of you attending church on Sunday, please see Annette, sorry Annette, as well as those of you who are interested in making plans for a quarterly fundraiser, please sign the book she has. Remember the fundraisers will help the school get another gym."

Stephon and Miles were making their second round to the buffet which was filled with fruit, croissants, muffins, eggs, sausage, sage, bacon, and grits. There was a chef available to make pancakes or waffles on the griddle that was set up at the table with the butter and syrup. The reunion committee gave the alumni a beautiful setting to spend their time together.

"Are the boys okay?" Miles asked passing the syrup.

"Yeah, they wanted to come with me. I guess they know when I come, I usually take them out even if it's just to the store."

"So this weekend they'll miss out huh?"

"No, I'll go get them tomorrow afternoon. I know after the dance tonight it won't be early. Plus my apartment is a wreck, so I need the morning to get things in order."

"How's the car riding?" Dante questioned as he nodded to passing classmates.

Stephon convinced both Dante', and Miles that his car wasn't the one they wanted to sport for the day. It was a 2010 Altima, but it didn't compare to the 2011 vehicles that Dante' or Miles owned.

"It's good. Hey, did Cherese say what Kyle did last night after she got home?"

"He didn't show up. She hasn't seen him and to be honest I don't think we will either." Miles answered curtly.

"Did she seem upset about him not coming home?"

"No, it seemed like she wasn't worried, but she didn't want him to catch her leaving either. I told her to spend the day with Kalliah and Brianne."

Stephon looked toward the table and noticed the women talking. The conversation had them laughing, and if he didn't know better Cherese didn't look like she had been abused. The men walked to the table and ate as they listened to Dante' explaining why he was late for the prom ten years prior.

"It wasn't funny then but now, I still laugh about it." Dante' responded unable to hide his laughter.

"So let me get this straight. You went to pick her up with the limo driver and you guys had to wait while her dad told you about the facts of life?"

"Miles man she was so embarrassed she wanted to cry. Her mother kept trying to interrupt and every time she interrupted his drunk ass started the whole speech again."

Kalliah threw in the thought she had held over the years. "That's what you get for asking a girl from the other side of town."

"Yeah what school did she go to?" Cherese thought she knew most of the girls from the neighboring schools.

"She went to that Catholic school didn't she?" Stephon teased.

"No, she didn't go to any Catholic school. What made you think that man?"

Stephon smiled to himself before answering. "You know what they say. If she had been from a public school her father wouldn't have been beating you over the head with the sex talk."

Brianne agreed with Kalliah. "Dante' was out of his league, and her father knew his little girl had stepped to the wild side."

"If Kalliah said yes I would have been on time." Dante' raised his brow at Kalliah.

"No, 'cause my father probably would have given you the short version of the speech; 'Boy don't make me have to come looking for you'."

Everyone at the table laughed. The talk of their memories continued until the hour of eleven. The friends gathered their brochures and other items that had been passed out during the morning. Cherese gave Miles a look of desperation, and he escorted her to lobby ahead of the others.

"What's wrong?"

"I don't know what to expect. I'm sure he was with that bitch, but what is he gonna be like when I get home?"

"Why do you put yourself through this?"

"I can't Miles. I can't"

"You can't what Cherese?"

Cherese began to cry. Miles didn't move. They were approached by their other friends who immediately surrounded the two so no one else would see Cherese breaking down.

"Let's get her out of here. We can go to the suite. We've got her Miles. You guys go on just in case Kyle does show up to play golf."

Great Expectations

Stephon and Miles began to walk slower as they approached the fifth hole. Dante' was ahead of them visually setting up his shot. It took them a while to choose each club hoping they would close the gap Dante' had made in the score. It was clear that Dante' played more golf than they had time for. Dante' stood waiting, laughing at them as they paused before preparing to play the hole. Stephon asked about Kyle's absence before taking his shot.

"That joker didn't even call you. I guess after this weekend, he'll be back to beating her with none of us knowing."

"He can't think that. I mean the only one leaving town is Dante' you and I are still here."

"Listen, I've only been here since yesterday and there's one thing I can tell you. That girl is scared to death of what he'll do. Stephon is right Miles. Kyle will probably lay low the weekend and then beat her ass just because. Cherese won't tell 'cause his threats will demand her silence."

"Dante' the call is made. He won't last a week."

"What call?" Stephon hoped Miles didn't ignite something he would regret.

"Let's just watch it play out. I'm gonna talk to Cherese about her spending more time with Brianne and Kalliah. I'm sure they will too, after this morning's episode. He's got her scared even when he's not around. Whose turn is it?"

The sound of an approaching golf cart stopped Miles from taking his swing. Kyle stepped out of the cart with a bag of clubs and thanked the caddy, giving him a respectful tip.

"I'm glad I got all the information from you. I'm sorry I'm late. How is everybody this morning?"

A unison answer of "awright" came from the trio. Kyle explained he knew little about the game, and the clubs belonged to a friend who played the game often. Throughout the game, there was no way anyone would say the four men weren't mutual friends. They went to the club house to drink a few beers while waiting for a second tee off time. They knew the second game would be different.

****

Kalliah brought another glass of water to Cherese, who was lying on the couch. After they arrived at the suite, Cherese confessed she hadn't taken her medication and just needed to take it and relax. The relaxing moment led to a two-hour sleep. Brianne and Kalliah worked on their laptops and avoided any conversation that would cause them to misjudge their friend. When she woke up screaming, they both ran to her side.

"Drink slowly you must have had a bad dream."

"Cherese you've got to remember to take your medication. What were you dreaming about?"

"Thanks Kalliah. I usually remember. I guess with the morning excitement I forgot."

"Cherese I wasn't going to get too deep with this but going to therapy, taking medication and drinking, is not going to solve your problems. You really have to decide what's best for you; not your marriage. You may think that you can be silent and get through this but look at you. You don't get any rest. He's still beating you, and because of it, you're scared to death. Cherese I deal with women like you daily, their families, their children, and it never changes until they decide not to accept it any more. I don't want you to say I guided you into any decisions, but you need to decide for your physical and mental salvation."

Cherese continued to drink the iced water avoiding the questioning stares from her friends. Brianne reached from her seat and affectionately tapped Cherese's leg as she continued.

"We love you Cherese. I love you. You need to love yourself." Brianne left the room. She returned to her bedroom and closed the door leaving Kalliah and Cherese to talk.

"She's right. I know she is, but I have so much to lose. All we worked for over the years is in my home. My parents will never understand me leaving Kyle."

"Cherese you can't work and haven't worked in more than a year. Your marriage isn't a marriage. Remember you said Kyle is openly cheating. I don't think your parents will misunderstand that. You have to get yourself together. The last two years have been rough for you, and I'm so sorry I haven't been closer to you to help you through this. I thought it was the miscarriage. Cherese please even if you go back to him, get out of the situation long enough to clear your thoughts and regain your strength. You can't live like this."

"Kalliah, you're right, Miles and Brianne are too. I just don't know what or how to get out without him stopping me."

"Listen he wasn't around today, maybe we can get you out of there for a few days. I'll think of something. You just go with it. The weekend will go as planned, so he doesn't think anything of it, and I'll talk to him on Sunday. By then the guys will have spoken with him. Who knows? Maybe something will sink in. Cherese, but that means after being here with us, you won't be going back there."

Cherese's silence underlined Kalliah's fear. It would take time to convince her that she was in danger.

****

"Women set the tone for the relationship, but if you let them think they run things, your manhood is forever gone."

The men finished their second round of golf. They entered the clubhouse to eat and have a couple of beers. The afternoon remained friendly with no mention of Cherese or their marital problems. Dante' began the conversation on relationships after they placed their orders.

"Kyle's got a point. Some of these chicks don't want you to be the man in the relationship other than in the bedroom."

"C'mon Stephon. You're only agreeing with him because of what ole girl did to you."

"Yeah, shit how'd you let her leave you with two damn kids, and she's in another state ready to get married? If your ass was the man in the relationship, she would have taken those brats with her."

Dante' and Miles knew Kyle struck a nerve. They watched for Stephon's reaction.

"Yeah, you're a typical nigga, you know the type, you would have beat her ass and made her stay, or beat her ass and made her take them with her. Fuck the bullshit Kyle, I ain't the typical nigga. Maybe you understand and live by that shit, but I don't. Make a mental note, I love my brats and whatever that bitch doesn't want to do for them is all good with me. Beating love in her head won't work. She didn't love me or them. I wasn't pushing it. Do you push for love Kyle, or do you go blow for blow?"

"What?"

"Cherese wanting the perfect marriage, paying for your sorry ass to look like the man, even wanting your child; but that wasn't enough. You couldn't have her loving a child over you, giving all she had to a child. You wouldn't be the man. The typical nigga, that's what you are. You killed your kid, and if she doesn't get out of there you'll kill her."

Miles watched as Kyle took it all in. He appeared to be too calm listening to Stephon's accusations, which would have caused any man to react.

"Stephon, you've got a few things confused. But you being the bitch of your little group, carrying gossip instead of truth, doesn't surprise me. Cherese fell and lost the baby. We planned to start a family. It was that lost that has caused her to have this breakdown, and other episodes of anger, fear, and fighting. Man you name it, we've been through it. I know you guys think I'm the one at fault, but I've been dealing with this the best I can. Miles I know I've been a real ass with you man, but understand she's my wife."

"And when did that matter Kyle. You've been beating on her for months, even the night of the so called fall. You beat her ass Kyle, and I thought about killing you time and time again. You know what saved you, that same line, understanding she's your wife. Do you know why we invited you out? Cause she's your wife."

Dante' picked up where Miles left off. "So understand this. Either the beatings stop or we begin. We'll be coming at you from all angles; the street, your job, and the legal system. Your sorry ass won't know which way to turn. So man to man, we want understanding. You beat on Cherese. We'll be meeting you again."

Kyle stood to his feet. He reached in his pocket and took out his wallet. He threw a twenty-dollar bill on the table. "Fuck y'all. Like I said, if they think, they're in charge; you can't be the man. I decide what will and won't happen in my marriage and my house. Not her or her friends. You've stepped over the line fellas, friends or not. Miles expect her to call you crying, 'cause if I need to beat her ass to keep my house in order, I will. You punk ass mother fuckers don't rule me or my marriage. Thanks for lunch and the game."

Stephon, Dante' and Miles watched as Kyle walked out the door. Miles banged on the table. "Well we just put her head in the noose."

"Maybe not, he might have second thoughts. He definitely listened, which was more than I thought would happen. Stephon, brotha I'm proud of you I thought you were going to jump up and beat his ass right here."

"Being locked up does wonders for impulsive reactions. I can't afford any trouble. Miles you okay."

"Yeah, I need to warn Cherese."

****

The call to Kalliah from Miles came an hour too late. Cherese left with the intentions of getting herself together for the dance. She had no knowledge of their confrontation with Kyle. She needed to get a few items at the mall to complete her outfit before going home. Shopping with Kalliah and Brianne would make them all late. She promised she would call when she got home.

Kyle hadn't called her all day, and she was grateful for an entire day of peace. She got home a little before six and was surprised the house looked as it had that morning. After going through the house Cherese's nerves made her stomach queasy. Whenever Kyle stayed out for days, his return was a drunken stupor, and she was attacked physically before he retired for the night. Kalliah's call didn't ease her nerves any.

"He hasn't called?"

"No, I don't know where he is. Kalliah is it wrong for me not to care."

"No, hell no." Kalliah answered knowing what Kyle told Miles. She didn't want Cherese to feel guilty and stay home waiting for him to arrive. "So did you get what you needed for tonight?"

"Yeah, shit it's almost six thirty. What time are you leaving? If Kyle isn't here soon I'll have to meet you. Maybe I can leave my car at the hotel, and we all ride together."

"We won't be leaving until about eight or so. From eight until nine is the cocktail hour. Can you be here by eight?"

"I'll call you when I'm leaving. If Kyle comes, I'll let you know I'm leaving with him."

Cherese put the phone in its cradle and listened closely thinking she heard the front door. **"Great, now I'm going to be paranoid all night."**

Face to Face

Kyle turned his front door key at seven thirty. There wasn't enough time for him to get dressed, and that's the way he planned it. He could smell Cherese's perfume as it permeated throughout the rooms. He went in the kitchen, and the odor changed to that of fried chicken. Cherese had taken the time to leave dinner cooked to avoid his complaints of her night out. Kyle had other plans for the evening, and they didn't include the McKinley High bunch. He grabbed a chicken leg and climbed the stairs heading for their bedroom.

"Hey I'm sorry I didn't call. Time crept up on me before I knew it."

Cherese didn't know how to respond. Kyle wasn't drunk or angry. He continued to eat his chicken, passing her in the bedroom. He went into the bathroom to wash his hands. Cherese dared to ask him if he was still attending the dance. She could barely hear him speak as the water continued to run from the faucet.

"Listen hon, you go ahead. I shouldn't cause you to be late. I mean it will be another ten years for a reunion. We'll be back to our normal lives after this weekend. Call Kalliah and Brianne maybe you can catch up with them. Oh, you better drive I don't know where the night will take me."

"Are you going to be here when I come home?"

"I don't know babe. It all depends on how things go. I've got some things to attend to. Came up unexpectedly; you have a good night, and I'll see you in the morning." He searched his closet raising her suspicions.

Cherese knew that meant his plans were preset. She felt like undressing and curling up in the bed. There would definitely be questions about her husband, and she would break down before the night was over. The phone rang interrupting her prelude to depression.

"Cherese, its Kalliah." Kyle handed her the phone as he passed her going in the bathroom with clothes for himself to change into.

"Yeah, I'm ready. No. I'll meet you at the hotel. Thanks, I'll be right there."

Kyle gave her a smirk as she tossed the phone on the bed. He was too busy preparing himself for a shower to be concerned with her leaving. Cherese finished putting her facial makeup in her purse and slipped on her silver sandals. She purposely admired herself in the full-length mirror hoping Kyle would comment about her efforts. He kissed her cheek and told her to drive carefully. The bathroom door closed before she could answer.

Cherese got into her Lexus confused by Kyle's mood. The mere mention of the reunion being over and getting back to normal living scared her. What was normal to Kyle was torture to Cherese. She tried not to remember the last blow that caused her to fall to her knees and beg him to kill her. He laughed, backed away from her cowering position and left. That was the last time Cherese questioned where he was going or where he had been. It had been three months and now after his remark, Cherese was certain he would kill her if she ever asked again. She looked in the rear-view mirror ready to back out of the driveway. Her eyes threatened tears. Miles would call her Puffy. The thought made her smile. The name always made her think of P Diddy or Sean Puffy Combs, whatever he was calling himself these days. Cherese continued down the drive thinking, **"Its funny how what Miles says always touches me."** She wiped the tear carefully that ran down over her makeup. **"Ten years, I don't think so Kyle. This is a new beginning."**

****

Kalliah looked at her watch again hoping Cherese wouldn't be much longer. She and Brianne agreed; calling could cause a problem. When her cell rang Brianne came out of the bedroom, her appearance was more than Kalliah expected. She dropped her phone as she checked the text message. "That's what I'm talking 'bout." She smiled at her friend adding a nod of approval.

"What? Was that Cherese?"

"Yeah, and is that all you? Girl you 'bout to turn some heads. I love that outfit on you."

Brianne twirled in the middle of the floor to give Kalliah a full view. Her entire outfit was taupe with matching sandals. Her size was held perfect in the linen pants and Sheer Lurex Halter. The gold and pearl accessories gave it a rich touch, and her hair and nails were flawless.

"Girl, I don't know if I can stand it! You look so good Brianne."

Kalliah's cream linen tunic suit would turn more than a few heads also but they both understood that Brianne never put herself in the limelight. It was obvious she wanted to make a statement.

"Thanks. Let's not have Cherese come up here. We won't get to the dance if she comes up to talk."

Cherese was standing by the front lobby smoking a cigarette. She quickly disposed of it in the receptacle before they came out of the door. Blowing the smoke out of her mouth, she fanned the air. Brianne and Kalliah gave her a bewildered look, and she pointed to her car.

"I parked over there. My car or yours? I kinda figured we could take yours. I need to get my drink on. Brianne, girl, that outfit is really working. I like yours too Kalliah. I had this black pants suit for months. I couldn't make up my mind about what color I wanted to wear. I love black and silver though it has a rich look you know?"

Kalliah could tell Cherese was talking to keep them from questioning her about Kyle. She shook her head and took the keys out of Cherese's hand as they walked toward her car.

"Cherese, what year is this, I wanted a Lexus, but I would have never bought one this color. Is this pearl?"

"Girl, I don't know. One of those I know I was wrong gifts from Kyle. It's a 2010, shit if I was really getting one for every time he could use that excuse I would have a fleet."

Brianne got in the front seat only after Cherese insisted. She was trying to avoid being a part of the conversation about Kyle. "Kalliah, I can drive there if you want me to."

"I got it Diva. Cherese is he meeting you there?"

"No, and you know what I'm free tonight so no more talk about him for the evening okay?"

"Okay, no problem."

Brianne closed her eyes hoping Cherese meant what she said.

****

Dante' answered his cell and heard Kanye West playing in the background. He looked at the caller ID and didn't recognize the number. The LCD light went out indicating the call was disconnected. Miles came down the stairs and interrupted his thoughts of who the caller may have been.

"Let's go man."

"Stephon need a ride?"

"Naw, he'll meet us there. You okay? Hey did you get a chance to talk to your mom?"

Dante' hesitated thinking the call was from his mother's new cell number. Shaking the thought he answered the question. "Yeah, she's fine. I promised her you and I would visit tomorrow."

"Did you? Hey, that's fine with me. I hope it's in the afternoon. This may be an all-night thing. Come on man, you're dragging."

"Listen, let me call Angel. It might take me a minute or two." Dante' went into the kitchen dialing Angel's number. The phone beeped and he answered the second line.

"Hello?"

"Dante'?"

"Yeah, who's this?"

"Man, hold on." The silence on the other end was making Dante' angry. Angel's voice brought him little relief.

"Dante', hi it's me."

"Angel? What's wrong? Who is that guy?"

"My cousin, I'm at my Aunt's house."

"So why didn't you answer your phone?"

"I think I left it at the doctor's office."

"When did you go to the doctor's office?"

"Today, earlier; I wanted to tell you but I…."

"What is it Angel? What's wrong?"

"I'm pregnant."

"Pregnant?"

The line was silent again. "Angel?"

"Yes." Her voice was faint. Dante' could tell she

wasn't telling it all.

"So, what else is wrong?"

"Dante' what if it's not yours?"

Dante' was shocked; she didn't let him say it. He would have felt better if he had.

"Are you saying that's a possibility? I thought that shit was over."

"Dante', you know it's over. I love you. Please don't let this destroy us."

"Angel, damn girl, what am I supposed to say? How do we find out?"

"Find out?"

"What you don't want to know?"

"We're getting married Dante'. I understand your need to know, but I don't really want to know."

Miles came to the door after hearing part of the conversation. Dante' raised his index finger, and Miles stepped back out of the room giving him privacy again.

"Angel, we really need to talk about this. I can't, no you can't expect me to tell you I'll marry you, and I don't know whose child you're carrying. This ain't good Angel, and you know it. I'm not. No let me change that to, I won't talk about it now. What made you go to your cousin's house?"

"My mom suggested I go there and talk to my Aunt. I didn't want to talk about it. My Aunt still doesn't know. No one knows but you and my cousin. Dante' I told him the baby was yours."

"Angel, why?" Dante' couldn't believe he wanted to marry her. His hands were sweating he didn't want to talk to her anymore. "Angel, I can't keep doing this. I gotta go. I'll call you tomorrow."

"Dante', promise me you won't do anything until we talk."

"Do anything?"

"Yeah, just promise me."

"The same way you promised me? Yeah, you got that."

Dante' hung up the phone.

Letting Go

Stephon made his way through the crowd to the bar to order Brianne's drink. Dante' and Miles walked onto the balcony overlooking the city. The reception was held on the top floor. The entire floor and penthouse were reserved for the gala event. White sheer drapes and balloons with white roses and rose petals in them added an air of elegance.

Stephon looked around the dance floor watching his classmates as they danced like they had many Friday nights during their four years of school together. Stephon asked the bartender for Grey Goose on the rocks to go with Brianne's Apple Martini. He smiled as she danced toward him in the middle of the floor.

"Would you like to dance?"

The music was beginning to mix with the three Martini's and continuous compliments about her outfit. Brianne's self-esteem had reached a new level.

"Sure."

They placed their drinks on the table where Cherese and Kalliah sat watching and returned to the floor. Brianne was light on her feet for a big girl. The couple danced in sync listening to the cheers from all who danced around them. The music went from hip-hop to club and then the pace slowed allowing old lovers to become reacquainted. Brianne was sure that was their cue to leave the floor.

"Can a brotha get close?"

Brianne was taken aback. Stephon held her gently as the rhythm rocked them. The music lulled Brianne as she felt herself relaxing, putting her head on his shoulder. Stephon readjusted his embrace comforting her with his touch. She hadn't danced slow or close with anyone since high school. It was another thing she avoided. The whispers in the ear, the warm breathing on the neck brought back the night of bad memories from the prom. Brianne stopped moving as the tears began, to roll down her face. Stephon kissed her cheeks gently.

"C'mon let's get some air."

The two walked out onto the balcony finding an area with two chairs facing the twilight image of the city.

"Are you feeling okay? Can I get you anything?"

Brianne's answer was barely above a whisper. "No, thank you. I'm sorry I didn't mean to ruin your moment."

"What moment? Oh, girl please; I didn't have a moment dancing with you. Is that what you thought?"

Tears began to flow again, and Brianne made no effort to stop them. Her cheeks glistened, and Stephon used his index finger to catch her next tear.

"Baby, what's got you so upset?"

"Stephon, I've held this shit for years and the more I want it to remain buried the more it resurfaces inside me."

"So what is it? If it's upsetting you this much you need to let it go. Is it something I did or said?"

"No, it's not you. Aw lawd, Stephon it's just …"

"Just say it."

Stephon waved for the barmaid, asking her to get a few napkins for Brianne. "Do you want a drink?"

"Yes, an Apple Martini please"

Stephon ordered another drink as well. He pulled his chair around so he could face Brianne. "Brianne I want you to tell me what's wrong. Does it have something to do with your job, your health, what?"

"I wish it was that simple. You know that I went to the prom with Kyle's friend Wayne. Anyway, I thought all along it was a setup, you know another joke on Brianne. Everyone had an idea about three weeks before the prom I didn't have a date. Cherese was going with that guy from college, you know her on again off again friend, and Kalliah was going with Curt. I didn't even have a prospect. Anyway, Wayne had teased me most of the year and we had been out a few times. He was cool but when he got with Kyle and the rest of them, he wasn't shit. Neither were they."

"Wayne went to Dunbar right? I only remember him vaguely."

"Yes, he died in a car accident about three years after we graduated. I think they all played ball together. It was about four of them, or it's only the four of them that have affected my life forever."

Stephon looked puzzled but didn't question her statement. The barmaid brought back their drinks, and Brianne took her glass drinking more than half before she continued.

"The night before the prom Kyle and his girl, I forgot that cows name too, they both came to my house. I should have known something was up then. Anyway, they came by to tell me about the plans that were made for after the prom. Kyle's girl was having a party, and I was welcomed to come along with Wayne. I didn't even question if Wayne knew about it. All went fine until after the prom. Kyle's girl told me the guys went to get the liquor for the party, and we would meet them there.

We went to some penthouse in Maryland with people I didn't recognize, supposedly friends of Kyle's. Anyway, they had food, drugs, and music. My dumb ass chalked it up as, what they said, a party. I asked for Wayne a few times, and they said he was on his way. Kyle and three others came in with the bags I thought had liquor in them. He came over and said Wayne went home. I asked him why. He just smiled."

The tears began to flow again as Brianne downed the rest of her drink. "Of course my question was how was I getting home? Kyle said when he got ready for me to leave; he'd make sure I got there."

"You and Kyle were cool in high school?"

"No, he was cool, or I thought he was with Wayne. They were into some old 'you my boy, but you do what I say do' type shit. Wayne's dealing with me was not allowed by the boys. That's why he only dealt with me off and on. You know on the sneak so his boys didn't know. Anyway, Wayne got his ass beat after the prom for being with me, and I was in for what they considered fun."

"Brianne, you don't have to continue. I don't want you to go into this; you don't have to tell me."

"No, I want somebody else to know this shit. It's been eating at me for years."

Stephon reached for her hand. He wasn't sure if it was to support her, or to keep him still as she spoke. Brianne held his hand tightly before she spoke.

"Kyle went to three of his friends, and they laughed and pointed at me. I got up looking through the people for Kyle's girl. Kyle must have known that was who I was looking for 'cause, he stopped me in my tracks. He told me she went home 'cause no woman of his would be partying and giving up ass to just anyone. I tried going for the door but was stopped by another one of his so called boys."

"None of the females tried to stop what they were doing, or speak up, knowing you wanted to leave?" Stephon asked trying to visualize what she was saying.

"They were too busy getting high, laughing, dancing or fucking. Right in the open; on top of the couch, on the floor, two on one, girl to girl; it was a damn orgy. I didn't know nothing about that shit. Shit I was a virgin, just graduating high school; it was my fucking prom night."

Brianne broke down completely. Stephon stood, not knowing what to say. He helped her to her feet so he could hold her. Brianne's voice was muffled by Stephon's chest as she cried while describing her torment.

"Kyle told the guy to take me in the back. Something about he owed Malik and Talib a round before I would be going home. Again, my dumb ass thought he was going to come to this back room and get me when he was ready to leave. I didn't know what the round was."

Brianne stepped away from Stephon and turned holding on to the balcony railing. She continued talking while looking over the city.

"The room was dark and soft music was playing. Kyle's sidekick told me Kyle would come and get me when he was ready. I took a deep breath as my eyes adjusted to the darkened room. There was a king-sized bed and a chair in the room. A light under the door near the closet caught my eye. I opened it only to find a bathroom. I began to relax thinking Kyle knew it wasn't my kind of party. It must have been thirty minutes later when the first of four came into the room. I had sat in the chair daring not to touch the bed for fear of falling to sleep."

Stephon noticed the tears were welling up in her eyes. He put his hand on hers as she clinched the railing tighter. Stephon felt each of her words as she described being raped and teased by four of Kyle's friends.

"They just kept saying they wanted to know what Wayne felt while riding a big girl. They wanted to know what Wayne tasted, did he go down like this; did he do it like that? The third one shouted while busting his nut that wasn't nothing better than virgin pussy. Kyle and the rest must have been at the door. Kyle cut on the lights and that's when they saw the blood. It was all over them, me and the sheets. Sperm and blood; I screamed for what I thought was to be the last time but Kyle jumped on me and covered my mouth with his. I shut up scared to death. Kyle called for Malik.

Malik never came to the door, and one of the other's who had their round with me told Kyle the rule was if he didn't want his, it was up for grabs. Kyle told him grab it then, 'cause I was Wayne's girl, and he couldn't fuck with me like that."

"So Kyle never touched you?"

"No, only to shut me up, that's when he put his tongue in my mouth. Anyway, the one who had just got up was rubbing himself saying he wasn't through. Kyle told them both to hurry up 'cause my nasty ass had to get home. They did what they were told. It lasted for another ten minutes. They took turns busting what they thought was the best. They didn't use condoms, and the contest was to pull out and watch the sperm flow. I tried fighting but after fighting each round I had little defense. I guess they were right, I just gave it up."

"Who told you that?"

"That's the lie that went through Dunbar High. Wayne never spoke to me about it. I didn't see him again until after our graduation. He said he didn't know nothing about a party, and he heard I gave it to up to them 'cause he didn't really want it. I've hated Kyle ever since. I never saw those other guys again. I don't even think they went to Dunbar. Anyway, the rumors or whispers continued. By the time I was over the trauma the truth was buried. When Cherese first got with Kyle, I wanted to tell her. Even then Cherese was and still is so insecure about herself I didn't want to hear her say 'I wanted her man'.

I've had problems coming home knowing that my Aunt and cousins wouldn't believe me then or now. Not to mention coming home only holds bad memories. To be honest, without Kalliah and you, I didn't have any good memories in D.C."

"I guess things went that way for a reason. I'm a little older now, and I've been to prison. I think I would have really hurt Kyle if I knew what he had done to you. Brianne, I've held a spot for you in my heart since our sophomore year."

"Stephon, you don't have to feel sorry for me."

"I really feel sorry for myself. I talked myself out of asking you to the prom. You know, wanting to take the girl everyone talked about instead of ... damn girl." Stephon couldn't finish his words.

He turned and walked toward the barmaid and stopped before getting to her. Brianne walked up behind him. The pain that Brianne shared had Stephon in tears. They held each other letting the silence speak between them.

****

"So baby what do you want to do? I can't make you leave your...."

"Miles, I don't have anything I've lost it all."

"Whatever it is you're not going to make up your mind tonight. Can we just enjoy the night?"

"Are you suggesting....."

"Cherese, I'm not suggesting. I'm saying it. I can go back with you. I'm sure Dante' doesn't mind driving my car; he can come back and get me in the morning. You can stay with Kalliah and Brianne tonight, or that's how the story will go. Stay with me tonight Cherese, let me show you what I know you deserve. Spend the night in my arms. If tonight is all you can give me and decide never to venture down that road again, I won't complain."

"Miles I don't want to go home, but what if Kyle suspects something?"

"Kyle knows I love you. He always has known, and I think he tortures us both for it. He knows you won't leave him 'cause, he thinks you still love him."

"Miles, I do love…"

"No, you love the idea of marriage. You love being called Mrs. Shit, become Mrs. Miles Baker, be my wife. Baby marriage has so much more than Kyle has given you. Look I've waited not wanting to push you, but I can't let him destroy you. Give me tonight, and let me give you forever."

Cherese closed her eyes as she felt Miles getting closer to her. He kissed her slowly teasing her knowing she wanted more. Miles respected her too much to kiss her in public that way. They separated and smiled as the music's pace caused other couples to part dancing to a new beat. Cherese threw her hands in the air and turned giving Miles a view of her perfect figure as she wiggled. As she backed her body into him dancing to an ole school jam, she allowed her butt to taunt and tease him, he got the message. It was time to leave. He touched her waist and closed his eyes as her hips moved in a circular motion. Miles leaned forward to whisper into her ear.

"So are you going to the suites?"

"If that's where you want me to be."

"Make the call to Kyle then, so there won't be any problems. I'll meet you at your car."

"I don't know if Kalliah and Brianne are ready."

"Are you ready?"

Cherese turned to face Miles. She stopped dancing and led him off the floor. Cherese went to the ladies' room to make the call to Kyle. Miles returned to the table where Dante' and Kalliah were laughing and talking.

"Is she okay?"

"Yeah, she's calling Kyle. Man you take my car when you're ready to leave. I'm riding with Cherese in her car."

Kalliah didn't understand. "She's letting you take her home?"

"She's not going home, not tonight. She'll be spending the night with you guys at the suite. I'll be getting a room there too. If Kyle looks for her, which I doubt, the car will be there. He won't look for my car so it won't matter."

Kalliah got up to go to the bathroom. She couldn't believe Cherese was letting go. She opened the bathroom door and didn't see Cherese.

"Rese, you in here?"

"Yeah girl give me a minute. Come round the other side."

Kalliah followed Cherese's voice, which led her to a sitting lounge away from the toilets and sinks. The area was quiet and Cherese was dialing Kyle's cell number for the third time.

"I don't know who he's talking to, but it's going straight to voice mail like he's on the other end."

"Is he home?"

"No, I tried that line first. Oh wait, I think I got through now."

Kalliah went to the other side to give Cherese a little privacy.

"Hello, Kyle?"

"What's up?"

"I'm still at the dance. It's really laid out nice. I was going back to the suite with Brianne and Kalliah. I wanted to let you know."

"Yeah, listen, the cops may want to talk to you. You don't know shit, if they call or come by the house tomorrow."

"Where will you be tomorrow?"

"That ain't important, the less you know the better. I made some moves tonight, and they may have me caught up for a minute. I ain't bringing the shit to the house so don't go tripping. Just do what I said. If they ask you don't know shit."

"Well that's for damn sure. I'm always the last to know."

"Cherese you been drinking heavy or something? You know you ......fuck it."

"Know what?"

"On those damn meds."

"I didn't take none of those damn meds tonight, and yes I've been drinking that's why I said I'll be with Brianne and Kalliah. I'll be home in the morning."

"So you got clothes and shit with you?"

"I got credit cards."

"Bitch, don't get it twisted. Just do what I said. Don't talk to the cops, or you won't have shit. Remember if I lose it all, so do you."

"Are you home?"

"No, that's too obvious for them. I'll be home in a few days."

"Days?"

"Listen if this shit works out, baby, we'll be sitting on top of the world."

"Kyle, I—" Cherese thought about Miles' offer. She could pack and get out while he was laying low.

"You what?"

"Nothing. I'll talk to you tomorrow. I'll probably stop at the house and get a few things between now and tomorrow. I'll hang out with Kalliah and Brianne and miss the cops completely."

"Listen just stay in touch. I'll stop by the house Monday or Tuesday, if it's all good I'll stay home."

"Alright." Cherese hung up the phone wondering what Kyle had done during the past few hours.

"Kalliah?"

Cherese put her phone in her purse and decided to use the bathroom before leaving. Kalliah was coming out of one of the stalls.

"You guys are going to meet us at the suite?"

"Listen, oh yeah. But tomorrow I'm going to the house and get a few things. I think fate has caught up with his ass."

Cherese went into the empty stall and continued her thoughts. "I'll call you in the morning before I go to the house though."

Kalliah listened not fully understanding Cherese's sudden courage. "So you're okay for tonight?"

"Yeah girl, safer than I've been in years, I think I'm going to stay that way." Cherese mumbled to herself although Kalliah could hear her. "Safer than before, that's for sure."

****

Kalliah returned to the table which had apparently changed to a private setting for her and Dante'. "Looks like everyone is making their way to the cars." She sat to finish the drink she left on the table.

"Stephon and Brianne left too. They looked shook up, but they left together." Dante' drank the last of his drink from his glass while scanning the room.

"I always thought about the two of them getting together. I mean, Miles surprised me after we graduated saying, he always liked Cherese but Stephon always had a thing for Brianne. He teased her enough, saying she was like a sister, but I always knew it was more than that. Brianne doesn't talk much about dating or her male friends, but Stephon always had a way of making her feel good."

"And what about you? Surprise me. Tell me who of our friends puts you at ease." Dante' asked causing Kalliah to smile.

"I guess that would be you, but we agreed a while ago not to chance our friendship, you do remember that don't you?"

"We were kids then and just like our friends maybe we ought to reevaluate our relationship."

"Dante' what are you talking about?"

"Us, is there a chance that we could reach another level? Lovers always start as friends, and we've been friends for damn near a life time."

"What about your girl?"

"What about your boy?"

"That's almost a done deal. Answer me, don't duck the question. Are you saying your relationship is done too?"

"I'm saying that she is not the topic, we are. I'm not trying to work her into this equation."

"There can't be an equation if you have someone else. I think you have some baggage to sort out."

"My love for you is a part of that baggage. I can't keep pretending I don't love you. It's more than just a friendship for me. I can't love someone else wondering if I'm making a mistake, because I do love you. Hey, let's get out of here. Can I interest you in relaxing with me?"

"Relaxing?"

"Yeah, c'mon Kalliah, tell me you don't feel what I feel."

Kalliah grinned and stood. Dante' followed her lead.

Confrontations

Kalliah was glad Dante' wanted to talk. They shared the same feelings. When she heard he was in what could be a serious relationship, she knew she wouldn't be able to replace his friendship. Men always wanted to be more than friends, and most women didn't want the opposite sex continuing any type of relationship with their man. Kalliah had questions of her own about how they would handle their relationship, now her questions could be answered.

Dante' opened the wine and poured it slowly over the ice cubes in each glass. Kalliah sat back on the couch adjusting herself for comfort and took a sip.

"Did Brianne say anything to you?"

"Anything like what? She just said she was riding with Stephon, and they would be here later. It's just one thirty I guess they'll be here shortly. Why are you worried? Your boy won't try nothin' slick, will he?"

"They're grown." Dante' laughed. "Brianne can handle herself, I'm sure."

"You know she can. So tell me, I know it's not my business, but you were talking like you were serious about this friendship versus love stuff."

"It's been on my mind a lot lately. We're not getting any younger and to be honest, Angel and I have had quite a few off and on moments. Kalliah, I really haven't had an open relationship with anyone other than you and my mom. You know, we can talk or joke about anything. I miss that. I want that in any long-term relationship, especially a marriage."

"You're thinking about marriage?"

"Don't you, I mean, I know you think about a family the nice house, and a good career. C'mon girl you've dreamed about it over and over. I just can't get a clear vision on whose face is under the veil."

Dante's vision had been distorted before Angel's call. Now he could only see himself lifting the veil, and it slowly descending to the floor meeting the hem of a beautiful white gown.

"You never thought about marrying Angel?"

"I did. But I don't think she's trustworthy." Dante' wanted to change the topic, or at least not discuss his issues with Angel. Kalliah could tell the conversation was making him nervous. She wondered how close he had gotten to the altar before finding out his Angel didn't meet his expectations.

"A marriage definitely has to have trust. I don't think I ever thought of marrying anyone. I thought of the concept, but it's funny I ….."

"You what, go ahead say it." Dante' hoped they were having the same thoughts. Maybe her vision included him.

"No. Forget it. Can you pour more wine please?"

He got up to pour the wine and Brianne and Stephon came through the door.

"Hey, is Cherese and Miles here? I saw her car."

"No, well yes. Miles got a room here."

Dante' and Kalliah saw Brianne's response. She left Stephon standing in the middle of the floor. Stephon followed her without any explanation.

"What's up with them?" Dante' asked, watching them retreat to the bedroom.

"That's your boy, you tell me."

Dante shrugged his shoulders and continued.

-"Anyway, tell me what do you see when you think of marriage."

"You won't let that go will you."

"Alright do you see Morris?"

"Maurice, and no I don't see him."

"So the face is blank or what?" Dante' sat next to her moving as close as the couch would allow. Her smile told him she wanted him, and he leaned in and kissed her. Kalliah held her wine glass higher, being careful not spill it. Dante' reached and took the glass from her hand as he kissed her deeper. Their bodies sunk into the assorted pillows on the couch. Kalliah opened her eyes and gently pushed Dante's shoulders. The kiss ended with the promise of more.

"Alright, so I see your face. I have for years; but listen, that doesn't mean anything."

"Say what you want." Dante' stood up and pulled Kalliah up from the couch. "I want you too I want our relationship to take another step. I know what we said but girl you've been on my mind for years. You've got me held captive."

Kalliah smiled, she knew Dante' was at a loss for words. She could feel the warmth of his hand in hers. The wine made her mind up for her. She led him into the bedroom where they both could get relief.

****

Miles smiled watching Cherese walk from the bed to the bathroom. Her bronze toned body made his mouth water. He rolled on his back looking at the ceiling as his manhood agreed he needed her touch again. The pulsating jerks from his penis made him want to call her name. He fondled himself anticipating her warmth and wetness.

Cherese walked toward the bed giving Miles a slow frontal view. Her nipples stood erect. She had no idea that her hormones would react to anyone other than Kyle. They had been married for seven years, and she hadn't had a different sexual partner since her sophomore year in college. Miles touched spots she didn't know existed.

Cherese got into the bed with a condom in her hand. She ran her hand over his assisting him in putting it on. She mounted him slowly teasing herself. The feeling of guilt crossed her mind once since they agreed to a night of pleasure. As he slowly took off her clothes she wondered how women cheated on their husbands and went home to them as though nothing happened. As he inserted his fullness into her, she understood.

As the pace caused her to relax, she couldn't imagine having sex with Kyle again. He didn't desire her and told her so as he humped his way to each orgasm. Her wifely duties weren't expected often but when they were she felt like a prostitute that hadn't been paid.

Miles rolled her off him gently putting her on her back. He kissed her lips and continued down her neck. Cherese's body trembled beneath him, and his touch eased her into feelings she never had before. She held his penis and inserted its head hoping he would push himself further. Miles let the head of his manhood tease her entrance. As it throbbed, he patiently waited to continue. Cherese wanted to beg him, but bit her lip and moaned. Miles took the cue and penetrated her slowly as her muscles relaxed. He then embraced her for the ride. Their pace increased as the sound of Cherese's moaning became the music they both needed to hear.

Miles exploded as the beads of sweat on his bald head told him the mission was complete. He remained still allowing Cherese to move back and forth completing her own orgasm. As he kissed her he pulled back gently.

Miles got up to relieve himself and remove what was the second filled condom. "Can I interest you in a shower?"

"Yes, I'd love to shower with you."

****

Stephon and Brianne fell asleep on the bed. The Martinis and Grey Goose eased them into slumber shortly after they arrived at the suite. Stephon felt Brianne sit up and opened one eye to check her mood.

"Why you looking like that?"

"Well, usually when you wind up sleeping with a woman and don't remember going to bed it can mean one of two things. One, you both were drunk. Two, you had sex, and it wasn't that good. Now if she gets up before you, and it wasn't good, you got to be ready to haul ass."

Brianne started laughing. Stephon continued with his reasoning.

"On the other hand, if you both were drunk you don't remember how it was. It gives you another shot at it."

"So I guess you're saying you want another shot?"

"No, my ass wasn't drunk I didn't get a shot. So the way I see it, you owe me at least two."

Brianne continued laughing as she went into the bathroom and closed the door. She didn't think Stephon was serious, and he was more than considerate not making an attempt. She wasn't drunk when they went to sleep. Brianne listened to Stephon breathe for more than a half an hour before she dozed off.

The conversation about Kyle and the prom night ended when Brianne agreed she would tell the others when they met up at the suite. Cherese and Miles never showed, and Brianne was okay without talking about it again.

"Bree? Are you okay?"

"Yeah, do you need to get in here?"

Stephon didn't answer, and Brianne came out of the room to find him still lying across the bed. The thought of a relationship with Stephon crossed her mind twice over the course of the night and watching his chest rise invited her to join him. Brianne's wall was breaking. Stephon knew her secret and hadn't criticized or blamed her for 'giving it up'. He only asked one question. He wanted to know did she feel better releasing the secret that had a hold on her emotions. She couldn't answer him because she didn't know how she felt. She was fine until she thought about Cherese and Kyle, or went to visit her family. No one else knew about that night, and if she could keep it that way she would.

Stephon told her Cherese should be told. Her friends would want to know. Dante, Miles, Cherese and Kalliah loved her and would always be her friend. They didn't say much more before Stephon closed his eyes.

Brianne looked at the clock. It read eight thirty. There was no sign that anyone else was up in the suite. She lay back down and Stephon turned repositioning himself so she could move closer to his bare chest.

"Relax. We'll have more moments like this. Close your eyes and relax."

Brianne didn't answer. They slept until eleven.

****

Dante's reaction to Brianne's shocking account of her prom night experience was the same as Stephon's. First, he felt anger and then pain. Kalliah was crying and hadn't stopped since she realized the story was leading to her best friend being raped. They allowed her to finish, as they took deep breaths trying to keep their composure. Kalliah got up and went to the bathroom unable to control her emotions. Stephon joined Brianne on the couch and held her close to him. She wiped her tears but kept her head up proud that she could finally tell the story without breaking down as she had done before.

When Kalliah returned, Dante' handed her a glass of orange juice. She took the glass and sat on the other side of Brianne on the couch.

"Why didn't you say something before now?"

"What was I going to say? It would have made things worse. Who knows, you guys may have felt like others in that damn school."

"Others like who? Brianne, we didn't know this happened." Kalliah looked at Dante' and Stephon hoping they didn't know what went on that night.

"No we didn't know about it, I don't think it got back to McKinley." Dante's words were reassuring.

"Well my cousins knew, and my aunt didn't want to hear it, since I didn't tell her that night. I went to Planned Parenthood about a week later and got tested. That was another ordeal. They called my aunt because of the bruises, and of course, they thought that I was being abused at home. The nurse threatened my aunt thinking it was my uncle and then when she found out he wasn't living with us, she accused my cousins. Of course, my aunt thought the accusations were mine. Something I made up to cover for some boy I was "laying up" with. To tell you guys the truth, I think that was more traumatic than the rape. I needed my aunt to believe me, talk to me, console me or even look at me. She called me a whore most of the time when she got mad. As soon as I could I left what you all thought was a loving home."

Dante' couldn't understand Kyle's actions. "What does Kyle say when he sees you now?"

"Nothing, you've seen him. He looks through me as I do him. I deal with it only because of Cherese. I love you guys like the family I didn't have, and that includes Cherese."

"Wow, I can't believe he has the balls to act like it never happened. I mean I knew you didn't like him, but I thought it was because of the shit between him and Cherese."

"Dante' that ain't none of my business. I talked to Cherese before she married him. I asked her about signs of abuse, emotional or physical. I came from the angle of my job, so she wouldn't suspect anything. I told her everyone asked those questions when they worked in my field. She denied it and told me I would be the first to know if he showed signs. We hugged, and she walked down the aisle to her "happily ever after." I think she called Miles when Kyle started his shit with her. The rest is history."

"What is Cherese gonna do when Kyle finds out about her and Miles? "According to her Stephon, Kyle won't know. He'll be away until Wednesday."

"Wednesday?"

"She called this morning saying she would see us here later this afternoon. She was going to get a few outfits and stay here with us until Kyle called her saying he was going home."

Stephon heard what Kalliah was saying, but he had a hard time processing Kyle staying away from his own home and Cherese not questioning it. Miles or no Miles, Kyle was into more than just trouble with another woman.

"Did Miles call?"

"No, not yet."

"Man you seemed worried."

"Dante' just call him."

Dante' didn't ask any more questions. He dialed the number on the phone.

"Hello, Miles? It's Dante', damn you still sleeping? Where are you? Oh, so when….Yeah….alright. You know what you're doing. Yeah, yeah that's good in a few, yeah later." Dante' hung up the phone and saw his friends staring at him.

"Noisy asses, look at you, you're frozen in time waiting to get the scoop." Dante' teased.

"Dante' where's Miles?"

Dante' smiled. "He's good he's leaving here in about forty-five minutes. Cherese left already. Stephon you brought clothes with you?"

"No, I've got to go and get my boys why?"

"I think Cherese and Miles need to know about this too."

"Well I'll talk to Cherese when she comes here. Kalliah you'll be here right?" Brianne was feeling better but still needed support.

"Yeah Brianne, will you be okay? Listen this is some shit. Does anyone know how Cherese or Miles may take this?"

"Look, Stephon and I can talk to Miles. What time are you picking up the boys?"

"I'll ride by there, after we talk to Miles." Dante' and Stephon stood preparing to leave. Everyone kissed each other goodbye. Brianne held on to Stephon's hand pulling him away from the door where her comment couldn't be heard.

"Thank you."

"For what baby?"

"Being you, I mean being a friend."

"Say I can be more."

Brianne didn't answer. She didn't know how.

"Thank you." Stephon broke the silence speaking with a smile.

"For what?"

"Your silence gives me a chance. We'll be fine you'll see. It will take time, and I've waited this long. We both have wounds that need healing." Stephon kissed Brianne catching the attention of Dante' and Kalliah.

"Hey, whoa, what's up with this?" Dante' smiled, winking at Kalliah.

Brianne blushed and pushed Stephon toward Dante' and the door. "He's crazy that's what."

"Looks like you both lost your minds." Dante' replied shaking Stephon's hand as they walked toward the elevator.

****

Cherese found her home secured but empty. It was obvious that Kyle had been back and took items out of the house. The clothes in the closet had been snatched off the hangers, and the suitcases were scattered on the floor. Cherese began to sob. She didn't know if her tears were from anger, fear, or the reality that her marriage was over. She wiped her eyes and kicked off her shoes while stripping to her bra and panties. The comfort of walking through the house picking up out of place items in next to nothing gave her the touch of freedom that she hadn't enjoyed for years. She knew Kyle wasn't about to come in the door arguing, accusing her or demanding sex. She sat on the couch and wondered what trouble he had gotten himself into.

It took more than an hour to put the house in order. Cherese began packing and then had second thoughts about leaving her home. There was no longer a need to run. A sudden calm came over her; Kyle wouldn't be back. She was certain of that. She ran up the stairs carefree and when the phone sounded, it scared her into reality. Kyle would control her from anywhere. Depression took its place again as she answered the phone.

"Yes."

"Hey, are you alright?"

It was Miles. Cherese sat on the bed to talk. "He's not here. Miles he took enough clothes to be gone for months. It looks as though he attempted to move out."

"Did he say he was moving?"

"No, but why would he take so much of his stuff."

"Cherese did you check the rest of the house. Maybe someone else came into the house. Didn't you say he told you he got into a little trouble?"

"I didn't even think of that. No, that wouldn't be what happened. There was no sign that someone broke in. The alarm was on. Kyle would have set the alarm when he left."

"Look, you need to get over to the suite. Are you staying there for a few days?"

"No, I think I'll hang around here; something's not right Miles. I don't know what it is but Kyle has done something, and I don't want my assets tied up in his mess."

"Okay, are you going back to the suite though?"

"Yes, will you be there?"

"I'll see you there later. I'm just leaving. I'm meeting Dante' and Stephon in about ten minutes. I'll meet you there later, okay?"

"Yes."

"Cherese, don't dwell on Kyle. Go hang with your friends."

Cherese hung up the phone, showered and changed into jeans and a sweatshirt. Something Kyle would have griped about. She picked up the suitcase deciding she would spend a few days clearing her mind. The door bell rang, and she peeked through the sheer curtains from the bedroom window. Seeing two squad cars parked in front of the house, she carefully moved away, hoping they didn't notice the curtains move. She dialed Kyle's cell number on her cell phone pausing at the top of the stairs.

"Kyle, they're here. They're at the door now."

The bell rang again.

"Okay so call me after they leave."

"What am I telling them?"

"Tell them what you want."

"I don't know what to say. Where you are or what's going on, what did you do Kyle?"

"Shit Cherese. Tell them what you know."

"I don't know anything."

"Exactly my point." The phone went dead as Cherese turned the knob to greet the officers who had their identification cards and badges out for her to view.

Reality

Miles waited for Dante' in the lobby; the weather promised to bring another day of seasonal warmth, and he wished he could spend the day on his deck enjoying the spring breeze. He allowed his thoughts to drift to what his future would be like with Cherese. He understood she would need time to adjust to being a single woman again.

Miles had no intention of creating a rebound love affair. They would have to talk. It wasn't as easy as he had explained to Cherese the night before. The plans of her leaving town and residing in his townhouse sounded so much better when they were face to face. It was easier as he gave her reassuring passionate kisses.

Now Miles wasn't sure that Kyle wouldn't confront him. Cherese living in his home in Atlanta would cause a problem between him and Kyle. He thought about it, and with a half-hearted laugh dismissed his thoughts completely. The call he made or the cops would keep him at bay.

Dante' approached Miles with his cell phone to his ear. Miles could tell from the conversation it was getting serious. He showed the car keys to Dante', who followed him to the parking lot to retrieve his car. There was no pause in his conversation.

"Ma, she just told me about it last night."

"Dante' I didn't call you for you to explain anything to me. Just know, as usual, she's complaining. She thinks I have some magic wand that I can wave to get you to do what she wants you to do."

"Mama, Angel knows better."

"She just ought to. Dante' is this child yours?"

The question struck a nerve. He would have preferred she asked what his intentions were; were they still getting married; was he home because he had doubts? His mother knew he had doubts. Dante' waited for her to tell him to be careful. He couldn't give her an answer.

"Dante' if the child is not yours, you've got to face what you're getting yourself into."

Dante' sighed. "Yeah that's another reason why I'm staying here a little longer."

"Another reason, you needed reasons? Oh, I forgot y'all just went to the reunion right? How is Kalliah?"

"She's fine. Miles and I might stop by to see you today or tomorrow."

"Come tomorrow, I'll cook for you, bring Stephon too. You call Angel now. I think she knows what your decision may be already."

"Why what did she say?"

"Dante' you knew that girl was crazy when you got with her. She's shown you time and time again who she is. Now she's pregnant? She knows you're gonna think about whose it is, and if the timing is wrong….. well baby you call me if y'all ain't coming by."

Dante' smiled to himself. His mother knew what his thoughts were. He was glad he didn't have to explain or make excuses. He did want to know what she thought would be honorable. **"Can I really love her and marry her and not know if that baby is mine?"** The question didn't need to be asked aloud.

****

Dante's conversation with his mother lasted the length of the ride from the hotel to Miles' home. Stephon's car was in the driveway parked near Dante's. Miles cruised to a stop in front of his colonial home.

"This reminds me of our college days, man driving home and seeing your cars in the driveway. It always made me smile knowing you guys thought of my house as your home."

"I think about that a lot too. The things we did before we graduated and got our jobs and so called status. You know that can make or break you."

"That's strange I never thought about us worrying about the Jones', why think about status?" Miles turned off the ignition.

"It just crossed my mind. I mean, don't you think women choose their men by their status?"

They got out of the car. The afternoon sun was blocked by the trees that outlined his large manicured lawn. The bricked walkway was lined with foliage. Miles squinted as he looked toward Dante' to answer his own question.

"Dante' some women need that just as men do. You know to boost their self-esteem or keep them motivated. I mean look, I've been blessed, but this is small compared to those dudes I work around. I'm comfortable with what I've achieved, and I prefer to take my time about moving on in my career. Women are a different breed, though I know I can't read them all. Some get a good man and do them wrong, and then others get the wrong man and do them more than right."

He stuck his key in the door and shouted for Stephon.

Stephon stepped out of the den meeting them in the living room. He smiled at Miles extending his hand for their morning greeting.

"What's up? Tell me, how was your evening?" Stephon teased.

"Yeah, I didn't even ask, how did you pull that one off playa?" Dante' and Stephon took a seat waiting to hear how the night ended for Miles and Cherese. He wasn't about to discuss any of the continuous replay in his mind from the night before.

"She needed to talk. Well, we needed to talk. I really think she'll leave him this time."

"How many times have you heard that before Miles? Well, it doesn't matter, Dante' did you tell him anything?"

Stephon was anxious to tell Miles about Kyle violating Brianne. Both Stephon and Dante' knew Miles had taken the night well beyond a comforting conversation. "No we didn't talk about it yet."

"Talk about what?"

Dante' wanted to tell another story first. He needed their advice. Kyle's problem wouldn't affect any of them as much as Angel's pregnancy would affect him.

"I got a call today from Angel."

Stephon frowned indicating he had no idea what Dante' was talking about. He and Miles sat back listening as Dante' told them of his recent problems with Angel, the proposal, her pregnancy, and his love for Kalliah.

"I'm not sure I'm the father, or if I even love her anymore."

"How long was she screwing around with this other brotha?"

"Stephon, I wasn't prepared for her answer. She said off and on for eight or nine months. We got back together. She promised it was over. I've been careful about using protection, and lately I've been pulling out. Our relationship has been up and down since then. She's really been trying to make me forget, but I can't get the thought of her and someone else out of my mind. I really thought about it more when I received the invitation for the reunion."

"Dante' did you just start having these feelings? I mean you just proposed didn't you love her then?"

Dante' asked himself the same question and still couldn't answer it. "Miles, I guess reality set in after I saw Kalliah on Friday. I was wrong for proposing. Angel accepted, and I think she knew she was pregnant then."

"So where does Kalliah fit in all of this? Did you tell her about the pregnancy?" Stephon knew Dante' hadn't told her.

"No and she doesn't know about the proposal either?"

They questioned him with their stares, waiting for the explanation. "I couldn't tell her and get an honest response about her feelings for me. I wanted to know if what we felt for each other was still the same."

"You and Kalliah are just friends, right? Man, it sounds like you set her up. If she didn't have feelings for you, then you'd still marry Angel? "

Miles sighed. "Stephon tell me you didn't know that Dante' has been wanting to get with her for years. Something like you and Brianne."

"Whoa man, I didn't propose to someone else. I didn't expect Brianne to be receptive to a relationship with me either. I went with fate. But Dante' man you knew that you were coming here to see where a relationship with Kalliah would go. That's different. You and Miles, man I don't know…."

Miles and Dante' responded in unison. "What?"

"Stephon, love doesn't have a time or a place. Shit, sometimes it doesn't even confirm who you'll fall in love with. I thought Angel and I were the shit man; that was until I found out that she was cheating. Okay, she laid a lame line of confusion, decisions, and I can't remember all of her excuses for being with that damn guy. Anyway, I didn't think that she would still be dealing with him after I damn near flipped."

"Still dealing with him?"

"Yeah, she had to be. I didn't ask how far along she is. She said there may be a chance the child isn't mine. Supposedly, she stopped dealing with him when we got back together. That's been over three months. She'd be four months pregnant if it was his, and they weren't dealing with each other. They show at about four months right?"

"True, true."

"Well how could it be less than that if she's questioning whether the child is mine or his?"

"Damn, so you were gonna get back with Kalliah and dump Angel at the altar?"

"Miles, that's some cold shit. I wish I thought of it, but I didn't think about it that way. I wanted to make sure that I didn't have feelings for anyone else. I knew Kalliah would always hold a place in my heart. If I was getting married those feelings needed to be settled. After talking to Kalliah, I know we both have those feelings. I can't tell her I proposed, and the condition my relationship is in. She'll think I'm looking for love on the rebound or something."

"You should have told her about it though man."

"Miles, what the fuck was I gonna say? I proposed to this bitch thinking we could make it after she cheated. She's pregnant, but the baby may be mine. Can we wait and see before we commit to each other? I really loved you the whole time I was with her. Kalliah ain't going for that b.s."

"I thought you had this great open friendship." Stephon raised his brow and tilted his head.

"And that's why I can't tell her that."

"You better tell her something before someone else tells it." Miles looked to Stephon and then to Dante.

"Who could tell her? We don't travel in the same circles."

Stephon shook his head. "Your mom."

Dante' couldn't deny it. Kalliah and his mother were close; a lot closer than his mother and Angel. Miles and Stephon could tell that Dante's plan didn't include telling Kalliah at all. They sat silently until Stephon changed the topic.

"That's going to take some thought man. Listen you've got a minute to think about it. But Miles, we need to touch a subject that needs to be addressed as soon as possible."

"Me?"

Dante' remained quiet, caught up in his own issue; he forgot the reason for the immediate meeting. Stephon ignored his silence and continued, repeating Brianne's story.

****

"They said Kyle may be connected to these people who are involved in taking the money, and they just wanted to question him. Kyle sounded like it was more to it, like he knew he would be going to jail. They didn't say that though."

Kalliah and Brianne didn't know what to say. Cherese had been talking for the past thirty minutes about the officers who came to her door. She wanted to know the details but neither the cops nor Kyle gave her much to go on, and they wouldn't explain things, so she could understand. She was obviously worried. Her friends thought she was holding on to the hope that Kyle would change. She wouldn't leave him while he was in a jail cell.

"What the hell does he expect me to do? I don't know what to tell the police, and if they do find him, will he be arrested? How can I prepare to get a lawyer or bail for him?

I'm his wife. Don't I deserve to know what I'm supposed to do?"

Cherese began to cry. "I can't leave him now. There's always an excuse that redirects my happiness. What will people think if I leave now? They'll think I waited until his ass was carted off to jail to leave him. Other than the two of you and Miles no one knows the real shit he's put me through. I know I need to understand that he's been through so much with the miscarriage; the ups and downs of our marriage; and me not working sharing in our expenses. I just can't see me leaving him when he'll need me the most."

Brianne couldn't believe what she was hearing. She looked for a sign from Kalliah to stop her from saying what needed to be said. It was an opening to finally tell Cherese about the man she married.

"Cherese, you can't possibly think that you leaving Kyle would be a bad thing. You keep mentioning what he's been through what about you? You lost a baby too, and he's the one who pushed you down the flight of stairs. He's been beating your ass since you got married. You've been physically and mentally scarred. Who cares what people think? Just like you said they don't really know what's been going on. Your attachment to Kyle has been and always will be what you can give. Kyle only becomes upset when he thinks he's left out of your giving. I really think that's why he pushed you."

"What? Brianne how can you say that?"

"Cherese, you would have grown to love that child more than Kyle. You would have embraced motherhood and healed a lot of those wounds that make you a slave to Kyle and what he calls a marriage."

"That's bull Brianne. Kalliah do you believe that too?"

"Listen, Brianne studied this stuff. Maybe she has a point. Besides, you don't know whether or not he's gonna be locked up."

"Why would he say what he said? He knows that they've got something on him or his boys. He's involved. That's why he didn't come home. Maybe the cops lied to me to see if I would convince him to come home. That's why I came here. I don't want him to think I told them anything."

"Cherese you really don't know Kyle."

"Brianne, you know you never really liked him. I can remember your reaction when I said I was going to marry him. Everyone else wished me well and you asked all of those damn questions about him abusing me."

"And as things played out, I was right. The bastard is abusive. He always has been."

"So you knew he was abusive?"

"Cherese, Brianne needs to tell you how she knew, but we need you to understand that it's something that's been a mental burden to her for years. It's not easy to repeat this over and over, and it definitely is not easy to hear. We all agreed you and Miles needed to know this before you left your home or your marriage."

"How is it that you're deciding whether I will be leaving my husband?"

Brianne was getting as angry as she had in the past trying to convince Cherese she could do better. But today she knew she couldn't just let her words fade at the end of the conversation. Cherese needed to listen and finally understand the extent of her husband's abuse.

A New Direction

Stephon took a seat at the far corner of the cafeteria as directed. He was to meet the two detectives who would give him the time and place for the setup. Stephon was told that they didn't expect him to get too much information from the marks. He would know enough to be recognized and respected. He would pretend to have connections with a buyer who was looking for a supplier. He would have to explain he had needy clientele.

The deal needed to go down within the next couple of days. The conversation over lunch would be short, but it had to look as though they were all just friends.

Stephon checked the cafeteria daily trying to pick the employee or employees who were a part of the dealings. The money stolen from Tucker and Sons was used to buy the drugs, that much of the gathered information was verified by the detectives. Stephon would need only to identify the employees involved, and be led to the major players. He didn't think that one meeting with the detectives would work and now after four days of meeting casually with them, he had proof, he was right. Two employees, one black the other Hispanic had approached him earlier that day asking didn't he know he couldn't just step in on Kyle's turf. He pretended not to know what they were talking about. He was certain he found who may have been stealing the money. He wasn't sure what department they worked in, but he knew their names. He knew his undercover job would be over if he gave them up too soon. He had a more important reason to withhold his findings. Stephon sat patiently waiting for the detectives to join him for lunch. He needed them to confirm that his supplier would be Kyle Taylor.

The two employees took their seat like clockwork at twelve ten. Stephon took a chance to talk with the runners. The detectives would be arriving shortly. He made his way to the salad bar to get condiments. He stopped by the table where the two employees had begun eating.

"Listen, I was waiting for my boys, and a thought came to my mind."

The detectives paused, watching Stephon's actions as they entered the cafeteria. Stephon continued to lead the employees into his trap.

"What would that be?"

"Why not hook me up with your boy Kyle? I need to make this happen, and if he's already got this covered why not sit and talk?"

"Why should he? You got a hook?"

"I am the hook."

The detectives got in line and tried not to look concerned finding Stephon talking to the employees their informant told them to watch. It was hard to not trust someone with Stephon's record. They knew it was a risk that would pay off. They would question him before giving him any information regarding the buy. Stephon had been at the top of his game before doing time.

****

Dante' invited himself to join his mother for an afternoon of shopping. After taking her out to breakfast, he still felt the need for her company. They walked the mall looking from window to window for an outfit she could wear to her church's twenty-fifth anniversary dinner. Mrs. Jefferson was a small woman in both height and weight. At a height of five feet and one hundred twenty-five pounds, size was not the problem. She was picky about the colors, the new fashions, and of course what the members of the church would think.

"You know how they talk Dante', that dress is beautiful, but look how low that thing is in the front."

"Mama, you're not that big it won't expose anything."

"Oh not that big, does that mean you won't look at a woman whose dress is cut this low?"

"Alright, Yeah I would look but…"

"See, right there, this is a church function."

"It's not at the church though, right. I mean you're an attractive woman. I don't know. You pick one, and I'll check it after you pick it."

"C'mon now don't get frustrated. You've got to snap out of this mood you're in, ease up. When you gonna bring Kalliah over or do I have to call her?"

Dante' didn't answer. He hadn't spoken to Kalliah about the pregnancy or the marriage. He hadn't thought much about it. He spent the first couple of days in the week going over the past four months of his relationship with Angel in his mind along with spending his evenings with Kalliah. They spent their time visiting old friends and Kalliah's relatives. Being with her gave him comfort. Their relationship wasn't strained.

"You can call her. I guess she's been catching up with old friends and relatives."

"You guess, you know 'cause you've been with her. Have you told that girl that Angel is pregnant?"

"No why should I?"

"Men, y'all sure are dummies sometimes. You want that girl to tell you how much she wants you and her to have a relationship right? I mean this way you loving her is not a problem 'cause God forbid if you loved her, and she didn't love you. Did she tell you that she's been loving you for years?"

"Not in so many words."

"Y'all been dancing around a relationship for years, and now you want to dance close without the right music. The beat you hear ain't for you and Kalliah. You've got to change the music first."

"Okay, I think I understand that."

"Understand this. Angel is not gonna wait for you to tell Kalliah if she really thinks that's who you'll be dancing with next. Angel will be playing the music for your ass to dance to. Dante' she'll tell Kalliah if you don't."

"What? Angel doesn't know Kalliah like that. What makes you think she'll tell her?"

"She told me she would."

****

Kalliah waited for Brianne and Cherese to return. The three of them had plans to join Miles, Stephon and Dante'. The evening included dinner and a movie. Kalliah wasn't up for shopping again. They had been shopping the entire week looking for jeans. Kalliah found a pair she loved and bought more than she intended adding a blouse, shoes and jewelry. Brianne had her usual difficulty complaining nothing really fit her, and Cherese was a shop-aholic. They all left the suite together but Kalliah spent the earlier part of the day visiting her family.

Cherese didn't have much to say in Kyle's defense about what Brianne went through after their prom. Brianne asked her if she already knew about it through rumor or Kyle himself. She denied knowing but her attitude toward Brianne changed, and it was noticeable. Brianne hoped it wasn't pity or in some way Cherese feeling that she needed to be nice because Kyle had been so cold.

Brianne called at two thirty to tell Kalliah she was tired as hell, and Cherese was in New York and Company looking for black jeans. They would be on their way after she came out of the store. Brianne found an outfit she liked and the three of them would be casually fabulous for the evening.

When the phone rang again Kalliah looked at the number and noticed the area code was the same as Dante's but the number didn't match any of his lines. When she heard the accent, she knew it was Angel.

"Yes, this is Kalliah. Who is this?"

"Angel. Dante's girl."

"Hi Angel. What's up?"

Angel hesitated. Kalliah's politeness threw her off guard. If a woman called her about any man she dealt with it would have caused serious drama.

"I was calling to see if Dante' gave you guys the news. He's so forgetful these days. I wanted him to announce it at the reunion, but he said it wasn't really the place for it. I mean after all he really didn't consider everyone from McKinley High his friends. But I figured you six were good friends, and I'm so happy about it, I wanted his friends to share in our joy."

Kalliah could only guess what the news would be, but Dante' not sharing the news meant there was a twist to the story.

"No, I don't think our circle of friends knows anything about your, what did you call it, joy?"

"He didn't tell you that we're getting married?"

Kalliah didn't get upset at hearing the news she smiled playing along with what she thought was an unsecured woman's bait.

"Oh, I see. When? He really didn't say anything about it. Maybe he told the guys though."

"Hmm, well if he told them he won't mind me telling you. Sometime next year I would hope."

"So you didn't set a date?"

Angel couldn't believe Kalliah didn't fuss about him not telling her. "Uh, no not quite, everything is happening so fast. I mean like other couples we've had our ups and downs. I'm sure you were around when we were on the outs."

Kalliah nodded her head. She wanted to tell her no, she was dealing with her own outs, but if Angel was playing the game, she'd let her make up the rules. Angel didn't wait for her reply.

"Well this last time he really wanted to be sure it never happened again so he proposed. Of course, I accepted, what else do you do when you love your man?"

Kalliah understood why they had problems. Angel couldn't be serious and Dante' couldn't be serious about her. Kalliah could tell she was the "cutesy" type, and she played a lot of games.

"Girl I said yes and we're expecting our first born too. I know Dante' was surprised when I told him. That's why I didn't come to the reunion. I just couldn't miss my exam. Kalliah, we want you all to be there. We'll probably be sending out the invitations soon. I really don't want to be pregnant in my wedding pictures."

Kalliah fell back on the couch. She was mentally repeating Dante's confessions of love, but his voice was fading as she digested Angel's words. She could barely speak without effort.

"Well congratulations. Angel how did you get my number?"

"I went through Dante's phone book here at the house."

Kalliah's anger was rising. The matinee was at five she couldn't wait to see her loving friend.

****

Miles had been exceptionally quiet since Brianne's story had been told. He didn't know whether he could face Brianne. He always thought she liked Kyle and that was why she couldn't stand to be around when Kyle and Cherese were together. There was a list of problems he thought she had, but he couldn't put his finger on the roots. Now he needed to apologize even though she had no idea how he felt.

No one would blame him or Cherese for acting guilty. It was understood that Cherese couldn't possibly consider going back to Kyle under any circumstance. Sitting with everyone at dinner Miles would openly apologize to Brianne. He needed to clear his mind about at least one of the issues.

Stephon and Dante' were talking about which movie they wanted to see and why. Miles entered the room and tucked his Sean John tank shirt in his jeans.

"You guys about ready?"

"Yeah man you alright? You look like you're tired."

"Stephon knows how my days go. Thursdays are the worse, and I guess with all of this other shit I'm dealing with it's got me looking this way."

"What other shit? You ain't still bugging about Kyle are you?"

"I just don't want that brother thinking he can get out of the truth when it slaps him in the face. Then too you know he might want to slap Cherese. There's my problem right there."

Stephon didn't want to get into the conversation. The setup was in place, and Kyle got a direct message that there was a guy looking to deal big. It wouldn't be strange at all for Stephon to show up. He and Kyle had done business in the past, but Kyle's status had climbed since Stephon's last purchase. Stephon kept what he knew would be the solution to their problems to himself. He needed the buy to go down as planned. It would be believable if Stephon remained unattached to Kyle's personal life.

"Maybe we can prevent that. Kalliah and I could take her home and help her get her things. Actually maybe a confrontation from Brianne wouldn't be bad for his ass, and it might help her close the chapter about this shit once and for all."

"Hmm, you might be right. Stephon what about you, do you think Brianne would go for that?"

"I don't know man. It took her years to even repeat it. I don't know if confronting Kyle would help her or hurt her. We can ask her though; maybe if she knows it would help Cherese. I can't go with you though."

Miles frowned and when he noticed it didn't faze Dante', he let it go. Stephon looked at his watch. "We better get going."

****

Kalliah updated Brianne and Cherese with Angel's news. Her venting caused her to be more upset than she expected. Cherese and Brianne understood her feelings for Dante' had resurfaced in the past few days, and her love life was on a new high. Angel's call put a damper on her feelings. They all had questions about Dante's intentions, but only Kalliah could get the answers.

"Men and their bullshit, what was he thinking? You were desperate?"

Kalliah's eyebrows raised, and she shook her head listening to Cherese, the new love counselor. "I don't even know if it's his bullshit Cherese. From what he's said about her, it could be her shit. What about her cheating? The baby doesn't have to be his?"

"Yeah, that's true, but Cherese is right he's got some damn nerve telling you he wants to get with you. He always loved you, why didn't he tell you he proposed?" Brianne shook her head and sighed.

Cherese chimed in immediately. "Why didn't he say she was pregnant?"

"Alright, you've both got a point. I don't know why, all I'm saying is I don't know whether to trust her or not. I know I'm not going to bail him out. He'll just have to see this through. If it's his child or not, I'm not getting in the middle of it until he has clearly made a decision. I don't want the blame falling on me."

"What blame? If she's pregnant by him, and he doesn't love her, he's to blame. If the baby is the guy she's cheating with, well the blame is hers."

"Cherese, either way she'll say I stepped into the picture if he walks out of the relationship, and our relationship begins."

"Kalliah, that's some dumb shit too. You and Dante' love each other and you're worried about that bimbo and her feelings? If the child's not his it only validates what he told you about their relationship. He can't trust her no matter if they stay together or not."

"Brianne, our friendship holds some trust too. He should have trusted me enough to know I would have understood if he told me the entire story; not bits and pieces."

"Tell the truth would you have listened if he told you the truth?"

Brianne's question was answered by a knock on the suite door. Cherese answered it and wrapped her arms around Miles while greeting him with a kiss. Dante' and Stephon pushed past the two of them with teasing frowns. The men made their rounds of cordial hugs and questions about what movie the ladies had decided to see. The place for dinner, Grillfish, was Miles' choice. Kalliah picked up her handbag unwilling to become a part of the small talk.

"Let's go see the movie. What are the transportation arrangements?"

"Why don't you and Dante' ride together? We'll ride in Stephon's car and meet you there." Miles quickly answered Kalliah.

Kalliah rolled her eyes at Miles knowing he had no idea what he had just done.

Raw Emotions

The movie was exactly what the critics promised, one of Will Smith's best performances. The group agreed to see "I Am Legend" and other than small talk their attention was on the screen. Kalliah waited after the movie for Dante' to announce his proposal and uncertainty of parenthood. He hadn't mentioned anything about her mood, which she deliberately displayed hoping he would dare to ask questions.

Dante' opened the passenger door for Kalliah to get in. Miles stopped him and Stephon at the rear of the vehicles, as Brianne and Cherese got into Stephon's car. Kalliah looked in the passenger side mirror hoping she could read their lips. She dialed Brianne's phone to see if their plans had changed.

"Hey, why are the guys at the back of the car, what's up?"

"I don't know, Cherese said something about, they wanted to talk and the restaurant might not be the place."

"Talk to who?"

"Us, I guess. Yeah, Cherese said us. I don't know what they're talking about, and neither does Cherese. I know it's time to eat though. You and Dante' talk yet?"

"No, and I don't think he'll say anything at the restaurant either. If they're saying they want to talk, it probably involves all of us. Alright here we go. They're coming to the cars."

Kalliah hung up the phone just as Dante' got in the car. He reached over to adjust the volume on the radio. The R & B station was playing a club remix.

"Kalliah, you haven't said much, are you okay?"

"I'm fine, what about you and the guys; what was that little meeting about?" Kalliah didn't want to spoil her appetite with any drama.

"Yeah, everything is cool. I'll follow them and then they wanted to go their separate ways."

"Oh, and you don't have any plans?"

"I hoped you and I could talk."

"Yeah, I think we should."

Dante' didn't want to say the wrong thing, so he turned the volume up and gave her a smile. Kalliah didn't allow his charm to budge her disposition. She turned her attention to the sights on the streets. They pulled into the parking lot three songs later without a word between them. The group took their seats, led by the hostess, and ordered appetizers and drinks. Kalliah watched Cherese and Brianne as they seemed comfortable with the new beginnings of old friendships.

She wanted to cry. Dante' had always been the man she wanted but couldn't have. She watched as he laughed enjoying the food and conversations as though his love life was stable. The same held true for all of them, Cherese and Miles didn't seem to care about Kyle or the problems they might face.

Brianne had a barrier around her heart while Stephon was willing to wait forever. Kalliah couldn't live that way. She couldn't pretend it was all okay. Dante' would be a father and a husband, and she would lose it all. She needed to know if he really meant to deceive her by not telling the truth.

****

"Brianne, I want to apologize. I don't want to go into details but over the years I truly misunderstood your conduct."

"Me too, I think I know what Miles means."

Cherese and Miles broke the laughter down to a serious moment. It was the first time the group was openly discussing Brianne's secret. Brianne listened hoping it would give her insight on her family's attitude toward her and her feelings about herself.

"I don't know how you went on holding a secret like that and seeing Kyle like you did."

"Cherese, that's what has stopped her from coming home all these years. It's not just us that made her feel uneasy, but her family too. They didn't believe you right Brianne?"

"Kalliah, I think it was a lot of other issues that made it easy for them to dismiss what I was saying. I don't know if I'll even sit with them and talk like this. I want to say thank you though. I wish I had the strength years ago to confront you all with this."

"Well, better late than never, you've got to feel better now right?" Kalliah asked.

"Girl you know better than anyone else I've had my bad and good days. Cherese what are you going to do? I don't want you making a decision based on my past. You know your husband better than all of us; I mean his bad and good characteristics. I don't think any of us wants to find you really hurt. You know emotionally and physically."

"I've been telling her that for months. Cherese you say you want out. Wouldn't this lead you out that door?"

Miles sat bracing himself for the dreaded answer while hoping she wouldn't make excuses again.

"It damn sure is a push, but I was telling Brianne and Kalliah, I don't want to walk out on him when he needs me now."

"Look, Cherese that shit played out years ago."

"What shit Stephon?"

"That damn, stick by your mate no matter what, nobody does that anymore. They don't need a reason to walk out. They do what is best for them, and it don't always benefit the one they left."

He was thinking about the twins and the situation their mother left them in. It still was a question in his mind, **"How does a mother leave two month-old twins with her aging parents and no word to their father."**

"I understand that, but it's not in me to leave someone like that." Cherese said taking a drink from her glass.

"You know you could get caught up and charged for his shit too."

"Stephon you act like you know something, what's up?"

The waitress stepped in passing plates and rearranging the items in the center of the table to make room. The food looked and smelled good. Plates began to get filled with buffalo wings, mozzarella sticks and other items from the appetizer trays. Salad was being passed to those who ordered it with their meals. Stephon didn't explain his statement.

The dinner went well. Small talk of future plans continued to be the topic, and they all were careful not to question Cherese about her leaving Kyle. Miles was waiting for the ride back to the suite to talk to her about her intentions.

****

Once in the parking lot the group divided into the cars they arrived in. It was agreed that they would meet again before Brianne, and Kalliah left to go back to Virginia. Dante' opened the passenger door and signaled to Miles he would call him later. The non-verbal communication was understood, and he replied with a nod of agreement. Stephon shouted his good-bye and told Kalliah he, and Brianne would check them out at the suite later. Kalliah smiled to herself knowing there was a big possibility that Dante' wouldn't be there when they arrived. Cherese was deep in thought, and never acknowledged the group's separation. She texted Kalliah after getting settled in the car to say she would be with Miles making some life decisions.

Kalliah forwarded the message to Brianne with a question mark. Brianne's reply was "I don't understand what the decisions would be, but we'll talk with her later. You try to clear things up with Dante'." After reading the message, she closed her phone, let back the passenger seat and closed her eyes. Dante' watched her deliberate moves It was then he realized the ride to the hotel would be done in silence.

Brianne read the message on her phone again and passed it to Stephon. He read the message with a frown in his brow. He decided he wouldn't speak about Cherese's choices either.

"Miles where did you say your time-share spot was?"

"Macon, Georgia it's not a time share. My Aunt sold me her house. I use it as a summer spot or a getaway. It's really nice. I was telling Cherese about it. I hope she considers it. Kyle won't bother her there and like I told you babe, you can really relax there."

"We've talked about it Miles. I know you all have good intentions, but none of you are married. It's not as easy as you think to dissolve a marriage. There's financial commitments and property involved."

"I think we all have watched you over the years dissolve or fade as a wife, a friend and a person. Cherese it's not leaving a marriage at this point. It's about regaining the part of you that you've lost or hidden out of fear."

Miles turned the volume on the radio up knowing his statement made an impact. Stephon and Brianne made small talk between them. Cherese used a tissue to wipe her eyes.

****

Kalliah kicked off her sandals and quickly excused herself as she went to the bathroom. Dante' checked the hotel's compact refrigerator and took out two small bottles of Zinfandel. The chilled bottles were enough to make the glasses of wine refreshing without ice. Dante' wanted Kalliah to be at ease when he explained his situation and why he hadn't told her earlier. She returned, talking before Dante' could finish collecting his thoughts.

"Dante', there's something I need to clear up between us before we go into any other conversations."

"Okay, I uh guess we kinda want to do the same thing."

"Well then you go first. You mentioned we needed to talk earlier."

Kalliah hoped Dante' would explain and satisfy her curiosity. She really wanted to believe he wouldn't ignore a wedding or a baby on the way. Dante' wasn't quite prepared to begin. He still needed more time.

"Listen, there's no rush. We've got the balance of the evening to talk and to be quite frank with you; I don't want to spoil this occasion."

"What occasion?"

"This one, us alone, wine, conversation, understanding, should I go on?"

"I'm not sure. Should you?"

"Alright, I'll start. I know you, and I have had this friendship agreement for years. One that has put a hold on what I consider something that could be, or could have been beautiful. Kalliah to be honest I don't understand why we thought our friendship would be at stake. Why couldn't we explore each other as more than friends? Maybe I wouldn't be here with you, scared to death of losing more than our friendship. The stakes now are higher."

"And why is that Dante'? I mean you'll always be a friend, my best friend, I would hope. What's going on in your life that would change that?"

Dante' took a sip of the wine and sat closer to Kalliah with his arm across the back of the couch. She didn't move nor did she feel uncomfortable. They looked at each other deeply. Dante' wanted to kiss her and let the kiss take them to another level, but he knew it would be temporary if he didn't tell the truth about Angelina.

"I'm not sure how to tell you this. I really thought that my search for that one love was over. I told you about Angelina, our relationship, the ups and downs. I stepped back after awhile to reevaluate my love life and there was no other woman I loved more. I never was the playa type, well you know that. I didn't want to walk away from what might have been or what was meant for me. So just before the invites to the reunion were mailed, I asked her to marry me. Kalliah I think she's still cheating. I don't know what to do, what to say, and I damn sure don't want proof."

"What, you're willing to marry her, even though she's cheating?"

"For a minute I was. I thought we'd get married. She'd feel secure, and the shit would be over. I loved her."

"Loved?"

"Until I heard your voice again, your laugh, and finally after this week felt your warmth and love, again. I thought I found your qualities in her. She's not a bad person, but she wants more than I can give, and obviously, I don't satisfy her needs as she does mine. She's been dealing with this guy off and on throughout our relationship. I don't want him in our marriage, and the funny thing is if she promised to leave him alone I wouldn't trust her. Remember when we used to say what was friendship without trust? Kalliah I love you. I always have and it was our friendship, or the promise of it being everlasting, that held me not to ask or tell you more about my feelings."

Kalliah knew he paused so she could respond. If she told him, Angelina called her, and she couldn't possibly stand between him and possible fatherhood, she didn't know what he would say. She couldn't tell him.

"I needed the time away to feel who I was again. The stress of our relationship is driving me mad. I don't know how I would survive a marriage. Anyway, I decided to tell her the truth, but I wanted you to know first. Yes, I was going to marry her. It would have been the biggest mistake in my life. I'm not marrying her. I can't. I love you."

Dante' downed the glass of wine and walked to the refrigerator for a refill. He brought over the small bottles and filled his glass again.

"Dante' I don't know what to say, other than you need to think this through."

"What is there to think about? You answered my question honestly. That's why I didn't tell you about the proposal. I knew you wouldn't tell me your true feelings. I can't marry that girl and love you. I won't cheat myself or you, for that matter. Can you honestly say that you could love me, and marry someone else?"

Kalliah drank the wine in her glass and passed it to Dante' for a refill. She would not answer that question honestly no matter how many times or ways he asked. Maurice was nowhere near the altar, and she didn't have a list of prospects. Dante' was right. She had visions of him at times when she and Maurice were intimate. She and Dante' got close once in high school, but his mother's voice coming through the front door redirected their seating on the living room couch. He got close enough with the wine glass to kiss her on her lips. He handed her the glass and sat back.

"Could you marry someone else?"

"After you marry Angelina, I guess I would have to move on with my life. The reality is that you're somewhat committed. You've given her a ring and asked her to marry you. What about the baby?"

Dante' sat upright. Her question was unexpected. He didn't want to discuss the possibility of a long-term commitment, even if he didn't marry Angelina.

"The baby isn't mine."

"Really?"

"Really, I can't prove it yet because I'm here."

"Yeah, how did you come here and stay knowing she had that examination scheduled."

"I didn't know, she just told me she was pregnant. Kalliah I wouldn't be sitting here with you if it all were good with my fiancé. She's trying to hold on because her lies are surfacing before the ceremony."

"Hmmm...."

"I can't prove it to you now, but trust and believe she's lying."

"And if she's not."

"I still can't marry her." Dante's tone changed bordering annoyance. "I don't trust her."

"What about the child?"

"I'll be a father, if I am. That's it. I can't love her just because she had my child. What about you? Could you still be with me if I were the father?"

"I don't know."

Kalliah felt tears welling in her eyes. She wanted to scream. He couldn't be the father of someone else's child. Her childhood dreams were fading fast. Dante' saw her tears and wanted to soothe her. He reached his hand out to her. She took it allowing him to help her to her feet.

"I'm not marrying her. The child is not mine. Time will tell. I'm quite sure she won't get a blood test now. I'm going to cancel the wedding. Kalliah I love you."

Dante's embrace and the wine gave Kalliah the warmth she needed. She looked at his face for sincerity and when she found it, she closed her eyes longing for his lips to touch hers. The kiss was all that was needed. They walked slowly to the bedroom.

****

Brianne stood gazing in the curio that held Stephon's pictures of his sons and other keepsakes. She smiled at the grins of the twins who looked like their father did years earlier. The décor of Stephon's apartment was definitely an indication that it was a man's abode. The colors were natural, and the furniture was bought for comfort. It was obvious that he had children. The toys were neatly stacked on a small toy chest in the hall leading to the back of the apartment. Brianne listened as he explained what he considered a mess. She visualized the organized chaos in her own house without small children. She laughed telling him she understood.

"Well this is home. Can I get you anything? I hope Miles and Cherese will be okay."

"What would make you think they wouldn't be okay?"

Stephon led the way back to the sectional couch in the living room. He waited for her to sit before sitting across from her.

"I just don't trust that Kyle won't show up. I don't think he'd appreciate Miles at his house. Cherese is still in fairytale mode. Did you hear her?"

"How old are you boys?" Brianne changed the subject.

"They'll be three this year. I've got paperwork in for custody."

"That's good; you would have to move then huh?"

"I want a house. I have to be off probation. I've got almost a year. They'll be four and wherever I move, they can attend daycare. I'm really trying to stabilize myself as soon as possible. I can't get them until my background checks out."

"Or you're married, or have a great job; yeah I know the challenges they give you. You look like you've got it together."

"Well I've got most of it. I don't have a stable relationship, and they always ask that question. That was the reason I filed the papers. I don't want that to be a deciding factor, I mean, what happens to my kids if I break up with the woman they met?"

"They probably wouldn't care."

"Well I don't want it to be in the equation. Let me get you something to drink."

"Do you have something stronger than juice or soda?"

"You drinking? Awwright now, maybe a brotha can get a chance."

"You wouldn't take the chance if you had it."

"Brianne, don't push your luck girl. Remember you owe me."

Stephon got up from the couch laughing and went into the kitchen.

"I've got beer, that Long Island Iced Tea mixer, and hey, I've got coolers."

"The Iced Tea mixer is good."

"So, tell me lady. Does a brotha stand a chance?"

"What you looking for a weekend affair? I don't think so."

"Who said a weekend affair?"

"I didn't want to say a one-night affair."

Brianne thought about her dildo. She couldn't remember if she brought it on the trip with her. After lying next to Stephon following the reunion dance and being with him during the week, she needed to be touched. Her last escapade left her horny for more than a week. The brother talked a good game. He ran the lines about being more than fulfilling for a big girl, but he didn't give any indication that he needed to be trained along the way. Stephon would be different. Brianne could tell. The way he danced, and walked showed a bit of sexual confidence. He entered the room with the two drinks.

"Alright now, don't blame the night on your drink, taste it and see if it's too strong. I can add more coke."

Brianne sipped it not really caring if it was strong. She needed the drink to keep her hormones down.

"That's a devilish smile."

"Oops you weren't supposed to see that. Listen, Brianne I want you to know that I don't think of you as just a friend. I don't think I ever have. And I'm not talking about that sister shit either. I know that I never really got to know you, but I always admired you. It's funny how life has given the six of us a full circle."

"Six?"

"Yeah you know Dante', Miles, Cherese, Kalliah, you and me. We were connected as couples even then and didn't realize it. Now look at us, time wasted, I guess."

"Well it could have gone another way. We could have gotten on each other's nerves as we were maturing and threw away what could be long-term relationships."

"I like the sound of that, long term."

Brianne looked at Stephon's lips. She couldn't believe she wanted to attack him. She could feel her body heat rising. She said a silent prayer that it wouldn't be just a tease. She had a need to be relaxed and satisfied.

"So who you dealing with, in Virginia?"

"No one special, I go out every now and then, nothing serious though; what about you?"

"My boys; no I'm lying. My boys, my job, my television, and excuse the expression my hand."

Brianne couldn't contain her laughter. She had named her dildo, "No One Special." Stephon raised an eyebrow at her outburst. She covered her mouth trying to control the giggle.

"Will Kalliah be upset if you stayed here tonight?"

"I'd be upset if I didn't."

Stephon moved closer so their lips could meet. He massaged her breast and began unbuttoning her blouse. Brianne smiled knowing there was no need to check her suitcase. Stephon laid her back on the sectional as his hands reached the button on the waist of her pants. She assisted him lifting herself as he rolled her pants and panties down. Brianne used her bare feet to take the garments completely off.

Stephon stood taking off his pants and briefs revealing a package that Brianne knew would satisfy her desire. She hadn't thought about condoms but trusted he knew one would be needed. He pulled his shirt off and threw it on the top of the other clothing. He held his penis in his hand massaging it back and forth as he walked away from the couch.

Brianne watched as the muscles in his butt flexed. He returned with a condom in one hand and his penis in the other.

"Almost forgot."

"Wait. Not yet." Brianne said softly.

Stephon smiled. The foreplay began. He started at her ankles and kissed her slowly. As he approached her thighs, his fingers fondled her breast until her nipples hardened with arousal. He wet his lips and suckled her breast loving the fact that she was a forty two D cup. Her hips moved to the intensity of his touch as he moved back to her waist. Brianne's size and shape turned him on, and he knew upon entrance he would explode. He deliberately stood again increasing the massaging of his penis. Brianne watched as the head of his penis began to shine. Her vagina began to throb.

"Touch yourself. Come on touch yourself. Lay there and touch yourself for me."

Brianne took her fingers and knowing where to touch, she began stimulating her clitoris. She could feel it increasing in size as the wetness began to build inside her. Stephon was standing over her moving like a dancer. He never stopped moving his hands slowly back and forth over his erected penis. She could see the sperm mounting on its head. Her vagina throbbed as his manhood glistened. She had never been a part of this type foreplay, but her body reacted to it well.

Stephon knelt and suckled her breast again sending a rush to her senses. His mouth touched her naval, and again, he spoke in a whisper.

"Slow down baby, rub it slowly for me."

As she obeyed his wishes, he took his tongue and like an artist with a paint brush, he painted around her fingers. He licked the lips of her vagina while she fingered herself to an orgasm. Stephon put the condom on and gently moved her hand away. Brianne spread her legs for the best entry she had in years. He penetrated her slowly touched the walls of her vagina, as though he were sneaking past. His penis began to pump, and he began to moan.

Brianne couldn't believe the pleasure she felt. He moved back and forth to the sound of their juices, and Stephon continued to moan as though he were singing her praise. She opened her legs wider and felt him going deeper. They quivered together. Brianne could tell he was coming. He was almost screaming.

"Awww...shittt...girl damn. Brianne, dammnn."

"Baby, it's all good take your time."

She felt his penis slipping and wanted to divert his attention to fulfilling her own pleasures. Stephon didn't fail her. He put his fingers in her vagina and spread the lips. Her clitoris stood waiting for his lips to kiss it sweetly. He got closer and blew gently. Brianne began her own song of praise as he finished their first romantic encounter. Stephon kissed her thighs and held her hands tightly.

"This can't be just for tonight. You do know that right?"

"No, do you know that?"

He took off the condom as he walked to the bathroom quivering. "Shit." Brianne replied totally satisfied, "I heard that."

The Truth

It was close to twelve noon before Kalliah came out of the bedroom to the kitchenette. She hung the "Do Not Disturb" sign on the door at four in the morning when she walked Dante' to the door. There was no indication when Dante' left that Brianne had gotten in. A definite sign there would be no breakfast at dawn. Kalliah could smell coffee brewing and Brianne was humming contently to herself, a tune Kalliah couldn't quite name.

"Morning girl, want a cup?"

"Yes, what time did you guys get in?"

"I got here about seven. Stephon had to be at work by eight. We ate an early breakfast and he dropped me off."

"Nice. How was your evening?"

"Girl, you'll need that cup of coffee. I definitely need to ask you questions?"

"Ask me questions?"

"Get your coffee. I had a strange, but fantastic evening."

Kalliah thoughts went to visions of her evening. Dante' was more than she expected. They fondled and caressed each other until they couldn't control their desires for more. Kalliah begged for him to enter her as she listened to him moan as he explored her with his tongue. Dante' was large and his sacs were full. Kalliah watched as he slowly approached her. His gentle touch was all she needed to relax. He fingered her as he put on a condom. She closed her eyes expecting the next sensation to be in her inner walls. Dante' pushed in and out until the rhythm matched his breathing. Her vagina and his penis pulsated together, and the quivers followed. The thought of his marrying someone else never entered her mind. She wanted all he had to give. They had oral sex again until his penis stood waiting to feel her tenderness once more.

"Girl, did you hear me?" Brianne's voice brought her back to the present time.

"Whew girl, I am beat. I mean, don't get me wrong, I slept good but shit; my body hasn't had a night like that in a while."

"So you and Dante'......"

"Girl, yes.....oh I'm sorry we were talking about your fantastic night and questions."

"No you go first. Where is Cherese?"

"With Miles, so Stephon and you got busy too? I guess we all scored."

"Kalliah, have you ever had a male dancer?"

"You mean sexually had one? No."

"He danced for me nude. Girl he did the damn thing, nude. I was so horny by the time he touched me, I could have melted."

"Danced, danced? Pumping his body and gyrating nude? How was that?"

"No, that sensual type dancing; slow movements, and constantly massaging his piece. In a way, it was beautiful. You know like the Geisha dancers do. Girl then he stood over me and asked me to finger myself while he continued to move and masturbate. Ain't nothing like it! I didn't touch him to arouse him, and he didn't touch me. We touched ourselves and then girl.....it was on."

"Shit, that's different."

"Get this; he didn't even make comments about my size."

"What? What does that mean?"

"Girl I've had brothers talk that big girl shit while we're in the mix. I get tired of hearing about my breast, thighs and hips. If you like it, get on it. Usually, they give up before they put in any real work. Stephon wore me down girl before he got near it."

"Well he said you owed him one."

They laughed. Brianne got up to get another cup of coffee. A knock at the door redirected her attention. Kalliah rose from the couch as Brianne waved her off, she went to answer the door.

"Who is it?"

"Kyle. I need to talk to Cherese."

Brianne whispered. "Go call that hooker. I'll get rid of him. He won't ask me too many questions."

Kalliah went into the bedroom and closed the door. Brianne opened the door and checked the neckline of her loungewear careful not to show any cleavage.

"Hi Kyle come on in. They're not here. I think Cherese said something about picking up items at the house."

Kyle stepped inside, but Brianne didn't move from the entrance. Her reluctance to step aside made it clear; he didn't have a welcomed invitation.

"That note was from last night. I found it this morning. I need to talk to her. She took a lot of shit out of the house. How long are you guys staying here?"

Brianne thought about what he was saying. Cherese must have decided to leave him; if that was her decision, he didn't need to know where she would be.

"A few more days I would imagine. Since we drove, we've been stopping here and there. I have family to see as well as Kalliah. Cherese has been with us most of the time, but I haven't talked to her this morning I just got in."

"They weren't here then?"

"No, I left them last night. I only know that after we ate, they went their way, and I went mine. Did you try her cell?"

"She left it on the table with the note and the keys to the house. I don't see her car in the lot outside either."

"She was driving her car when we separated."

"Brianne, she mentioned that she doesn't want our marriage because of things I've done, even before we married. I hope you didn't influence her in anyway."

"Kyle cut the bull. You and I both know that the shit you do, you've been doing and probably will continue to do. If I had any influence over Cherese, she wouldn't have married you trifling ass. She's been with you all of these years, so obviously what happened to me had no effect on her so called love for you. What did you do to her?"

"Fuck the dumb shit. You told her during this little road trip, and the bitch thinks she's got a way out. You and that damn Kalliah, the two of you on a Thelma and Louise adventure, and now you want to include Cherese. You won't leave town with her. I'll see to that. Get it fucked up. Remember I've got boys that like a big black pussy."

Kalliah came out of the bedroom hearing Kyle's venom building. She walked between them and opened the door.

"Get the fuck out of here, and don't bring your sorry ass back unless you want the cops to find you. Trifling mother fucker."

Kyle gave Brianne a piercing look. "Bitch you lied!"

Kalliah pushed his shoulder. "Nothing that you don't do!"

"I have the right to know where my wife is!"

"Finally getting what she deserves." Kalliah slammed the door behind him. Brianne hung her head. Kyle's words repeated as they had the day she was raped, **"I've got boys that like a big black pussy."**

Kalliah called the front desk telling them that anyone wanting to come to their suite needed to be approved and that Kyle was not a wanted guest.

****

"Bree, I am so sorry. I left that note at the house thinking he wouldn't get it until tomorrow. He said he wouldn't be coming to the house until later in the week. I should have called you and Lillah before I went to Miles' house."

Brianne sat on the couch where she had been since Kyle's visit. She cried silently off and on while watching the television. She told Kalliah she would be okay. He had hit a soft spot. Kalliah knew it was more. She left her friend to herself to call Miles and Cherese. That had been an hour ago. Miles understood Cherese's need to leave and promised he would talk with her later. She now sat waiting for a response, but Brianne wouldn't acknowledge her presence.

"Kalliah, I don't know what to say or what to do. She hates me because of him." Cherese exclaimed leaving Brianne and joining Kalliah in her bedroom.

"No she doesn't, but what he said was fucked up. He didn't know I was here. I got scared for her. I didn't want it to go any further, and I didn't know if he would try to get physical. Cherese he's crazy. So did you leave him for good?"

Kalliah stopped getting dressed and waited for Cherese to answer. Cherese took a seat on the bed before speaking.

"Kalliah, you know I love Miles right? But I don't want to jump from one relationship to another. I don't know, but if I take up his offer, it's like I'll owe him. What would I owe him? Me. I don't want to ever have to give me as a token for a man again. I don't know about living in his house. I can't tell him no don't come. Shit it's his house. Suppose I want to entertain someone else. So here I am, stupid me. I left the only home I know going into seclusion to get myself together and still allowing a man to have some control over what I can or can't do. Kyle's going to jail. I can feel it. I want to sell the home and start over. I'm done. That rape thing tore at my soul. I've cried every night for what happened to her and knowing my husband was a part of her pain makes me sick."

Kalliah sat on the bed next to her and put her arm around her shoulders.

"Cherese, it's gonna be okay. You've got to believe that. What about your family? Can you stay with them?"

Cherese sighed. The thought of her family taunted her. Her family worshipped Kyle. They had no idea he was abusive. They didn't know she had been a victim.

"Kyle wouldn't stay away from them. I don't want him to have an advantage. You know my mother and them talking about holding on to our love, our marriage. They'll think it's about the miscarriage. And to be honest I haven't told them anything about how that even happened. Kalliah you and Brianne know that nigga pushed me. I'll take Miles up on his offer for now, but I can't stay there long. I just can't."

"You won't have to. Kyle won't come to my house. We have the room."

Cherese and Kalliah looked up at Brianne standing in the doorway. Cherese jumped up and hugged Brianne as she continued.

"You'll be safe as long as you need to be. You don't have to worry about owing me anything. Just promise me you'll take your time and get your life together."

"So, you'll leave with us on Sunday? That gives you a few days to take care of transferring doctors, banks and any other personal matters."

"I think I'll have my lawyer handle most of it while he prepares the divorce papers. I can't stay married to that ass.""Did you tell Miles you accepted his offer?" Kalliah asked as she stood looking in the mirror making final touches to her hair.

"No I avoided his question all night. We had a few drinks and took advantage of each other."

Brianne and Kalliah smiled. Cherese questioned them with her look.

"Tell me there were others that got taken advantage of."

Brianne sat on the other side of Cherese. "Girl, have you ever…?"

****

Stephon arrived at the cafeteria thirty minutes later as planned. The detectives sat waiting patiently for his arrival. At one o'clock most of the workers were reporting back to their offices causing the three men to have the area to themselves.

"Do you have an idea on how this is to go down?" Ryan Smith, the lead detective, questioned Stephon after every direction. "Yeah, the only thing I don't understand is, why can't the arrest be made there?"

"We'd have to arrest your ass too. Maybe you'd understand that." Juan Rivera, Ryan's partner, had been quiet at each meeting. He had a deep accent, and Stephon couldn't tell if he detected a bit of an attitude as well.

"So I'll be walking with drugs on me?"

"No, I doubt if Kyle brings the shit with him. You go with what we told you and guaranteed he'll set up a pick up for later. Just meet him when and where he says."

"Ryan, man, I've got a lot to lose here. I don't need to get caught with shit on me."

"Did I mention that you're protected? Trust me Stephon; this will work in your favor. You'll get that new job and things will be different for you and your boys."

"What do my boys have to do with this?"

"You want your boys to have a stable home, a father who can provide, and most of all you want to move on with no blemishes on your jacket right?"

"Listen my boys aren't in this, and neither is their stability. I've been doing everything according to the rules, and then you show up, now I feel like you're threatening me or something."

Juan leaned across the table getting close to Stephon's face.

"What my partner is trying to say is we can give you what you need to get on and pretty much guarantee your future or you can fuck this up and relive your past."

Stephon didn't understand Juan's attitude. He watched him as he sat back and stuck a toothpick from his sandwich in his mouth.

"I don't know how or when I rubbed your ass or fucked your bitch, but you're gonna stop talking to me like I owe your ass some explanation or apology. The two of you approached me. I've been doing things legit, and here you come with this bullshit. The funny thing is you want me to do the same shit that fucked up my record. I suggest one of you talk to me man to man, or fuck both of you. My life can't be any worse than it is now."

"Look man calm down, Juan isn't happy about this sting. He had another method in mind you know, but this is the way they want it to go down."

"Yeah well maybe you ought to do things his way then and leave me the fuck out of it. I don't want to carry no shit, period. I don't trust you or Juan, and I sure don't trust the others that don't really give a fuck about who I am."

Juan stood up. "Ryan fuck this nigga. I told you he wouldn't be worth a damn to us. The Feds can use their guy."

Juan walked away from the table toward the cashier to pay for the lunch. Ryan sat back and sighed. He pulled out his cell phone and dialed a number. He handed the ringing phone to Stephon.

"Hello."

"Yes, this is Stephon, who is this?"

"Ahh Mr. Drake, Detective Miller, I believe Mr. Smalls may have mentioned my name to you."

"Yes he did. What's up?"

"You tell me, I thought we were making progress. I told them to call me if there was some confusion. Do you have questions you need answered?"

"Yeah, listen call me on my cell."

"No problem." The phone went dead and Stephon's phone began to ring. He looked at the LCD display for the name of the caller, it stated unknown. Stephon looked at Ryan as he grabbed his cell from the table. He got up and left the table walking to join Juan, who stood in the lobby outside of the cafeteria.

"Mr. Drake. Is this better?"

"Well, now I'm not sure. Who are you?"

"Detective Miller, I'm with the FBI. This matter is delicate, and I understand your concern, but you'll be protected completely. Just follow the instructions as given. If you should deviate from the instructions, it could cause a problem from other agents who have no knowledge about your involvement. Mr. Drake, I can guarantee you that you're in better hands than you ever were. We'll talk more, after this is over."

Ryan came back to the table with Juan and sat down as if on cue. "Mr. Drake I'm certain you'll be more than satisfied with your new job and pay. Mr. Smalls is more than happy to compensate you for doing this job for him, and so are we. We'll talk more afterwards, thank you."

Stephon closed his phone and listened again to the instructions. He was to meet Kyle at eight o'clock that evening.

****

Miles and Dante' decided to play a round of golf. Dante' would be leaving Saturday or Sunday, and the opportunity to play then would be slim to none. They had lunch at the club house prior to the game, and headed to pick up their cart afterwards.

"So what do you think Kyle will do now?" Miles stood by the cart as Dante' loaded the back with his clubs.

"What can he do? Cherese has decided to leave him, and that's it. You aren't worried about him, are you?"

"We're supposed to leave to go to the house on Saturday. I'm really looking forward to her being relaxed. She needs that to get on with her life."

"Alright so why the question about Kyle?"

"Cherese admitted he was violent. I know he's stupid. I don't want him to get violent. His dumb ass might try to come to my house for her."

"I don't think that will be a problem unless Cherese tells him where she's going and with who."

"Dante' I didn't think about it until Cherese said what the inside of her house looked like the other night. She thought someone had been in her home and ransacked it. I didn't plan on moving to Atlanta with her or anything, but I don't want her letting him in either."

"You don't sound too sure about a relationship with her."

"It's just when she talks about him. One minute she sounds sure of herself, but then there are times when I can't tell if she's even thinking of moving on. We both agreed to remain close. I don't want to push her into a relationship until she regains her self-worth. I think she needs that. I'm willing to let her stay there, but I don't want him attempting to come there."

"Tell her then, straight up, you don't want Kyle in your home. I'd let her know, man tell her."

Miles picked up his bag and put it in the cart. They rode to the next hole before he responded.

"So how straight were you with Kalliah?"

"Not straight at all. I couldn't admit that the baby may be mine. I did tell her my feelings about the wedding and Angel being pregnant. It must have eased her mind, we spent the night together."

"So you and Kalliah had sex?"

"Yeah, shit we're grown."

"You're engaged."

"Miles, you can't be for real. You and I both know the shit I've been through with Angel. I called there last night and didn't get an answer. You want to know what I think?"

"No."

"You damn real. She's still with her baby's daddy."

"Why don't you tell her straight up?"

"My plans exactly; I'm not marrying that damn hooker, baby or not."

"So what do you do, come back after the baby is born to see if you're the father?"

"My first thought was to leave her ass at the altar. I wasn't gonna agree to change the date either. Let her ass waddle down the aisle, but then I want to be done with her as soon as possible."

"So when do you find out if you're the father?"

"I guess after the baby is born unless she agrees to a test before. I don't even know if they'll do that. I'll find out though."

"And you and Kalliah start from this week forward?"

"I don't think so. We really didn't talk about it. I have some baggage, and she's dealing with some lost soul."

"Some lost soul?"

"He's lost as far as I'm concerned. Her reaction to me in the bed said he wasn't a factor. I'll stay in touch, visit and move on from there."

"Hmm. I wonder how Stephon and Brianne made out."

"To be honest I'm surprised Stephon still made a move on her."

"Why? He's always liked her. Why wouldn't he?"

"After finding out about her past, man I don't think I could. Maybe at another time but her past is new to us. It had to affect his performance."

"Performance, they got busy too?"

"Miles, you know us. You know how we do it. What sense would it be for us to split up and not get busy?"

Miles smiled and took the first swing at the tenth hole. It was a concentrated effort, but the ball rolled down the hill into the trees that lined the course. Dante' laughed and set his ball on the tee.

"You know you ought to give this up. You can't win this game."

"Man, we've got eight to go."

"Yeah and you can't win."

"So is Stephon meeting us at the house? Did you speak to him? Hey, did someone tell him about Kyle coming to the suite?"

"He said he'd catch up with us later. No, I didn't tell him. I don't know if Kalliah called him or not. I didn't speak to her yet either. I'm going to talk with my mother for a minute after I dust your ass off, then I'll call Kalliah. I don't know if I'll see her before I leave."

"Yeah, okay. Maybe I'll take your advice and talk to Cherese and see what she's really gonna do."

"The way I see it, there's not much she can do. She needs to carry out her plans and don't look back."

Choices

"Mrs. Jefferson this cake is sooo good."

"Y'all take as much as you like. When Dante', Miles and Stephon get here I'm gonna tell them to take the rest with them. I don't need a whole lot of sweets just sitting here."

Brianne put her fork on her plate, and wiped the corner of her mouth. Cherese chose not to have a piece, while Kalliah took her time with each forkful.

"I'm so glad you ladies stopped by. So you leaving on Sunday you say?"

"Yeah, we've got to get back to work."

"Brianne you still working at the same job? You know I haven't seen your aunt much, how is she?"

"I spoke with her last week. All was well. My cousins still live with her. They're all fine."

"Did you stop by and see your family Kalliah?"

"Everyone is doing fine. My mother sends her regards."

"I don't get over on that side of town much. I need to though, that's where all the good shopping is. Cherese you mighty quiet, you okay?"

"I'm doing a lot better; better than when you saw me before."

"Did you tell Kalliah and Brianne, we spent many a night talking about them and the friendship you have? It seemed to calm her nerves.

We would talk about the things that she loved the most, and you two would always be a part of the conversation."

"Well we're taking her home with us for a while."

"Really Cherese, you leaving town?"

"Mrs. Jefferson, I think it's time. I need to find myself."

"Sometimes women need that. I'm glad you have somewhere to start looking. Listen there are so many that don't have a soul to search, or the will to embrace what's left after they've lost so much. You'll be fine, you'll see. A different environment brings different feelings, wants, and needs. Embrace it, and claim the blessing in it. God gave you strength enough to keep a level head. So, you look this in the face and smile at the goodness you find."

Cherese and her friends listened as Dante's mother spoke about what she needed to start her life over.

"Mrs. Jefferson, I don't think I'm coming back here. I may visit from time to time, but I can't live here."

"Does Kyle know that?"

"No, but I wanted you to know where I'll be. Kyle won't come to Brianne's house. I'll be staying there until I'm well enough to get a place of my own. My doctors and other matters will be handled by my lawyer. If you don't mind I would like you to be my liaison. I would ask my family, but I think they would eventually tell Kyle. He won't ask you."

"Girl he wouldn't know to ask me. I can't remember Kyle talking to me through your whole ordeal. Now that fella Miles might ask me….."

"He'll know. Even if Stephon or Dante' ask that's okay. But they'll know on Saturday when we go to dinner again."

"Saturday, I thought Dante' was leaving Saturday. I may be wrong though. He's got his own drama too."

Cherese gave Kalliah an **"ask her"** look and Brianne added a simple nod.

"Well I know that look means there's some questions. Y'all ain't changed a bit."

Mrs. Jefferson stood and cleared the plates from the table and covered the remaining cake that sat on the crystal plate. For years Dante's mother was an outlet for many of the youth who reached adulthood quickly, and found it difficult to talk to others. After becoming an ear for the church, and many of the member's prayer partners Mrs. Jefferson learned not to force conversations, she just listened.

Kalliah talked slowly and deliberately. "Mrs. Jefferson, I think Dante', and I are in love. He's told me about his engagement to Angelina. We've discussed her pregnancy, but he says it's not his child. He even said he can't marry her. I want to believe him but…."

Kalliah's voice faded. She took a napkin from the table to wipe her falling tears.

"Mrs. Jefferson, Angelina told Kalliah before Dante'."

Brianne held Kalliah's hand as she completed the small details for her. Mrs. Jefferson wiped her hands on her apron before reaching across the table, wiping it with the dish cloth.

"Now I can't say that I'm surprised. Angelina is a trip. I've never liked her. It's just something about her ways, but Dante' has been with her off and on for…. I want to say more than four years. Anyway, baby you have to go with your feelings. You and Dante' have been life-long friends. I want to tell you trust your friendship, but as his mother, I can't say that the child ain't his. Anything is possible. That's what that gal is banking on."

Cherese shook her head. "Mrs. Jefferson, does it matter though?"

"Does what matter? Yes, if that child is his, Angelina will be a part of his life. He's got to deal with that child as a parent. She will be the other parent. That's where young folks go wrong. It's bad enough that the children aren't raised with both parents, but the parents have to maintain a relationship."

"Dante' told me he'd be a father, and that was it."

"Baby I'd be a fool not to tell you that being a father includes being a parent, and being a parent means you've got to work with the other parent. Now don't get me wrong, they don't have to be intimate, or have that type of relationship, but they sure have to be more than that baby daddy, baby mama mess."

"That Angelina sounds like a piece of work."

"Brianne, she is. I don't know…..well that ain't for me to say. Kalliah I'm sorry if I didn't help you with making a choice. I think that's what you wanted, a direction to steer that love you have. You've got to go with your gut feeling baby. My son ain't no better than any other man out there. He should have walked away from her years ago, but he stayed, asked her to marry him, and now he has no idea if that child is his. Well, Angelina ain't changed since they been together, Dante' did."

"It seems as though I stepped in and changed his mind. That's all I keep thinking. If it wasn't for the reunion, he would have married her. Now there's a child that may not have their father constantly in their life because of me."

Cherese got up and went into the living room. The talk of an unborn child brought thoughts of her being pushed by Kyle and losing her baby. Mrs. Jefferson watched her walk out of the room. She motioned for Brianne to go with her leaving her and Kalliah to finish their talk.

"You know sometimes things happen for a reason. We don't always know what part we play in altering lives. Just like me sitting here with you. We may not know how this little conversation will affect your life until years from now. You'll reflect on it, and say if it wasn't for Mrs. Jefferson and me talking. Well, you may have been the spark that Dante' needed to redirect his life. I don't want to talk bad about nobody, but that Angelina is a mess. I really thought Dante' was gonna do some jail time over her and that man she was or is dealing with. Kalliah if you changed his mind about marrying her, it's a good thing. Now we'll have to wait to see whose child it is. If Dante' claims the child is his, all I can do is love that child. You and Dante' have to make a choice to love the child too. Baby you know that choice has to come first."

"Thank you so much for listening. You're right. We've got to wait and see."

"Chile don't you get caught up in that mess. That's baggage he needs to deal with not you. Let him deal with Angelina. You don't want either of them saying you made the decisions. Be a friend as you have all these years. Your friendship will mean more to the both of you after it's all said and done."

Kalliah stood refreshed. She was more than grateful that Mrs. Jefferson took the time to listen. The two ladies walked into the small living room where Brianne and Cherese were talking. Cherese looked better than she had when she stepped out of the kitchen.

"Well Cherese, you call when you get settled. Did you leave anything you'll need shipped to you?"

"No, I've got most of my things. I've been packing things over time and putting them in storage. Items I knew Kyle would give away or sale. I do love my black art though, but the lawyer said that could be looked at as mutual property. Anyway, I have a meeting with my lawyer, and I'll have him contact you."

"You sound determined. Something you've been missing over the past few months. I like that. Yes, I like that. Ms. Brianne, you stay in touch don't let it be so long. I want to hear what you're into."

"I will keep you updated from time to time."

Cherese and Brianne rose to their feet. They each embraced Mrs. Jefferson accepting the motherly hug and kisses. They stepped out the front door saying their goodbyes. Kalliah and Mrs. Jefferson held each other in silence. They both understood the strength that was passed during the exchange of unspoken love.

"Baby, keep your faith first. Let God take care of the rest."

"I will and thank you."

****

"Miles this is Stephon, listen, I won't be by tonight that thing with the job came up. I'll check you and Dante' out in the morning, but I need a favor."

"Anything, other than driving you to work for a week."

"Funny man."

"What do you need?"

"Listen; tell Brianne that I need to see her before she leaves. She didn't know whether they were leaving tomorrow or on Sunday. I tried calling her. I wasn't able to reach her. I'm probably gonna shut my phone off for a couple of hours. I don't know how long this thing is gonna take."

"No problem, hey watch your back man."

"I'll try."

Stephon hung up the phone and turned the television to the six o'clock news. The meeting with Kyle was at eight. He thought about the clientele he had before Washington D.C.'s finest caught him with enough CDS to have him charged with possession and intent to distribute. After being released, he vowed to walk away from the street game and never return; he didn't feel good about Kyle, Juan or Ryan. He needed to talk to someone other than Miles. Stephon was scared. He didn't want Kyle to sense there was a reason for his fear other than blowing his probation. Kyle wouldn't make a deal if he smelled trouble.

When the phone broke the silence in the room, Stephon welcomed it. He had all but convinced himself that the deal would be botched. "Hello."

"Hey Stephon."

"Bree, I'm glad you called. Are you okay?"

"Yeah, did you speak with Miles?"

"About an hour ago why?"

"Kyle came to the suite."

"For what?"

"Cherese. I told him she was with Kalliah. It got ugly. Kalliah came out of the room and threw him out."

"It got ugly? What does that mean? Wait, I thought you said Kalliah was with Cherese."

"I lied. I didn't want to tell him she was with Miles. He had gone to the house and found her note that she was leaving him. Anyway, he came over here I guess to talk to her. I got the blunt of his fury."

"Where is she now?"

"She's here with us. She's leaving when we go. I offered her a room in my home. She'll be fine."

"What about you?"

"I was shook. I'm not gonna lie. But you know what? I got the last laugh, and I did something good for myself and Cherese."

"Okay so I guess it helped you close a chapter."

"I hope so. I'm going to see my Aunt tomorrow. Then the chapter will be closed."

"Oh, okay. You sure you're alright?"

"Yeah, I'm better than I was earlier. And talking to you always helps."

"Brianne, what happens after this weekend? I mean, you leaving town, me being here. Don't get me wrong, I understand you're going home, but tell me you'll allow me to come see you, or you'll meet me every now and then. It doesn't have to be here."

"Stephon, Kyle has nothing to do with us. Of course, I'll be in touch with you."

"What if the chapter with your family is final?"

"It's pretty much that way now. I want my aunt to understand me. Brianne Gibson the adult; the child that was left because of her parent's death; the teen that was raped and whoever else she wanted me to be, is dead. I buried her, and she needs to know that. You were right I can't continue to hold on to my past."

"Well you know I am a part of your past too. I don't want to be a reminder of what you want to forget."

"I'm not confused. You are a part of the sunshine in my clouded past. I need all the sunshine in my life that I can get."

"I'm glad about that. I was worried for awhile. I don't want to lose your friendship again." Stephon looked at the clock on his wall. Although Brianne had calmed his nerves, he had to leave. "Can I call you later I have an appointment to keep?"

"We're hanging out tonight can I call you after I see my Aunt tomorrow? I probably will need to."

"Sure you can. I'll talk to you tomorrow." Stephon glanced at his watch, comparing the time to the clock on the wall. It was close to seven o'clock. He'd needed to leave in fifteen minutes.

****

"Dante' are you coming home in the morning?"

"Angel, where have you been? I've called three or four times today, and no answer."

"You couldn't have called. I've had the phone with me all day. What time will you get in? I want to meet you."

"Sunday 'bout twelve, no make it two."

"Damn, I would think you wanted to get here tomorrow."

"I made arrangements with Stephon and Miles for tomorrow. I probably won't see them for a minute, so I'll be there Sunday." Dante' thought how he wanted the dinner to go. Hopefully, his mother put in a good word for him. Kalliah had to understand the situation he was in. He would talk with her again after they all had dinner. Kalliah loved him, and that was all that mattered. Angel would be history after Sunday.

"Dante' I'm glad you're coming home. I missed you."

"Why did you call Kalliah; what was that about?"

"She should know Dante'. Maybe we'll be friends later, who knows, but she should know who I am, and that I am gonna be with you."

"Funny how you couldn't tell that nigga who was humpin' on your ass that. You got some shit with you."

"I didn't lie to her."

"No, you lied to me. To me Angel, I took your trifling ass back, and you're pregnant with his child. How fucked up is that?"

"It ain't his child!"

"How many months Angel; how far along are you?"

The phone went dead in his ear. It didn't faze him. He yelled for his mother to join him in the living room. She left the room when she realized Angel was on the line. The aroma from the kitchen spoke as though it were reading a menu. Fish, collard greens, macaroni and cheese, and cornbread would be ready to be served shortly. Jennifer Jefferson didn't interrupt her final touches to return to the living room.

"Dinner's almost done, c'mon in here. You can eat now too."

"You know what? I think Angel has lost it. I was asking her how many months along is she; she just hung up the phone. Now she just told me the doctor said she was pregnant. If the baby was mine, she'd say, four weeks, eight weeks or whatever. She can't tell me Ma 'cause the kid ain't mine. And I'm supposed to accept this, and marry her?"

"No. Get your plate from that cabinet, pass me one too. What happened to Miles, I thought he was coming with you?"

"He wanted to talk to Cherese. He offered her his home in Atlanta. I think he changed his mind."

"Why do y'all do that? Don't you think about these things before you put your foot in them? That's why they say you men think with the wrong head 'specially you young men. Now you caught in a proposal, and you don't bit want to marry that girl, and never did. You telling me Miles offered his home to Cherese and what? He remembered she married a fool?"

"Yeah, that's it."

Jennifer reached for her son's plate while taking the top off the pots letting the smell of a down home meal fill the small kitchen.

"It's nice this time of evening. You want to sit on the porch? I've got television trays that I use when it's like this."

"I'll set them up. Where are they?"

His mother pointed to the closet in the hall and continued preparing their plates. They sat on the porch reminiscing Dante's high school years, and the girls he dated.

"I guess the only one you see now from those days is Kalliah huh?"

"Ma, we were never a couple. We've always been friends."

"A lot of us sure thought it went further. Your father swore she would be your wife. You remember when I came home early and y'all liked to killed yourselves jumping up off that couch."

"You would have killed us if we didn't."

They both found the memory funny. Dante' paused in thought. He remembered his father using that incident as his prelude to their discussion about sex. Although Dante' didn't need the talk, it was one of the last father and son moments they shared.

"Kalliah and the other girls were here this afternoon. I guess Miles will be surprised to know Cherese isn't accepting his offer."

"Really, wow, I think he'll be hurt. He's confused."

"He's confused? What about you?"

"I'm not confused. I'm not marrying Angel."

"What if the child is yours?"

"I'm not marrying Angel. If I have to, I'll raise the child by myself. I am not going to be committed to her the rest of my life."

"Your commitment won't be to her. It will be to that child."

"Listen Ma, I know what you're trying to say, or make me understand. I am not going to abandon my responsibility to that child. First, I need to know that the baby is mine. Second, well, that step doesn't include marriage, at least not to Angel."

"So is Kalliah willing to marry you if the child is yours?"

"I didn't ask her. And it's okay if she doesn't. I'm not rushed to marry her."

"Oh, so you'll wait until she will marry you. Suppose she won't Dante'. I'm trying to make you see that no one wants to settle. They want what's real. Will you be rushing into a relationship because you're a single parent?"

"That sounds like a question for the mothers?"

"Why, you don't think you'll be considered a single parent?"

"No, I don't. Father's aren't looked at like that. I'll be a man with a son or daughter. I don't need a woman to handle the parenting, you know like women do."

"What are you talking about?"

Jennifer put her fork on her plate after putting a forkful of macaroni in her mouth. She chewed slowly savoring the flavor and smiling at her son.

"Why are you looking at me like that?"

"I'm waiting to hear this mess you talking. Go ahead explain this old wise one."

"Listen, women or I should say young women that I know about, hunt for the other parent in the men they date. They're always looking for fill-in daddies. Men don't look for fill-in mothers, why should I? I can handle a child, how hard can it be?"

"You'll see won't you? Do you want something else? Give me your plate."

"I'll have another piece of fish please, and macaroni."

"And you can handle a child huh?"

"Ma, that's different. You handled me."

Jennifer didn't understand her son's feelings about single parenting. She didn't become a single parent until his father passed, Dante' was sixteen. It was different raising a child alone from birth. Reality would shock him as it had done so many young single parents. She closed her eyes and prayed before preparing his second helping.

****

Stephon watched his rear-view mirror; unsure of the direction Kyle would be approaching his vehicle. He would see the White BMW as it crossed the intersection. He chose to park where he had a good view of the area. The spot was as it had been in the past; well lit, plenty of traffic, both vehicles and pedestrians, and close to public transportation. Stephon's shady past gave him experience in needing all of these factors. He and Kyle understood why their place to meet would not change. Stephon found it strange that he wasn't questioned about his return to the streets.

The white luxury car pulled into a parking spot under the street light. It was half past eight, and the lights glistened on the hood of the well waxed vehicle. Kyle got out of his car dialing on his cell phone. He made his observations of the area as he leaned on the hood of his car. Stephon decided it was the perfect opportunity to get out of his car while Kyle's back was facing him. He closed the car door and stood debating whether to wait or walk up to him.

Kyle turned before Stephon made his decision. He waved when he spotted him crossing the street. Pocketing his cell phone, he extended his hand to greet his supplier.

"Yo man, I thought you was running late or somethin'. What's good? I couldn't believe you called me through those jokers on your job. Man you could have hooked this up without them. You know that right?"

Stephon listened trying not to show any signs of nervousness. He could feel the presence of Juan and his partners, although he had no idea where they were.

"Yo man, you alright or what? Listen you want a piece of this? I may have to lay low awhile, and I need someone to do this. Tell me somethin' though, why you street runnin'?"

"I'm good man. I'm tired though, you know, working and keeping the man off me. But I've got to find a way to build man, something for my boys. You got to go with what you know. I've got some of my peeps on standby so I won't be doing the street thing, but I need some weight." Stephon was glad the question was put in the open. He didn't need Kyle to be suspicious.

"Well I've got it, but you know damn well it won't go down here."

"How much?"

The question was one Juan told Stephon to be sure he asked. Kyle never suspected he was wired and the conversation continued.

"The price depends on what you want. You said you had the cash right, listen you want to follow me to Eleventh Ave? You know the house where we got the set up right?"

"I think so, is that the black and white one on the corner past the church?"

Stephon wanted the cops to be set up before they left where they were standing.

"Naw man it's the next block over you got to go past the school. Just wait there bring, the money to the door and my boy will bring you the goods. Oh yeah, it is a black and white house, my bad, it's the third one on the block. Park your car in the driveway so you can get loaded."

"So I just give the money to whoever answers the door? How do I know my shit will be delivered?"

"Have I ever stiffed you before?"

"Kyle, it ain't done this way. If I wanted to deal with some punk at a door, I wouldn't have contacted you. I agree I don't want my hands in this shit either, but just like you, its business. Do business, like a businessman bro!"

"Listen, bring the money. How much you buying?"

Stephon smiled as he answered, the hook was almost ready to be reeled in. "Fifty grand, and another fifty grand drop next week, we'll talk about where then."

"What does that mean?"

"It means you set this shit up this week, and next week I'll set it up. I trust you now you trust me later."

Kyle had no choice but to deliver.

****

Eleventh Avenue was quiet. Juan, Ryan and the local police had set up surveillance while waiting for Stephon's car to arrive. Kyle had pulled into the driveway, and his car was now hidden behind the three-family house they used to run their operation in the neighborhood. The house had been raided a few times with only a promise that they would catch the dealers one day. The detectives hoped Stephon had accomplished what they couldn't.

Kyle flagged Stephon as he backed his car into the narrow space between the two homes. Ryan couldn't hear any voices over the mic taped to Stephon's back, and he couldn't read their lips. The actions of both men indicated that the house wasn't ready for entry. Juan punched in the address on the laptop in the car and four faces flashed on the screen. Kyle's was the first to appear.

"Yeah this is the spot they hit about six months ago. They got nothing according to this report but look at the precautions. Full riot gear was necessary that day. I don't know if we want your boy involved in this. The arsenal inside is probably well stocked. He may catch a bullet."

"What makes you think they're gonna shoot?"

"So we sit here right?"

"Rght, we sit Juan!"

"You cover his ass then when the bullets fly. I might just shoot his ass."

"What's up with you? Why you got a thing for this guy?"

"Ryan read his shit. Stephon Drake is no angel."

"And he served his time; we're using him to get the more popular asshole, Kyle Taylor!"

"This shit just don't seem right."

"Well we're here closer than where we've ever been. The casualty of war man, he should have known the risk. Besides their friends, Kyle won't let them shoot him."

The detectives watched as Kyle did a sloppy check of the car for any tracking devices. He smiled again as he returned to the start of his search. "Put your hands on your head."

"What are you looking for?"

"Stephon put your fucking hands on your head."

"What is this Kyle?"

Stephon knew the rules hadn't changed, "no one tells on another." Kyle did a quick pat of Stephon's legs, and waistband. Stephon held his breath certain that Kyle would find the mic that was taped between his shoulder blades. His idea of wearing the Redskin's football jersey helped hide any bulge. The mic sat perfect between his name and the number eighty eight on his back. Kyle never touched it. Stephon decided acting agitated may cause him to search further he stood still realizing he had passed the sloppy frisk.

"So can we get on with this or what?"

"Man, I just had a feeling that's all. Let me get your shit. Where's the money?"

Stephon opened the car door and pulled out the satchel that carried the money given to him by one of the other Feds. He followed their orders handing him the satchel carefully making sure a visual could be made of the hand off. Kyle took the money smiling, and Stephon grabbed his arm.

"You ain't leaving me standing here while you walk away with fifty g's. What you think I'm crazy?"

"Man my boys don't know you, and I don't want them to. Let's keep the honesty between us. Fuck, you know where to find me if you don't get yours. Where am I gonna disappear to? Check the back out man. It's boarded up, bolted purposely. The only entrances are this door here and the side. Trust me bro, we'll be doing business again. I ain't messing that up."

It didn't matter to Stephon; he was making it look good. If the Feds didn't lock Kyle up Stephon would be sure to get one of his boys to off him. He decided Kyle didn't deserve to live the night Brianne told him what he did to her. Cherese's marital problems added to his anger. The sting with the cops saved him the trouble of owing one of his boys. Kyle's days were numbered.

There was a breeze and Stephon tilted his head back enjoying the momentary silence. He took a deep breath preparing himself for the turmoil that he knew all too well would begin once Juan and his boys spotted the goods being loaded in the car. Stephon opened the trunk and made sure the device hidden inside still had the red light flashing. Kyle returned with two of his guys holding forty caliber handguns pointed at Stephon.

"Step away from the car, now!"

"What the fuck is wrong with you?"

"What's in the trunk Mother Fucker?"

"Nothing I was opening it for your boys to put my shit in it."

"Man you got to understand this here. Get the fuck away from the damn car."

Stephon moved while one of Kyle's boys took his arm and the other peeked into the trunk.

"He ain't got nothing, tell 'em to load Kyle."

The packages started coming out of the house Stephon was moved on the front lawn, and the drawn weapon was put in his ribs. Ryan could see through his binoculars that their opportunity to seize may cause Kyle to be shot. Juan pointed to one of their shooters who was positioned on the roof of the garage at the next house. He had a perfect shot of the man covering Stephon.

"We're good man, call it."

Men in black D.E.A. and S.W.A.T. gear flooded the area as the man covering Stephon fell to the ground after being shot in the shoulder. Stephon stepped back into the arms of an agent who snatched him away from the scene putting him into an over equipped black van. Stephon watched, surprised at the adrenaline rush that overcame him. Detectives and police collected evidence and the rest of the suspects in the house. The arrests totaled eight including Kyle. He looked over the area as he walked with the others to the large SUV. There was no sign of Stephon, and he wasn't in the vehicle. Kyle realized he had been set up.

Juan and Ryan got in the van after taking off their ballistic jackets. Their smiles told Stephon everything went as planned. Juan extended his arm with his fist clenched, and Stephon gave him "dap" which was both an apology and acceptance.

"Good job man, you did your thing. I like the way you roll."

Ryan shook his hand and nodded to the driver.

"Your car will be impounded, we tried to get in there before they put anything in the back, but it's all good you'll be furnished with a vehicle, as soon as we check in. You'll have to ride with us if you don't mind. We could have it dropped off to you, but Detective Miller wants a word with you."

Stephon was proud of himself. He nodded his head in acknowledgement. Brianne and Cherese would be glad to know Kyle met his match.

Forever Friends

Dinner reservations were made for seven o'clock, and Kalliah was starving. She hadn't stopped to eat all day. Her day included saying her last farewells to family and friends, a trip to the mall and finally packing. She hoped everyone would be on time she had plans on pigging out.

Her conversations with Dante' had been short, but she had to admit, she agreed with the way he wanted to handle Angelina and the pregnancy. After hearing how she hung up the phone without giving him an answer, Kalliah had her own doubts about the baby being Dante's child. She couldn't imagine not telling the father how far along she was, what would be the secret?

Dante' wanted to spend another night of intimacy with her, but she declined. A decision she regretted after their conversation ended. She had a need for his touch without the drama that might follow. Facing him, while eating dinner would be a different situation, she would definitely have to fight her own itch.

The outfit for the evening was form fitting, outlining her shape. She decided on a two-piece peach skirt set. It was double breasted with gold buttons, and the tunic top was scalloped around the neckline. Kalliah's breast and thighs added interest to what would be a simple outfit. She picked her gold accessories smiling as she went to the mirror to redo her hair for the evening.

Brianne and Cherese were assisting each other at the other end of the suite. Brianne chose her favorite lilac linen slacks with a multi-colored blouse. She was attempting to put her hair in a neat bun. She had been fussing with it for more than ten minutes.

"I need hair like you and Khalliah, but no, I'm the one who has to have a beautician do it everywhere I go. I can't even get this bun thing to work."

"Girl, let me do that for you. I love that outfit, reminds me of summer. I didn't know there were that many shades of purple."

Cherese was dressed in a rust Capri two-piece suit. Her makeup added a pleasant glow. She had been ready for hours. She spent most of the day writing her to-do list and calling her lawyer with business she needed him to handle. It was easier than she thought. She was tempted to call Kyle to tell him she was leaving, but the lawyer told her to leave that up to him. After hearing about the marriage, the problems and her concerns that he would be arrested, he told her it would be best not to associate with him. Everything was falling into place. She made her last visit to her doctor during the week. She filled her prescriptions, wished her well and gave her the name of a physician in Virginia once she got settled.

"There, that's gonna hold. Its six fifteen, are we meeting the guys there?"

"Stephon is picking me up here. Has Miles called you?"

"No I'll check with Kalliah maybe Dante' called her."

The two women walked into the living room together where Kalliah was checking her purse.

"What time are we leaving in the morning y'all?"

"Early, Cherese already asked. We're packed and ready."

Cherese plopped on the couch. "More than ready, I wish the movers could pick my stuff up from the house and move it all right now."

"Girl our house ain't as big as yours. Did they get it all in storage?"

Brianne called the storage company for Cherese. She would need a larger space until she could move her things with them in Virginia.

"Cherese, are you planning on moving the furniture out of the house?"

"Kalliah, if Kyle gets locked up, I'm selling the house. I'll give him his cut and whatever is his, he can say where he wants it to go. That would be the easiest way of handling things. If he doesn't go to jail, we'll have to fight it out for the furniture and other items he'll argue over just for spite. Brianne was right about enlarging my space that I already have then I don't have to worry Ms. Jefferson or Miles with that. I'll come back to oversee them moving what's got to be moved later."

"Alright now. Well, Ms. Thang is waiting for Stephon, you riding with me or waiting for Miles?"

"He didn't call so I guess I'm riding with you."

****

Dante' checked his messages at his home and was pleased. He would leave D.C. without work that needed his immediate attention when he returned to his job on Monday. Angel hadn't mentioned any calls during his mini vacation. Since she wouldn't answer her phone he'd just have to trust that his clients had their matters handled by other staff. He was determined not to call Angel again. Their next conversation would be face to face.

He buttoned his shirt and looked in the mirror; he didn't want to be over dressed. He paused taking the shirt off sighing. He was caught between thoughts. Leaving Kalliah without knowing that they would continue their relationship on a new level was wearing on him. Dante' wanted to start what should have been years ago. If he could turn back the hands of time, he would have told her he couldn't be just a friend. After dinner, he would explain she was who he needed in his life.

"Dante', did Stephon call you last night?" Miles entered the large guest room from the hall.

"No, he called this morning though. You were in the shower."

Miles leaned on the wall looking at Dante' with a question on his face.

"What? I didn't like the white shirt thing."

"Where's the tat you got for Kalliah? You got it removed?"

"Tat? Oh, no one knows it was for her. It's just initials man. Here on my shoulder." Dante' turned so Miles could see the fancy tattoo with the letters KC separated by hearts and doves followed by DJ. The letters were entwined with a vine of smaller hearts and doves. His caramel colored skin made it easy to be seen.

"Kalliah didn't see that?"

"You know what man…" Dante' took another shirt out of his garment bag and started putting it on. "If she did she didn't say anything. I got this tat in college. I forgot about it until you said something. I mean I didn't even think about mentioning it to her. I damn sure will tonight though, it will give me a reason to take my shirt off and work some magic."

"Yeah even if it is the last time."

"It won't be trust me. We're gonna be together. What about you and Cherese? Hey, c'mon Stephon is picking up Brianne; we'll meet everyone at the restaurant. Now what's up with you and Cherese?"

They left the house continuing their conversation. Miles stopped at his car. "Yours or mine?" Dante' went to the passenger's side of Miles' car.

"I have to make that drive in the morning. It's on you tonight man." They got into the car and closed the doors simultaneously. Miles turned the key to the ignition and lowered the volume on the radio.

"I thought about it man, Cherese and I haven't really had a chance to talk. She hasn't said anything about my place or leaving. That's the problem with her. I guess it's what she's going through or has been through. To be honest, a relationship with her may be harder than I thought. She's alright for dating and she totally satisfies my sexual needs, but man, I can't deal with her indecisiveness. She's too dependent. I don't really think it will work out.

"Really, you were so determined to make her yours though."

"Dante', I don't want to make her mine. I want her to want me too. That's the problem I just don't know what she wants. She thinks Kyle is going to jail, so now she wants to run? What is she running from? What people might say, or the fear that she'll be at the visit hall every weekend? She'll be sending money and waiting on his letters until he gets out. I guess that scares her, so she's moving to Georgia. I don't know man; I guess it's like what you said about Angel."

"What's that?"

"I can't trust how she feels about that dude. Kyle's got a hold on her mentally. That's a chain she's got to break before I commit to a relationship with her."

"So, do you just date her and have sex while he's in prison?"

"No, that ain't my style. He gets out, or comes home, and the drama starts over, and my heart is pierced. No man. I think we're better as friends. I'll talk to her tonight. What about you and Angel, did you get things straight?"

"No she won't answer the damn phone. I told Kalliah my intentions. I will tell her over and over again."

"Who are you trying to convince, you or her?"

"Get outta here man I don't need to be convinced, I'm done with Angel. Like you said I can't trust her, it doesn't matter who the guy is. Sexually, we're done. Every time I think about her being pregnant by someone else, or what I know happened in the past, man, I just don't desire her that way anymore. I was trying Miles. You know, trying to look over the obvious. She claimed it only happened off and on. It shouldn't have happened at all. This baby thing has me trippin'. I asked her how many weeks. She hung up the phone."

"So you don't know. The child could be yours."

"It's not. I'm sure of it, but she's got the upper hand. Without testing, how would I know? I'm not willing to take this shit to court unless she does some stupid shit about child support. I'll find out how many weeks and go from there."

"What? Dante', I ain't trying to throw dirt, but she could have been fucking both of you at the same time. So even if she's, what, four weeks pregnant it still could be his. When was the last time she claims she dealt with him?"

"She admitted to three or four months ago."

"They supposedly broke up then?"

"Yeah according to her she hasn't seen him since."

"They've been dealing with each other off and on throughout your relationship and old boy didn't try to get back in? I don't know man. I would have the test done regardless."

"I see what you mean. Hey there's Kalliah's car pull in right next to her. There's a spot."

Miles followed Dante's directions and parked next to Kalliah. They both got out of the car looking for Stephon's car. As they entered the door Stephon was greeting them.

"What's up guys? Step outside a minute."

****

"How'd you get here man? Don't tell me your car is down again?"

Stephon smiled and shook his head not replying to Miles' questions. They stepped out into the parking lot away from the door. Stephon checked the area, allowing those that parked the opportunity to pass before he spoke.

"What's wrong with you? You act as though there's a problem."

"Nah, no problem, listen Miles you know some of what I'm about to say and Dante' please just listen I don't want the girls to suspect anything I'll explain it all to you later. Kyle is locked up, and he'll be there for some time. Cherese hasn't got the call yet."

"So how do you know?"

"That's what I'm saying, I'll explain that later. Also if all goes well between me and Brianne, I'll be relocating."

"What?" Miles had no idea what he was talking about. "Did you forget you're on parole? You can't leave the state following a sexual twinge?"

"Oh man Miles that's low. Brianne ain't a sexual twinge and there's a reason behind the move. I'll explain that later."

"What about your boys, the job? Man, you can't afford to do another bid."

"This one I can afford and I'll be moving with my boys. I just didn't want you guys to look at me crazy when I ask Brianne to marry me."

"Whoa Stephon, what the fuck are you thinking? Don't get that girl all happy, and you know you can't fulfill that commitment."

"Miles, damn man, I'll explain that later."

Dante' took a deep breath and followed Stephon, who left them standing in the parking lot. Stephon opened the door to the restaurant. He waited patiently as they entered without any comments.

Dinner was filling and everyone had the same appetite as Khalliah. The group laughed and teased as they enjoyed their dessert. The discussion changed from the past, to future plans and goals. Brianne began the conversation announcing her offer to Cherese. The conversation went silent when she repeated the reasons for her offer and Cherese's acceptance.

"What? Did I bring this dead sound to the table? I thought this would be a happy note for everyone."

"I didn't tell Miles yet." Cherese reached for Miles' hand. He kept his hand on the table not responding to her touch. Cherese moved her hand. His unwillingness to react was a message that would have to be addressed later.

"Yes, I've accepted her invitation. I want to start over without being a burden to anyone. I guess I can say this, we're all friends. Miles was gracious enough to offer his home in Atlanta. I wouldn't dare compromise him or his house to the problems my marriage would bring. I'm still trying to get a grasp of the effects it has had on me. I'm getting better with it, but I'm willing to admit, I've got a ways to go. Miles I don't want to hurt you or ruin our chances for a future, if that's what God has in store for us. So yes, I'm leaving with Kalliah and Brianne in the morning. This would be a start for me, a start for a distant healing. My lawyer is taking care of my matters here, and if I'm needed, I will come back. That's if Miles will have me. I'll be his house guest."

Cherese added a slight smile to her statement and again placed her hand on Miles' hand. He took her hand and kissed it gently.

"I'm sorry Cherese, I thought Miles knew. I was enlightening Stephon and Dante'. I apologize Miles."

Miles nodded accepting Brianne's apology.

"Well things will change for Cherese, and that makes me happy. I've also decided to write to my family expressing my feelings. I've tried over the past two weeks to visit, but I still couldn't do it. After talking with

Stephon, I agree it's gonna take more time. Depending on the response I will decide if I'll sit with them face to face. I want to thank you all for understanding and supporting me in conquering my fears. I don't know what I would have done if I carried what happened much longer."

"Whatever happened to the other guys that were involved?"

"I don't know Dante'. I never thought about asking who they were. I didn't really know them. I'm sure Kyle remembers them and there were others that were at that damn after party who may know. I guess if I hadn't seen Kyle after graduation, I would have been able to hide the pain forever. I told Cherese part of the pain was it resurfaced whenever I saw him. But I'm okay now."

Stephon wanted to break the news about Kyle's arrest. Juan and Ryan told him it would be best for no one to know about his involvement. After meeting with Detective Miller, he understood the reasons why.

"Well I have plans to add to Brianne's. We've decided to continue seeing each other seriously. I finally won her over. I mean without her laughing in my face thinking I was just teasing her. I want to make a toast to us if you all don't mind." Stephon stood, holding up his glass waiting for the others to raise their drinks.

"To Brianne, let this be the beginning of the better things in life for the both of us. I want my best friends and you to know; I love you, and I intend on showing you how much as time goes on."

Stephon leaned toward Brianne and kissed her slowly on her lips bringing cheers and the tapping of glasses with the silverware.

"My next bit of news is I am transferring out of D.C. I'm moving to Virginia as well. Not with Brianne and the ladies but into a home for me and my boys. Hopefully, in a year, I don't think I could wait any longer than that, Brianne will join us."

Brianne turned to face Stephon, who had dropped to his knee with a box and ring in hand. "Brianne, I know it's sudden, but girl I won't be able to live without you. Will you marry me?"

"Oh Stephon, yes I'll marry you."

Kalliah and Cherese were crying with and for their friend. Dante' and Miles stood to shake Stephon's hand. Kalliah needed air and left the celebrating table to walk out a nearby door onto the veranda. The air hit her face as she held her head back preventing the tears from falling. Dante' excused himself to join her in the night's air. The sky was clear giving way to the galaxy of stars. Dante' put his hand around her waist placing his head on her shoulders.

"Baby, I wish it could be us. Are you okay?"

Kalliah tried not to cry. "Dante' I...."

He kissed her as she spoke. It was a kiss that told her he understood and wanted to make her feel secure in his arms. The kiss was filled with the emotions they shared for years. It was all Dante' needed, all Kalliah wanted.

"So what do we do now? Our future is at a standstill. Dante' I'm scared that I'll be the blame for what may be a major decision for you."

"It's my decision. C'mon, let's talk about this later I have something to show you."

Kalliah stopped and gave him a questionable look.

"Girl stop; I know better. I would have to make sure of your answer. But will you be my girl?"

"Dante' you got someone filling that spot. I'm not willing to share."

Kalliah walked away from Dante'. As they joined the others at the table, there were no questions or strange looks. The check had been paid and they all agreed to stop at a jazz spot not far from the hotel.

Zanzibar on the Waterfront had a comfortable setting where they could relax, listen to good music and talk intimately. Miles was pleased to know they entered during a break in the jazz group's performance.

"Who's playing tonight, does anyone know?"

Miles enjoyed contemporary jazz, and didn't see any headliners posted on the walls.

"Most of the groups here are good. How much music do you really plan on listening to?"

Stephon asked his question in passing Miles. He pulled out a seat for Brianne. Miles didn't comment. He needed the music to soothe his emotions that were playing a tug of war with what he knew may be reality. Cherese had no intentions of them being together after the weekend. He liked it better when he was giving her the option. He wasn't a part of her thought process. It was obvious she didn't need his help in making decisions for herself. His emotions told him she was still attached to Kyle.

Miles looked at Cherese as she talked with Brianne admiring her engagement ring. She was beautiful, and she knew it. Miles couldn't imagine her living in Virginia. They had been closer friends in the past year than either of them thought possible. Since the reunion, he had found the softness in her touch was more than a momentary thrill. He thought about her leaving Kyle, but he never thought about her living anywhere but in Atlanta. He was wrong; she was more than able to claim her independence.

"Cherese, would you like something to drink?"

"Yes, wine. I don't want to drink too much tonight."

"Will you walk with me to the bar?"

Cherese looked at Miles. His caramel eyes were pleading with her. His expression said he wanted more than the drink. She knew they needed distance from their friends to talk. They excused themselves and walked toward the bar disappearing into a group of people standing and talking near the dance floor. Brianne watched and noticed Stephon watching the couple too.

"What do you think that's about?"

"Babe, he's hurt. I know he is. He really didn't expect her to leave, and if she left, he thought his home in Atlanta was the safe haven. You know he actually thought she would stay with Kyle while he's locked up?"

"Kyle's locked up? When did he get locked up?"

Stephon looked around like someone else told her where Kyle was. He leaned to her and whispered, "You're not supposed to know that."

"How do you know it? Does Dante' and Miles know?"

"Kinda, listen it really doesn't matter how I know right now."

"Stephon, when will Cherese find out?"

"When they call her; the police will contact her eventually."

"Kyle doesn't have her number."

"Someone will contact her."

"Damn. What is she supposed to do now?"

"Brianne, now she can live, and so can you. He'll be in jail for a while."

"Wow, how do you know Stephon? What happened?"

"Not now. You'll have to know soon enough, just not now."

Brianne looked into the crowd, as though she could see Cherese and Miles. "You know she may have second thoughts about moving if he's locked up?"

"Babe, she needs a new beginning. She'll still move, trust me."

"What are you two love birds whispering about?"

Brianne looked at Stephon allowing him to answer Dante's question. "Nothing man. We're good. Kalliah you ready to go home?"

"Well, we gotta go, so I guess I'm ready. When do you think you'll be moving our way?"

"In a few months, I'll definitely be there before the end of the year. I have a job lined up for October, so I'll take the summer to travel and get this custody thing straight."

"That's really quick man. I thought you had some time before you could even deal with that."

"Man, things have changed. I got a new job, a fiancé and my boys. All I need is a home for them, and I'm done."

"Stephon what is the court saying about all this?"

"Kalliah, believe me, it's being taken care of. My job is handling the paperwork for the transfer. I'll be dealing with the government, and before I agreed to take the job, I requested a few perks."

"Damn, you got it like that, how's that?"

"I saved them some big money. I stumbled on some problems at the job, told the right people, they investigated and found out. I saved them a fortune. They repaid me by cleaning up the mess I made of my life and giving me a new start."

The sound of the band stopped the conversation and Dante' called over the waitress to order the table drinks. Kalliah gave a smile thanking him for the needed drink. She knew he would wait to talk to her after they were alone. It would only take two more drinks, and they would be communicating a lot better.

Cherese and Miles found an area to sit in the rear of the lounge. The plush love seat sat close to the floor, and the dim

lighting added a touch of intimacy for the customers who wanted to get acquainted before leaving. The music could be

heard softly, and the plasma television flashed news clips and sports results from an earlier broadcast.

As Miles led Cherese to the seat, they passed a few men who smiled admiring her beauty. Miles held her hand until she sat down assuring the spectators he was with her.

"You've got a few admirers."

"Hmm….. if they only knew."

 "If they only knew what?"

"If they only knew how much I care for you."

Her response raised his brow. "So when were you going to tell me about your decision?"

"Tonight, I didn't expect Brianne to tell everyone. Really, I wanted us to talk and come to an understanding."

"What is there to understand Cherese? I offered you my home. You could have told me you made other arrangements."

"You sound angry. What does this change? I actually think it's for the better. I'm not obligated to you for the wrong reasons, and you're not obligated to take care of me while I try to get myself together."

"Is that how you felt; I would be obligated to care for you? I would care for you 'cause, I love you Cherese."

"I know Miles. I don't want that confused with pity, guilt or blame."

"Blame, guilt what does that mean?"

"I don't want you to blame yourself for me leaving my marriage, or feel guilty later about our relationship. I've done a lot of thinking about this. You were right, I need to get away from Kyle, but I don't need to run into anyone's arms because I'm scared to stand on my own."

"So what's up now? What about us, our relationship?"

"We still have a chance at loving each other. I think a better chance. We can see each other just as planned. When you want to visit, we can stay at your place."

"Cherese, what about Kyle?"

As though on cue, the television flashed a "Breaking Report". Kyle and seven others were named in a drug bust, and their photos were on the seventy-two-inch screen. Cherese held Miles' hand tightly as they listened to the report. Kyle and the others were being held for the manufacturing and distribution of drugs as well as weapon charges. During the bust there had been two fatalities one being a Drug Enforcement Agent the other had not been identified as of the broadcasting. Kyle was identified as the shooter. The full story would air on the morning broadcast.

"Oh my God!

"Are you okay?"

"I guess so. What the hell was he thinking?"

"You knew he was tied up in this shit?"

"No, I've been so busy trying to get it together. I didn't know what his ass was into. We went through this shit before, early in our marriage. Off and on for small packages, but never like this. What the hell?"

"Well I'm glad you know now?"

"You knew he was locked up?"

"Yeah, Stephon told me. We didn't want to tell you until the authorities told you. I guess the news broadcast is just as good."

"That's fucked up Miles. Why wouldn't you say something?" Cherese got up from the couch leaving him looking up at her.

"I didn't want you staying here with him."

"What?" She paused. He stunned her with his statement.

"Cherese, he can't love you, in jail or out. I didn't want you to be confused, and like you said pity him, blame yourself, or feel guilty."

"You must really think I'm one sick bitch, huh? Let him whip my ass, force me to lose my child, and then play the forgiving wife when he does what, twenty years? Miles, do you give me any credit?"

Cherese's body language spoke loudly. Miles stood offering his excuse.

"You always said you were devoted to your marriage. I'm sorry I misjudged you."

"You damn sure did."

Cherese walked away just as Miles attempted to embrace her. He reached for her hand, and Cherese walked quicker making certain he had to quicken his pace to keep in step. As she approached the table, Stephon stood thinking she would want to take her seat.

"Brianne when you guys are ready to leave, I'll be at the bar. Good night Miles. This dumb bitch has some other decisions to make." Cherese pushed pass Miles not looking back for his response.

****

Dante' took her abrupt statement to mean their evening out would be ending shortly, he was sure Miles wouldn't want to stay. His disheartened friend could be seen at the far end of the bar sipping on his drink. It was apparent that embarrassment kept him from joining them at the table.

"Damn, I guess that didn't go well. Cherese can ride with us if you and Kalliah want. It's not a problem."

Dante' ignored Stephon's comment uncertain if Kalliah was willing to share the night with him. "What are you driving; I didn't see your car?"

"My car, uh, I have a loaner. It's outside though. A black Mercury Sable. It was parked near Kalliah's."

"Oh, why the loaner, is yours down again?"

"Yeah, I had some problems with it last night."

Stephon hoped the excuse would sit well, but Brianne was trying to connect his answers with the information he had given her about Kyle's arrest. She looked his way and noticed the broadcast airing on the television behind the bar. The band was playing Paul Taylor's "Steppin' Out" causing her to speak louder for Kalliah and Dante' to hear her. Her voice was still inaudible, but when she pointed to the television, they understood what she said clearly.

Kyle was arrested. Kalliah showed her surprise immediately moving closer to the edge of her seat as though it would help her hear the commentator as they showed the men who were arrested arriving at the precinct. The spokesman for the D.E.A. was shown with the evidence that was apprehended during the bust. The broadcast was live from the house on Eleventh Avenue with the police and investigators still on site.

"Oh my God, does Cherese want to leave now?"

Brianne was standing waiting for someone to say they should leave. Miles returned to the table and received dirty looks from both Brianne and Kalliah.

"Listen, it looks like the broadcast is going to ruin my night. I told Cherese I knew he was locked up. She's pissed. Can one of you tell her to call me before you leave tomorrow? She probably won't want to talk to me, but I really want to talk with her before you leave in the morning. I need to apologize."

"What are you apologizing for?"

"Kalliah I don't know. Being an ass for loving her, I guess. I just want her to know, I'm still her friend, and I still love her. Not matter how this turns out."

"What?"

"I told her I didn't know what she would do if Kyle got locked up; now that it's a reality, well she took it wrong."

"Yeah, but you just said no matter how this turns out. What is going to change?"

"Kalliah, you don't think she'll leave with her husband being locked up do you?"

"She's going with us tomorrow Miles. She'll call you in the morning. I'll make sure of that. That's all that needs to be said for tonight."

Brianne spoke with an undertone of disgust. Miles pulled Dante' away from the table; he didn't want to test her apparent anger. Stephon read the expression on her face.

"Babe, you okay?"

"I'm fine. It's just I could tell where he was going with that "her husband" mess. Miles is full of shit. He had so much to offer her as long as she was tied to Kyle. Well, she's free and she doesn't need his implications to retie those knots of pain and suffering. Cherese will be fine. He need not worry."

Stephon had no clue what she was referring to, and he didn't want to spoil his night. He walked toward Dante' and Miles to see what their plans were.

"Kalliah you understand what I'm saying right?" Brianne sat back down as she caught Cherese's attention at the bar. She waved and pointed to her watch a signal that she was ready to leave, if Cherese was ready to go.

"I guess I do. How could Miles think Cherese would want to be here for Kyle?"

"Things Cherese has said. When we are hurt, we try to clean it up by saying you know, woulda, coulda, shoulda shit. Cherese has said it to us, and I know she probably has said it when talking to Miles. You know the ways she would have saved her marriage, questioning whether or not she could walk away, and not certain about what to do."

Brainne drank the balance of her Martini before continuing her thoughts.

"Miles and Cherese got closer because of what their relationship looked like compared to her marriage. She's longing for love, intimacy, and support. Miles did that these past two weeks. Now he's worried? No, now he wants to back off because she may need more. He's not ready. I'm glad she realized she needed time to heal, time to get herself together before being involved. Miles is not scared for her. He's scared for himself. I deal with his type daily. Women get caught with his kind, time after time. The rebound lover, he's the arms women fall into during the healing process, and then he's gone too."

"I don't know Bri, you know more about that mess than me, but Miles offered his home."

"I don't think he ever thought she would move. Why be upset about her moving with us? Why want to question her being with Kyle? Believe me Kalliah he's better as a part time lover. I won't be the one to tell her though. I've done enough fortune telling as far as her love life is concerned."

"I know that's right. She can ride to the suite with us though; you and Stephon can leave if you're ready to go."

"What about you and Dante'?"

"I don't know, with drinking and all, I don't know how much talking we'll get done. Nothing will be solved. If anything I'll get another night of quivers and fulfillment, not a bad ending for my vacation, but I'm not dealing with coming between him and a baby. He needs to clear that up before we can seriously deal with each other."

Cherese took a seat and placed another Apple Martini on the table. Her face was glowing apparently from her downed drinks. Her smirk told her girlfriends that she didn't care that she looked tipsy.

"So what are they planning on doing now? Helping Miles explain his sorry ass reason for thinking I'm stupid as hell."

"He said that?" Kalliah couldn't believe what Cherese said.

"No, maybe if he had balls, he would have. I'm done with men for a while. Y'all ain't got to worry though; I've never been into women."

Cherese laughed heartily at the thought of her being with a woman. Both Brianne and Kalliah knew she would be talking most of the night. The question was who would be listening. Dante' and Stephon returned to the table as Miles headed for the nearest exit.

"Miles said to tell you all good night and have a safe trip home."

"Humph, he sent a damn message to me?"

"Actually he asked for you to call him when you got up tomorrow morning." Stephon reached to get the beer he left on the table, finishing it as he prepared to leave.

"Stephon, picture that shit!!"

****

Dante' rode with Kalliah and Cherese, as expected Brianne and Stephon left Zanzibar before them. They promised to meet them for breakfast in the morning. Cherese didn't say much until the radio in the car aired the report of the biggest drug bust in Washington.

"Damn I'll be glad to get away from that."

"Did they call you Cherese?"

"Who?"

"Stephon told me and Miles they were going to be contacting you that's why we didn't tell you about it."

"You all knew? How did Stephon know?"

"He said he would tell us later." Dante' changed the station as the names of the suspects were being announced.

"I don't want to know. No, whoever "they" is, didn't call. They don't have my number. I wonder if Kyle tried calling the hotel, why didn't he call you Kalliah?"

"Maybe they only gave him one call. He may have called the hotel. Do you want to talk to him before we leave tomorrow?"

"No. I'll wait and talk to my lawyer. I don't think I should. I don't want to give the impression that I know anything, and I'm running. They can't stop me from moving can they?"

Kalliah slowed down, stopping at a red light. She could tell by her tone Cherese was upset. "They won't stop you. They can't think you're involved. We'll talk to your lawyer in the morning. Don't think about it tonight."

Dante' listened remembering what Miles said. He could hear the doubt in Cherese's voice as she spoke. He hoped Miles was wrong; **Cherese couldn't possibly feel obligated to Kyle or her marriage, could she?**

What Is Real?

Kalliah talked to Cherese until she felt herself dozing. The conversation was beginning to fade to a murmur, and the clock was reading three-thirty. Kalliah told her they would talk more before they left for Virginia.

She excused herself realizing she promised to talk with Dante' and hopefully get some sleep. Cherese reluctantly agreed. The conversation held more questions than answers and wouldn't bring her peace of mind now, in the wee hours of the morning.

Dante' was sprawled across the bed. He obviously had been watching the television waiting for Kalliah to come to the room. He left them in the living room after Cherese broke down crying when another clip of the news appeared on the television. Kalliah stood admiring his body. He had removed his shirt and was lying on his stomach sleeping peacefully. The drinks she downed earlier in the evening lost their effect when Cherese began to question what she should do about Kyle. Her seductive mood was returning causing her to tingle as she visualized herself mounting him one last time. She fought the temptation turning her back to the bed and slowly removing all but her thong and bra.

Kalliah tried not to wake Dante' while getting comfortable on the open side of the bed. He responded to the touch of her body by putting his arm around her. The sensation between her legs had her full attention, and she sat up hoping Dante' would awaken.

"Is she okay?

Kalliah smiled knowing the conversation would be short. Dante' wouldn't ignore the heat from her inner thighs.

"I told her we could talk before we left. I think she just needs to know what's going on with Kyle. Once she gets the facts she'll be fine."

"Are you okay?"

"I will be."

Dante' rolled on his side to kiss her understanding her words were an invitation. After minutes of foreplay, Kalliah mounted Dante'. He closed his eyes as she moved slowly up and down moaning softly as she satisfied her heat. Dante' could feel his sac filling, and he hadn't put on a condom. He thought about the release and the feeling it would bring. His penis began to throb.

He lifted Kalliah placing her on her back as his penis spat sperm across the bed. The sight of his pleasure made her throb. Dante' wanted her to enjoy the encounter as much as he had. He spread the lips of her vagina and began to please her orally. Kalliah quivered as she reached her peak. He inserted his hardened rod touching her clitoris while he moved quickly in and out.

Kalliah saw herself in this position many times. They held on to each other and kissed passionately as Kalliah's juices flowed. Dante' pulled himself out knowing he would cum again.

"Whew girl, you tryin' to kill a brotha?"

"No, I think I'll keep you around."

"Are you okay?"

"You asked that already."

"Kalliah, why this? I mean I wanted this too, but I didn't think you would."

"You said you're not the father right?"

"No, I can't be."

"Would you tell me if you were?"

"Would it change things?"

"Would you tell me?"

"Yes, I would tell you."

"Dante' that's important. I want to know if you're the father of that child. I don't want you neglecting your responsibility just to be with me."

"Kalliah, if I was, would we have a future?"

"Why are we going back and forth with this? Just tell me when you find out."

Dante' thought about the tone of her voice and decided not to ruin their last few hours together.

"Look, let me show you something." He turned showing Kalliah his shoulder, and the tattoo that Miles questioned him about.

"I didn't notice that before. How long have you had that?"

"Since college, I needed something to remember you by. Miles asked did you see it and I thought you should know my thoughts about us went further back than this reunion."

"What did Angel say about it, or did you give her some lame excuse for my initials?"

"She never asked. I think she's always known how I felt about you. Another reason for her cheating, she claimed she wanted me to know how it felt."

"What?"

"Yeah, she would cheat whenever she thought I was visiting or calling home. She really thought you lived in D.C."

"So now that you have come home and got with me, what do you tell her?"

"Nothing, I'm done with her. Really, it has nothing to do with you. You did add another reason I don't want to be involved with her. I won't risk losing my chances with you again."

"We've got some issues to clear up before we start a committed relationship. I would love to say it's all good but I would be lying. I don't want my past or yours to interfere with our future. We can stay in touch and see how it goes."

"So what you saying, 'Thanks for the time we spent together?'"

"Sort of, but I'm not trying to be so cold. Angel is still your fiancé. That needs to be dealt with, there's a child to be born, and on my end, there's Maurice. I think we both owe them, the truth, and we owe that to each other. Our relationships were ending, but there was someone else in our lives two weeks ago. I do love you Dante', but I can't hold your hand while you tell Angel it's over baby or not. I won't be in the middle or be your excuse."

Dante' wanted to interrupt, but Kalliah kissed his lips and continued.

"She'll think I am; believe me, I'm a woman. She'll think you got pussy whipped in two weeks, 'cause that's all we did during these weeks, and you're trying to get back at her for cheating. She'll be willing to forgive you for the sake of the child, and the marriage. Dante' don't include us. If you're leaving her for the reasons you told me, tell her. Don't mention your love for me, how long you've loved me, or what pleasures we've discovered with each other. We're friends, and friends understand the others' feelings. This is important to you and me. Don't use our relationship to bury your relationship with Angel."

"I understand. I'm really glad we're friends."

"Friends before lovers."

****

Miles couldn't wait for Cherese to call. He left his home Sunday morning determined to speak with her before any of his friends thought of getting out of bed. Dante' hadn't returned to his home, and he was sure Stephon was still with Brianne. Cherese couldn't use the excuse that they were leaving shortly to keep from talking with him.

He paid close attention to the news before going to bed. Kyle's face was shown on his television three times before he finally understood the entire story. The media gave bits and pieces in each broadcast, and now Miles understood that Stephon had been a major part in breaking up a large drug trafficking ring. There was no mention of how the D.E.A. stumbled upon the sale, but Kyle's involvement, and the shooting was enough to give him a lengthy sentence.

Miles would ask Cherese to join him for breakfast and he'd explain himself. She misunderstood his comments, and actions. He didn't want to be the one left holding on to a love that would be attached to her past. He looked at the clock in his car where he sat parked in the hotel parking lot.

Six-thirty was early; he would wait for another thirty minutes. He needed the time to get his thoughts together.

The morning air brought a warm breeze. It was air he needed as he thought of the words he would use to convince Cherese his statements were an attempt to protect his heart. He longed for her. His emotions were tattered. He smiled to himself as he thought of what Dante' and Stephon would think of him begging Cherese for her forgiveness. **"The hell with their thoughts."**

****

Cherese hadn't slept. She laid in the bed tossing and turning thinking about what the detectives could hold against her. She changed the channels on the television again hoping to hear more about the bust. She called her home number for messages only to find more of Kyle's family had called than hers. She hoped to get out of town before her family called about the arrest. Mrs. Jefferson called leaving a message for her to call before she "got on the road." Cherese decided that would be the only call she would return. It was seven o'clock when the news broadcasted their top story again. "Washington D.C. drug ring is a major break for the D.E.A." Cherese listened closely as they named all seven of the men who were arrested. Kyle and his friend Tarik Bateman were charged with the murder of the D.E.A. agent and an officer on the D.C. police force. Cherese wiped the tears from her eyes. It was confirmed Kyle would be in jail, and she would be free of his abuse.

Her cell phone rang. The sound was muffled; her phone was inside her purse. She rushed to get out of the bed not wanting to miss the call. Cherese wasn't ready to deal with any legal matters, but she hoped it was the police or detectives who were involved with Kyle's arrest.

"Good morning baby. I didn't want to wake you, but I wanted to catch you before you left."

"Good morning Ms. Jefferson. I'm the only one up this morning. Kalliah and Brianne are still sleeping."

"Oh, I see. Well, child have you seen this mess on the news? I just need to know, will you be changing your mind about leaving?"

"I wasn't sure what the detectives may do or if they wanted me to stay. What do you think?"

"Call your lawyer. He called here, but that was early yesterday. He said he was checking the numbers he had for your contacts."

"I'll call him about nine. I'll probably have to leave a message being it's Sunday. Ms. Jefferson, do you think I ought to stay? I don't want to make them suspicious about something that I don't know anything about."

"Cherese, follow your lawyer's advice. He's the one who may know what the officers would want. Get him involved on your behalf. They may not want anything."

"I will. Thank you. I'll call you before I make any decisions."

"What time do you think y'all will be leaving?"

"To be quite honest they may have to leave without me now. I want to be sure I won't be in trouble."

"Yeah, you call your lawyer. Call me later now."

****

Stephon brought the coffee he made to the kitchen table. Brianne was dressed and ready, waiting for a call from Cherese or Kalliah. She insisted on making the bed and cleaning the bathroom before leaving. Stephon could tell she was in a good mood. She was humming to herself, content with the new direction her life was taking.

"Bree, the coffee is ready do you want breakfast?"

"No, I'm sure they're not up. We can go to the hotel and eat the buffet there. I think I got hooked on the fresh fruit."

"So fresh fruit in the morning; is there anything else in the morning that quenches your appetite?"

Brianne entered the kitchen smiling. Stephon met her in the center of the floor. "I know tasting you in the morning quenches my taste buds." He kissed her softly and talked into her neck. "Thank you for making my life complete."

"Stephon explain this Kyle thing. I'm sure you have your reasons for not saying anything last night, but can you ease my mind?"

While drinking their coffee, he explained the job he was offered, and the reason he took it. Once he met with Detective Miller, he was offered a job doing the same type stings at government offices throughout the United States. He could pick where he wanted to relocate with his children. He would be trained, and his court papers would disappear in the system. He talked it over with his lawyer and decided it would benefit him and the boys.

"I prayed that I had shown you a better man than the rumors may have led you to believe I was. I took a chance in asking you to marry me. God saw fit for that to work as well. I'm blessed, now I realize it. I do have a reason to be here, my boys and you."

"Stephon, do you think Cherese will hold this against you?"

"What?"

"Setting up Kyle."

"I'm not telling her."

"I didn't think so, but I think Kyle would."

"She'd be a fool to try to get with him again."

"Stephon, she always says that's her husband. I don't know. She's stuck by him in all the mess that he has done."

"He'll be looking for a way out. Cherese needs to stay clear if she doesn't want to be blamed in any of the dealings."

"You'll tell her that right?"

"No."

"Stephon. Why wouldn't you tell her?"

"Brianne, I can't let anyone know who I work for or why? Kyle may be affiliated with other transactions. Cherese is free; it's up to her to stay away from him."

****

Miles woke up worried that he had missed Cherese. He slept deeply for forty-five minutes, fifteen minutes longer than planned. He entered the lobby and quickly stopped the elevator doors from closing. There were only a few guests in the lobby checking out, a sign that most were still enjoying the comfort of their beds. Cherese opened the door never asking who, or looking in his face once he entered the suite.

"Lock the door behind you."

"You knew I was at the door?"

"I looked through the key hole. Why didn't you just call?"

"Cherese, can we just talk? Can we go in the room a minute?"

"No, talk right here."

"I want to apologize. I shouldn't have implied that you didn't have a grasp on things, or didn't know what you wanted. It was just that I didn't have an understanding of what…."

"What it took to deal with a battered, abused, and confused wife of a drug dealer? I was that same woman two years ago Miles. The same woman when you offered me your home for refuge, and the same woman you made love to. What changed your thoughts, or were they always the same? I make the decision to get myself together, and you're threatened by that? Tell the truth Miles, Kyle was a threat when I was with him, and he's a threat now because of what?"

"It's like you said, you're his wife. I realize what I knew all along. I can't compete with your husband. He has a hold on you. I thought it was control by force, but it's just a hold on you period. You care about him because he's your husband, but it's more than that. I can't compete with that type of love. I can respect it though, but I can't compete with it. I don't know what to do, what to say, how to react. I love you Cherese. I just don't know what to do."

"Miles, I have to close this chapter of my life before I start a new life with you. That's all I wanted to do. Separate the old from the new, and heal. I'm worn mentally and physically, and you don't deserve me as a burden. I love you, and want to be at my best for you."

"Are you leaving?"

"I don't know now. I need to call my lawyer and find out what I can do, or what is best in this situation."

"You're not in this mess; I mean Kyle didn't throw your name into it, did he?"

"I may not find out any information until tomorrow."

"Will you let me know?"

"Yes."

Miles got up to leave feeling awkward now that he understood her feelings. Cherese was more certain about herself than he was about their relationship. He needed time to get himself together. He would make sure he gave her enough space.

Splintered

The ride home was long, and filled with unwanted thoughts for Dante'. Miles' summation of the possibilities of him being the father of Angel's baby was haunting him. The truth was he wasn't sure if the baby was his or not. Angelina played between Dante' and whomever throughout their relationship. He accepted her infidelity, and looking back in their relationship, he didn't understand his reasons.

Dante' made a stop to pick up groceries and got a strange feeling that Angelina would be there waiting to smooth things over. It was one o'clock. He remembered telling her he would get there about two so that gave him a little time to prepare for her lies. As he opened the front door, he could smell the Sunday dinner cooking. The house had that "just cleaned" odor and Dante' knew Angel planned it that way.

He began to unpack the groceries while the aroma spoke to his empty stomach. "Hey, I hope you're hungry." Angel entered the kitchen in one of Dante's football shirts and a pair of shorts.

"I thought you would be meeting me. I didn't expect for you to be here."

"I stayed here a few days, so I came back to pick up a little. Also I figured we'd have a nice dinner, and I can answer your questions about our baby."

"We don't have to wait for dinner to talk about that. I think that needs to be talked about now."

"There's no rush Dante', it's not like the baby is due this month. Where's your bags, I'll unpack them for you."

"Funny you should mention the baby being due. When is the blessed date?" Dante' paused to hear her answer. Angel hesitated smiling before giving him one.

"I'm going on my sixth week. I made arrangements for an appointment for us to see the doctor. I'm sure you want blood work done as proof. Dante' I have to admit I gave you every reason not to trust me."

"So this blood test is for me, or is it for you? You sound like you're unsure."

"C'mon', how many times have you said you don't trust me? You need proof, so we can move on with our lives."

Dante' didn't know what to say. Angel wouldn't take the test if she knew he no longer wanted to marry her. He needed to know if he was the father.

"When is the appointment?"

Angel turned to the stove checking on the food that was making the pots sing as they boiled. "Are you saying you can't go?"

"No, I need to make arrangements at the job. I'll need to take a day off."

"Hmm.....You probably won't need a full day, just the morning. The results come back about a week later."

"Okay so when. I agree. We need to move on with our lives."

"The appointment is at the end of the month."

"Why so late? Didn't they have anything sooner?"

"My next appointment is then. I only go once a month. I told her you probably would want to have the test done because of how our relationship was at that time."

"Or how it is."

"Whatever Dante'! I can't convince you that I love you, or that I've been committed to you since that time."

"Well I think you need to have the test as soon as possible. The longer it takes, the longer I have to think about what may be the truth...."

"Wait, so you think you're gonna throw this shit in my face all month, or all nine months?"

"All I'm saying is why wait. I need to know Angel. I don't think I should have to wait."

"The appointment is at the end of the month. I ain't paying for another appointment to satisfy your suspicions. You want a blood test that bad, then you pay for it. You really should be paying for the appointments anyway."

"Here we go, here we go, what the hell makes you think I'm paying for his responsibility."

"The baby ain't his, but you know what I'm done with both of your asses. He wants to know if the baby is his, and I told him the same thing I told you, the father is Dante' Jefferson. I don't have to prove shit."

Angelina cut the pots off and left him sitting at the kitchen table listening to her rattling in Spanish throughout the house. He knew her routine. She would curse in Spanish knowing he only understood a few of the words she was spewing. She would gather her clothes, or belongings that were visible and slam the front door as she was leaving. The ritual usually took no more than ten minutes. Dante' let her walk out the door determined she would have to call him before he called her.

****

Kalliah called her relatives and Maurice when she returned to Virginia. She was happy she could leave a message on his phone as she had most of her vacation. The ride home cleared her mind about the on again off again relationship they shared over the past year.

"Maurice, don't worry about returning my call. It's obvious that things between us aren't working. It's been real, but I gotta think about me. You understand because through it all, you've been only thinking about you."

As she hung up the phone, she sighed with relief. She could only hope Dante' could express his true feelings to Angelina without putting her between them. She unpacked her clothes, and headed toward the kitchen to prepare a late lunch.

"Brianne, I'm making a sandwich do you want one?"

"No thanks."

Kalliah smiled to herself. Brianne had announced her diet would begin immediately. She wanted to slim down for her wedding date. The date would be determined after she lost at least twenty-five pounds. Kalliah agreed the wedding could be the motivation she needed.

As she sat at the kitchen table eating her sandwich, she read the mail that had accumulated while they were away. Her thoughts between the bites and reading drifted to Dante'. She wanted to call him but decided not to. The phone rang redirecting her thoughts. She was guessing if Maurice had the nerve to call back. She let Brianne answer the call.

"Kalliah it's for you."

"Got it, hello."

"Kalliah, hi this is Angel, Dante's fiancé, I hope I'm not disturbing you."

"No you're not, what's up?" Kalliah was beginning to be annoyed with her calls. She recognized the game. If Angel was determined to include her in their relationship, she would tell her what she really needed to hear from Dante'.

"I think we need to be honest about the situation your relationship with Dante' is causing. As women, you know, we need to be blunt about what goes on in our affairs. I don't like the idea that he is as close to you as he is. I don't think it's good for us or our marriage unless you and I have an understanding about where you stand."

Angel paused as though waiting for Kalliah to respond. Kalliah had no response waiting for her to get to the point.

"I know you're aware of my pregnancy, and if I know Dante', which I do, he told you about our past. Kalliah that was the past, if you're waiting in the wings, don't wait. He's the father of my child, and we're a family, complete with marriage. I won't allow the "baby mama" label to be placed on me. I will be wifey 'cause just like you may have had plans, mine have been in the works for the past few years."

"I think you have the wrong idea about our relationship, and if I know Dante' like I do, he didn't tell you shit. He let you talk just like

I did, and you walked away with your own conclusion. But I guess if you called me again you're still insecure about who I am, or what my so called plans are. First, let me tell you there were no plans. Secondly, your relationship with Dante' is between the two of you, don't look for me to step in, or out of my relationship with him to give you security. And finally, if the baby is his, he can choose to do what he wants. What others label you as, well that depends on how you carry yourself. Dante' didn't say much about your wedding, or the pregnancy. What he did say…. Well, you know him. Why not ask him? I am his friend, and I will always be his friend, until he decides otherwise. Talk to your man."

"You're his revenge. He got what he wanted that's all, revenge. You fucked him didn't you? That's what he wanted; to hurt me, like I hurt him. He thinks the baby isn't his, so he reunited with you just in case. Dante' always said he could be with you whenever he wanted. Why did he wait until he proposed? 'Cause that's what he chose for revenge, I knew there was more to it. Two weeks, I worried the whole time he was in D.C. about something that he couldn't avoid. You wanted him too right? Even after I told you we were getting married. What was on your mind? Did you think fucking him would be a commitment? He used your ass to prove a point to me. Well now his ass will really feel it. He won't know if he's the father, and he won't have me. Fuck both of you."

The phone clicked in Kalliah's ear.

****

"Brianne, I don't know if they'll even tell me what I really need to know. If I leave now Kyle may not get a fair chance."

"Cherese when did he give you a fair chance. I don't understand you. I understand love, marriage, and commitment, but I also understand that to go both ways. Kyle has never done anything close to what a loving husband would do. You worry too much about what your family and friends may say. Cherese you have told us more than once, you're the one who's married. Do what's right for you girl. You deserve it."

"I don't know. I understand but there is something tugging at me saying I should see this through. At least until he's got representation."

"Well that will be in a few days. That will give you time to get all your business in order. Are you still filing for a divorce?"

"Yeah that I'm certain of. I don't think I ever was a wife to him, but I do believe he loved me. I guess that's what kept me holding on. I'll stay in D.C. until I get things cleared with him, and my business matters."

"Then what, you and Miles still considering getting together?"

"I'm not. I learned a lot about him, too much. He's not the strength that I need. He's a friend, and we should have kept it on that level."

"Did you tell him how you felt?"

"In a way; Miles won't push it though, and we'll be friends anyway."

"Well you know where to find us if you need us for anything."

"Brianne, tell Kalliah that I'm glad we're friends. Thanks for all you've done. I'll be okay and if not I will call."

"You better. Don't wait until you fall girl, call us while you're stumbling."

"Love you."

"You too."

Brianne hung up the phone feeling better about Cherese's decision to stay in D.C. They didn't leave the suite until Cherese spoke to the lawyer. By noon, she knew where Kyle was being held. His bail was more than she, or any of his family was willing to pay. Her lawyer explained the charges, and told her she would have to get him another lawyer. Since he was her lawyer for their divorce, defending him in this case would be a conflict of interest. She decided to get her extra keys to her home from her mother and stay there.

Stephon promised he would come to visit at the end of the week, and Brianne loved the feeling of anticipation. She was in a good mood, and glad to be back in her home. She walked into the living room to find Kalliah with her eyes closed lying on the couch.

"I know that's right girl, between the ride and the vacation itself you need another week."

"Girl if I had another week, I'd probably be wanted for murder," Kalliah replied never opening her eyes.

"Murdering who? Maurice, his sorry ass ain't worth doing no time."

"I wish it was his sorry ass. No, that damn fiancé of Dante's, that bitch is sick. Or maybe I should say slick. That was her on the phone."

Kalliah repeated the conversation she had with Angel hoping Brianne had another way of looking at it. Brianne sat in the lounge chair listening to her friend and watching her emotions build.

"Kalliah, you can't possibly believe what she's saying. Dante' wouldn't use you like that. I don't think she knows him the way she thinks she does."

"What I know is Dante' didn't tell me about the wedding, or the pregnancy. He didn't tell her that he didn't want to marry her. She said he wouldn't have her, or the baby. If Dante' told her regardless to who the father was, there would be no wedding she wouldn't think she was walking out on him. Brianne, he sat there and listened to her talk about me, and what we had done for two weeks, and didn't open his damn mouth. Where's the friend in all that? I didn't seduce him. We made love because we love each other, not because it was some damn plan."

"Call him. Talk to him before you come to the conclusions, she wants you to come to. She fed you that information for a reason, otherwise why didn't she just leave him, and that be it?"

"I told him no drama. Don't include us in your reasons to leave that dipsy bitch. Damn. He just sat there, and didn't say shit. I should have told her ass about what she called fucking. I should have given her explicit details to the best damn lovemaking I've ever had. That's what she wanted, to ruin my memories of it."

"Looks like she's winning, call him Kalliah."

"I can't Brianne. He knows what they argued about, if it's what she said, as a friend he should call me."

****

Cherese dreaded going to her mother for the extra key, but fate saw to it that she wasn't home. Her brother didn't ask any questions, and she didn't stay long enough for anyone else to see her there. She left her mother's and took the scenic route home. The days were beginning to get longer, and Cherese noticed she was watching nature's changes more than usual. The budding of flowers and new lawns always gave her peace. The home she and Kyle shared had a large yard lined with beautiful foliage. Now that the weather was warmer, she would spend many hours sitting in the yard enclosed by a stockade fence. The decision to stay would depend on the news coverage of Kyle's arrest. If it drew attention to Cherese, or their home, she would move.

She entered the home and stood looking around the house as though in shock. She almost forgot there were pieces she had placed in storage. The vacant spaces in the rooms gave the house an abandoned look. If she were staying longer than a month, she would get the items out of storage, and return them to her home. She would have more than enough time to prepare for her next move. She flicked the light switch hoping the power hadn't been disconnected and checked the phones. Both were still working. The light on the phone was blinking indicating voice messages. She pushed the speaker on the phone and let the recording repeat the calls.

Her mother, Ms. Jefferson, the law office and Detective Ryan Smith, who left his number, called. She didn't need to speak to Ms. Jefferson, and she spoke with her lawyer. Her mother would have to wait, and she really wasn't ready to talk to any of the Detectives. She decided to start a cleaning project to calm her nerves, and past the time away. Monday morning would be soon enough to deal with business.

It was close to seven when the door bell rang. Cherese couldn't imagine who would know she was home accept her mother. She cautiously went to the door removing the rubber gloves she had put to scrub the bathrooms. Miles stood with his back to the door. Cherese recognized who it was before he turned to face her with a dozen roses.

"I come in peace."

"Come in." Miles handed her the flowers and entered. He looked around the home that was decorated with what he was sure was her touch.

"Your place is beautiful, really nice."

"Thank you. Why'd you come here Miles?"

"To let you know that our friendship means a lot to me."

"I understand that."

"Well, I don't know Cherese really. I wanted to make sure you were okay. Have you found out anything else?"

"No, other than his bail is close to five hundred thousand, and I'm not putting up my home for him."

"So that's why you stayed?"

"Yes, I need to make sure he doesn't manipulate my, our money. I need to keep a closer eye to what's going on. I've got to play the loving wife until he's sentenced. Then I'll do what I need to do."

"Play the loving wife? I thought you were the loving wife."

"Don't push it Miles. I have been thinking about the way things look, but you should know better."

The phone rang interrupting their conversation. Cherese excused herself while offering Miles a seat in the living room. She picked up the cordless phone from the table that sat in the hall leading to the back of the house.

"Hello, yes I'll accept."

"Hello, Cherese?" It was Kyle. She let out a deep sigh, and returned to the living room sinking into the couch's pillows.

"Yes, this is me."

"I knew you wouldn't leave. Thank you baby, listen; there's a number in the box on the dresser that I need. It's for a lawyer. I don't remember her name. Make sure you call the woman, not the man on the card. Tell her I need her to work on getting me out of here."

"Kyle you killed a D.E.A. agent and shot a cop. Not to mention all that other shit. What makes you think you'll be getting out?"

"Cherese trust me, I'll be out. I'm glad you didn't leave baby. There's a lot for us to clear up, and this mess is just something else we need to discuss."

"Kyle don't call back, or I'll change the number. I'll call the lawyer for you, but don't expect me to get involved in this mess."

"Cherese, you've never had a back bone so who is your support now, Miles and the gang, who?"

"Kyle is there anything else."

"Come to visit me, or I'll tell them how you knew this shit was going down. I want you to visit me every week until I get out, or your pretty little ass will be sitting across from the judge explaining how we bought all those pretty pictures, your expensive ass clothing, and whatever else I bought with drug money. You can't explain how your sick ass has made out above it all for the past two years without working. I'm glad you stayed by my side."

"Fuck you Kyle."

Cherese pushed the disconnect button on the phone. She couldn't help but cry. Miles joined her on the couch and took her into her arms.

"It's gonna be okay." Miles didn't know what Kyle said, but this time he was willing to fight.

****

Stephon reported to work earlier than usual. He was asked to attend a meeting that had been scheduled with Detective Miller and Mr. Smalls at eight o'clock in the Administrator's Board Room. He was told to dress casual because he would be spending the balance of the day with Detective Miller. He didn't really understand the need to meet before work; since he had been informed it would be weeks before they could get all his paperwork in order.

Stephon pushed the button for the ninth floor, and waited for the elevator doors to open. He followed the signs directing him to the board room. There were more people than he expected seated at the large conference table.

"Good morning Mr. Drake. Have you had breakfast?"

Stephon was a little slow in answering Mr. Smalls, who greeted him at the door. "I had coffee."

"Well if you want anything, there're bagels and doughnuts along with coffee and juice in the back. We'd like to get this meeting started. We've prepared your package and seat here." Mr. Smalls noticed Stephon's hesitancy.

"You'll be introduced to everyone as we go along." Stephon recognized his Parole Officer, the counselor from Family Services, his lawyer who sat next to him, Ryan Smith, and Juan Rivera. There were two other men he hadn't met and a woman who was obviously taking notes, for the record. She had a laptop opened and wasn't sitting at the conference table. Mr. Smalls asked everyone to take their seats. It was then that Stephon noticed Tracy's parents were present also. He walked over to help them to their seats greeting her father with a handshake and holding the coffee for her mother as she sat down.

"Good morning, Mr. Lawson, Mrs. Lawson. Where are the boys?"

Mrs. Lawson smiled, which immediately gave Stephon relief. "They're with one of the counselors in the other office. They're fine. We were told we were to bring them. I think they want to tell us what you tried to explain."

Stephon hadn't gone into details, but did inform the Lawson's that his custody papers were being considered, and would probably be complete within the next year. The grandparents had only one concern. They wanted to remain in touch with the children. Satisfied that the couple had not been upset, and the boys were okay Stephon took his seat.

The meeting began with introductions. Stephon was introduced to Detective Miller, who did most of the speaking; the second man was Detective Craig Moore and the lady as he suspected was a recorder for what they called the official procedures.

"We all know the circumstances that have brought us to this meeting. Stephon, Mr. and Mrs. Lawson, there has been a hit put out on Stephon, and his family. This could include yourselves, as well as the children. The characters we busted have the capability to carry out the threat, but we have been two steps ahead of them in the case. Therefore, we're obligated to protect you Mr. Drake, and your family, as we promised. There will be paperwork that has to be done immediately, allowing you to move as well as having the Lawsons relocated. Our questions, as presented to all of you, should be answered truthfully so we can accommodate your needs. Before we begin with the paperwork and explaining our procedures do you have any questions?"

"You said we'll be relocating? Why? We're the children's relatives not Stephon's. I'm sorry Stephon. It's just I'm retired and all my life, I've lived here in D.C. I'm not sure I want to relocate."

Mrs. Lawson sat ready to hear the answer to her husband's question. They had no idea what Stephon's involvement was in the bust.

"Stephon has helped us bust what could be a larger drug ring. Meaning, it may be more people involved who are not locked up and are on the street. We have taken a large amount of their money and drugs off the street and others may retaliate. They may want some sort of revenge. As of this morning, I've been informed that the word is a hit is out for Stephon and his family. Unfortunately, that includes the children, and they know what your relationship is too. Your moving is a precaution. But if you refuse to move you will only have to sign documents stating we offered you the opportunity to relocate. It's for your own safety."

Tears were rolling down Mrs. Lawson's aged face. She took out a tissue from her hand bag and wiped her eyes. "Do we have a chance to talk about it? Can we talk to other members in our family?"

Detective Miller changed his professional tone as he spoke to the woman who appeared to be older than his mother.

"Mrs. Lawson, we're going to fill in all the blanks. Yes, you can make contact with whomever you need to talk to, and we'll put you in another home, wherever you choose to go. We just want you and your grandchildren as well as Stephon to be safe. There may be a time where you can return and be guaranteed your safety. Today, you're safer with us."

Miller focused his attention again on everyone else at the table asking again if anyone had questions. When no one responded, the representative from Family Services took the Lawson's to another office while Stephon remained in the conference room.

"Detective Miller is it really necessary to uproot them? I mean can they have protection for a couple of days and then you guys just back off. That's a major move for people their age."

"Stephon, how do we know when? How do we know someone else won't try this if we don't do something now? We're sending a message. They're under our wing just as you are. You're one of us, and that extends to your family. They can choose where they want to go. It will shake things up for whoever set up the hit."

"Damn, I didn't mean for them to get caught up in this shit. I was looking for a better way, not putting anyone in the line of fire. I mean I'm willing to put myself in harm's way, but I don't want them to be put in the middle every time I take on an assignment."

"Even if you don't take another assignment someone assumed you were a part of that hit. Kyle has a way of getting rid of his fears. We believe he's ordered a few hits in the past. But his case is behind you now. We want to move you as soon as possible. You won't be returning to your home."

"What about our belongings? How will we get our things?"

"It will be packed and shipped through our people. Unfortunately, that's the only way we can guarantee your safety. You will be living in an undisclosed location until your move is complete. That's why we're here today, alright, if that answers your questions let's get your end started."

Stephon wanted to apologize to the Lawson's. He didn't intend to infringe on their liberties. He sat with Smith, Rivera, and Moore, as they explained how and when his training would begin, and what his job would include. He would be assigned to Detective Moore once he arrived in Virginia. Stephon tried to stay focused but kept wondering about his court papers and Family Service. In the past, he had been frowned upon by both offices and separated from his children. He knew the move would upset the normal routine for everyone, and he didn't want the bureaucracy to add stress to a stressful situation.

"Moore, Smith, listen, I need to be honest. Can we talk about this after I know what's going on with my boys and the Lawson's? My mind is drifting, and I don't want you to think I'm not concerned about the position I'm taking."

"Sure man, take a minute, but there're some things that have to be done before we leave here today."

Stephon smiled and nodded his head. He could tell he and Detective Moore would get along well. Juan and Ryan left them at the table with Stephon holding his head.

"Listen man, I know this is a lot, but it gets better. You get used to the adrenaline rush, the long hours and the threats. I hear you're looking to get married."

"Yeah, this is a lot to take in all at once. I thought it would be a minute, you know, time to grow on me. Can I even talk to her about this?"

"Sure, call her about it. How many of your friends know you're leaving?"

"Oh, five that's it. I didn't go into detail with anyone other than my fiancé. I'll call one guy, and I'll talk to everyone else later."

"Yeah man, make your call. Go deal with the family and I'll be here to talk with you afterward. Before you know it, you'll be getting married. You and your family will be okay."

****

The week passed and no call from Dante' could explain why Kalliah hadn't heard from him. Angelina's conversation kept replaying in her mind. Each time it brought up new questions that only Dante' could answer. Brianne's reasoning no longer helped the moments of anger Kalliah battled with. She wouldn't wait any longer she would call Mr. Jefferson when she arrived home, and hear his side of the story.

It was close to three o'clock, and the anticipation of her planned call was aggravating. She looked at her Friday's schedule, and decided she would leave work early. The ringing of her office phone stopped her as she was clearing her desk for the weekend.

"Phillips Marketing Group, Ms. Carter how may I help you?"

"Hey, girl it's Cherese."

"Hey, what's up?"

"Bullshit as usual."

Cherese sounded different. She sounded as she had years ago before the pregnancy, the therapy and the drugs. Kalliah sat back in her seat ready to listen without distractions. She was hesitant about complimenting the differences she made a mental note of. Cherese always wanted her friends to think she was in control. Kalliah wondered what the problem was.

"I know that's right. How are things going with Kyle?"

"He's been calling everyday threatening me. I've talked to my lawyer and according to him; he'll be serving time for sure. But the threats continue. That fool wants me to do the bid with him. I thought about it, Kalliah, I was stupid enough to tell him I would be around. Now the bastard is making demands."

Kalliah didn't want to remind Cherese that his demands didn't just begin. Kyle was doing his usual, and he expected his wife to respond as she had in the past.

"Girl I told him to stop. I would be there to see him on Saturday, and we would talk about this thing in person. I don't know what came over me. I don't even know what I'm going to say, or why I'm going to a jail to visit his sorry ass. But that's what I told him. Kalliah, I'm scared. I don't even know why, but I know I can't live in fear. I think living here is a mistake. You and Brianne might be right. I need space to heal. Kyle being in jail isn't enough he still can reach me."

"What about the house and your other business matters? Did you talk with the police? Will you be questioned?"

"The lawyer will be handling everything. Kyle threatened to use everything against me. I told the lawyer, and he said it wouldn't matter. Kyle is looking at twenty-five years or more. My marriage is over either way, but I can't live being scared that he will carry out his threats somehow."

"How, if he's doing time, he can't hurt you, can he?"

"He'll find a way Kalliah. I know he will. I'm going to try to reason with him tomorrow, if not, I'll be moving."

"Where will you go? Will you come live with us?"

"That's the other problem. Kyle knows that I'll seek you or Brianne's help. I think Miles may have been right. He won't know where I am if I take his offer."

"But Cherese…."

"I don't know, maybe I'm just talking to fast. I don't want to involve Miles either. I don't know what to do. This is the bullshit I was talking about…"

It was at that point of the conversation that Kalliah realized her friend was having a breakdown. She continued to talk about where she could hide from Kyle's threats until she broke down crying.

"Cherese, Cherese, Cherese, please listen. Where are you? Are you alone?"

"There's no one here for me Kalliah. You and Brianne are there. Miles kept his word. He's only called once this week. I pushed him away Kalliah. I don't know if he'll let me stay at his home. There's no reason for him to want to help me, the bitch. You know maybe Kyle is right. I don't deserve anyone but him."

"Cherese did you take your medicine today?"

"Medicine can't help this mess. I thought him being away, locked up would be a help. I can't do this. I can't keep being scared like this. I don't want to live like this."

Kalliah got scared with Cherese's last words. She would call Miles or Stephon. Kyle had got his wish. Cherese was still under his control.

****

"Miles, you have to go to her. I don't know what she might do to herself."

Kalliah told him the last words said and the rest of their discussion. She began quickly gathering items she was taking home, as she listened to his rationale.

"Calm down. If she called you, it was a cry for help. I'll call her, and keep her on the phone until I get there. She'll be fine. What would make her think visiting him at the jail would change his threats?"

"I've never been able to figure out their love, or marriage. I can't let her kill herself. She survived living with him and his abuse. Miles she can't kill herself over this ass hole. Call me on my cell. I'm leaving my office. Please call me when you get to her."

"I'll be leaving here in less than five minutes. I'll call her from my cell. Don't worry, I'll be with her."

Miles hung up the phone and dialed Cherese's cell phone number. After four rings her voice mail picked up. He hung up and tried again.

Again, it rang without her answering. Miles jumped up. He began to get nervous. He left his office jogging down the hall to the elevator. He pulled out his phone again and frantically dialed her number. When he reached the lobby he paused to dial the house phone. There was no answer.

"Cherese answer, damn it, answer the phone!"

****

Kalliah drove home with tears in her eyes. Miles was right. She reached out. This call was not the only time she reached out. As Kalliah remembered the abuse Cherese had endured over the years, guilt tugged at her heart. She felt she should have done more. As she pulled into the driveway of her home, she checked the clock as she had every five minutes. She grabbed her cell phone, purse, and keys rushing inside to tell Brianne that they needed to be on the alert.

Brianne was sitting on the couch crying while watching what appeared to be a special report from the news. Kalliah sat next to her as the commentator explained what was so important to break the regularly scheduled programs.

"We're interrupting the regularly scheduled programs to bring you this story relating to one of the largest drug rings that got busted last week in the D.C. Metro area. There has been more arrest made in conjunction to the case. One Stephon Drake......"

"Stephon? What the hell, Brianne, what the hell?"

"He lied Kalliah. He had to. They've arrested him. Why? Why lie to me? I was ready to marry that man."

"Has he called you?"

"No. Not a damn word. He called saying he would be here next week instead of this week. He was coming to look for houses and some paperwork or some shit. Lies; the bullshit they put us through. I'm done girl. I was ready, you know, ready to begin what I thought was meant for me. You home early, what's up?"

"Oh shit!"

Kalliah checked her phone. She hoped she didn't miss the call with the volume of the television being higher than normal.

"Girl, listen, I had to call Miles to check on Cherese. She called talking about Kyle and his threats as usual, but she sounded so desperate I was worried about her harming herself. I don't know what to do. Do you think we need to go back and get her? Brianne, she sounded so desperate, saying she had no one. She's weakening to his comments about her, calling herself a bitch that no one would want."

"Damn. I thought she was over that."

Brianne sighed looking at the television and shaking her head. "Kalliah, what are we gonna do?"

"Somebody's gonna tell us something. I know they will. You'll see.

The two friends cried together waiting for the phone to ring.

****

Dante' watched the news Friday evening and immediately dialed Stephon's number. He stood pacing the floor and after several attempts, he gave up calling and dialed Miles. Miles had alerted him of the problem with Cherese earlier. He hadn't heard anything since that call and now Miles wasn't answering his phone. He would have to wait to speak with him later. Dante' had avoided calling Kalliah since his argument with Angel. He knew she would ask about the baby. He had no answers. He needed to talk about Stephon and Cherese. He took the chance that Kalliah wouldn't be home and dialed the number. The television became the background to the ringing of the phone as it revisited the arrest of Kyle Taylor and the others explaining the events that led to the day's arrests.

Brianne turned the channel when the phone rang hoping the call would be from Stephon explaining his current status. Dante's voice brought a smile to her face as she mouthed his name to Kalliah. She shook her head no mouthing back, "Did he ask for me?" Brianne had to be honest and just raised her eyebrow with a smirk. Kalliah understood her non-verbal communication and walked into her room to get into a more comfortable outfit.

"Yes, it's playing down here too. You haven't heard from him today?"

"No, I spoke with him, I guess on Tuesday. I know Miles was with him on Wednesday. He's been packing since you left; I guess he didn't pack quick enough."

"Dante' I'm not understanding didn't he say he saved his job money? How did drugs, guns and murder come out of saving that dead ass job he had? He was a clerk in the mailroom right? Maybe I'm wrong but how much could he save them from holding a clerk's position? I was a fool to believe that shit."

"We both were. I believed him too. Maybe Miles can explain it. Uh, he went to Cherese's house did you know about her?"

"Yeah." Brianne almost slipped and said Kalliah told her, but she knew she was supposed to wait until he mentioned her name. "He hasn't called with an update yet."

"I hope she's okay. She's been through enough."

"We all have. That's why you can tell your boy whenever you talk to him he better come straight cause this is bullshit. I don't want a life that's an open door for the police because of the criminal antics my husband may be involved in."

"I can understand that. Did they say what his involvement was? I missed part of the broadcast."

"No. Just that he was listed as one of the additional people who was arrested. I guess he made his one call to Tracy's parents, since they have his kids."

"This may ruin his chances to get them or for him to move."

"Oh well. You do dirt. You bury yourself. I just can't bury myself in his dirt. That's not my thing. So what's up with you? How's things?"

Kalliah had come back into the living room and plopped on the couch snickering. Brianne put the phone's speaker on so she could hear his response. Dante' wanted to answer truthfully, but declined knowing Brianne would tell her friend. He would call back and talk to Kalliah.

"Things are things. I'm getting back on schedule with work and other than that everything is good. I was hoping your girl was around. I haven't talked to her, and we really need to talk before we both get caught up in our schedules."

"I can tell her to call you, but I doubt she will. You know she's been waiting for you to call."

"Really, I thought I blew it. You women are difficult to deal with when it comes to emotions. I'm trying to be nice but, well, you know. It gets you nowhere."

"So you're not sure what you want to do?"

"No, I know what I want to do. It's just I can't do it the way Kalliah wants it done. It's just not gonna work that way. Angel ain't trying to listen to me, and I still don't know much more than I knew before."

"So you need to get with her and talk about it."

"Who?"

"Kalliah. You know I wasn't talking about Angel."

"Oh, I don't know if I can bring this to her with no answers. Kalliah ain't like Angelina. I've got to come straight with her. Angelina's playing games, and I ain't for that either."

"So you do nothing?"

"Is that what you think?"

Kalliah shook her head yes prodding Brianne to say it to Dante'. Brianne covered the phone and replied. "Talk to him!"

"No, he should have called me."

Brianne moved her hand and took the phone off the speaker mode. "You really need to get things in order Dante'. I mean unless you like the games. I know it drives us women crazy." She shot her eyes to Kalliah, who waved her hand, as though she didn't care.

"You're right, but Brianne, suppose the baby is mine?"

Brianne got up from the couch and walked into the kitchen and turned on the faucet to drown out her voice.

"You still don't know if you're the father?"

"She wasn't going to the doctor until the end of the month. We argued. She left, and I haven't heard from her."

"I thought you told Kalliah the baby wasn't yours."

"I know, but I really don't know. I doubt it, but I don't know."

"Why did you say the baby wasn't yours?"

"I love Kalliah."

"Damn Dante'."

The call ended with Brianne suggesting that Dante' call back, and speak to Kalliah if he wanted their relationship. She hoped there would be no questions about whether she thought he would really call. She returned to the living room with a tall glass of Iced Tea and the phone in her hand. Kalliah didn't ask any questions, and Brianne smiled telling her friend they both would be waiting for the phone to ring again.

Rainbows

Miles turned into Telford Street. He tried to breathe calmly as he parked his car in front of Cherese's home. He rushed to the door and rang the bell. He tried looking in the window but was unable to determine if she was home. There were no sounds coming from inside. He rang the bell again. There was still no response. He began banging on the large door with his hands and feet.

Cherese rose from her bed in a dazed state. She heard the banging and immediately the fear of Kyle's threats became a reality. She remembered there was a locked box in the bedroom closet that held Kyle's gun. The kicking and banging continued as she moved frantically searching for the keys. The keys were where they had been for years on a hook inside the closet door. Cherese smiled remembering Kyle telling her she wouldn't remember a thing if she was pushed to use the gun.

"I'll show his black ass."

She went down the stairs creeping, hearing the ringing of the bell now blended with the rhythmic banging. The person at the door couldn't be seen through the small windows that crossed the top of the door. She had no way of knowing who the intruder was. The news showed new arrest. Stephon had been included. Cherese didn't know who to trust. Stephon pretended to be her friend, Kyle could have sent anyone to harm her. She wasn't taking any chances.

"Get away from my door, damn it! Who sent you here?"

Miles could hear only bits and pieces of her screaming at the closed door.

"Cherese it's me, open the door. Are you alright?"

"Me who, who is me? I'll put a cap in your ass get away from my damn door!

Her hands shook. She was scared of the gun, and the person who was at the door. Her fear didn't allow her calm down, or recognize Miles' voice.

"Cherese. Open the door."

"Get away from the door."

Miles tried the doorknob. Cherese saw it turn, and pulled the trigger. The gun went off. BANG!! Miles broke the door open, and she fired the gun again. BANG!!!

"Cherese!! Put the gun down!"

Hysterics took over. She held the gun toward the floor. The shots fired had gone astray. One hit the ceiling above the door and the other shattered a lamp that sat on a coffee table.

"Put the gun down baby."

"Baby? Are you here 'cause he sent you? Miles are you? I'll shoot your ass. Don't try me, damn it! Don't try me!"

Tears rolled down her face as she waved the gun at him again. She turned her back walking away from the front door. Miles stepped slowly toward her trying to get closer. He could tell by her appearance, she had taken more than her share of medication, or alcohol, and maybe she had both.

"Cherese listen. It's me, Miles. No one sent me. You called Kalliah remember?"

"Back the fuck up, I said!" Cherese turned with the gun pointed directly at Miles, causing him to put his hands up in the air. She began laughing at the sight of his fear.

"Yeah, tell Kyle that. I didn't forget where the gun was, and I ain't scared to shoot it."

The sound of sirens caused her to get nervous and she gripped the gun with both hands.

"Tell them I didn't do it. I wasn't with him. Miles you know that! He wants me to do time with him."

"Put the gun down Cherese! Someone heard the shots. Drop the gun before they come in."

"If they come in I'll shoot."

From the partially opened door, Miles could see four police cars parking strategically outside.

"It's the police Cherese."

"They're here for Kyle. He's not here, and I didn't do anything. He left this gun for me to protect myself. Don't come in here, damn it!!"

Miles didn't know what to do. The cops were cautiously approaching the front door; he could hear their radios and conversation as they got closer.

"Officer she's got a gun. I think she's had too much medication. She's not talking right!" Miles yelled out the door, hoping they heard and understood his message. The officers slowed their walk placing their hands on their weapons. One officer waved his hand at one of the parked sedans. A voice came over a bullhorn startling Cherese again.

"Ms. Taylor put down the gun. We're here now. We've got him."

Cherese screamed, "No. I can't!"

The gun went off. Bang!! The officers took cover. Miles yelled, "Help, get an ambulance!"

****

Stephon and Detective Moore pulled into a rest area off Route 95. They left Stephon's home shortly after the news media, and camera's taped his planned arrest. Stephon was assured his furnishings, and belongings would be shipped to him through the office of the DEA. The movers would be dressed as DEA agents. The staged performances would spread throughout the neighborhood, and Kyle's connections would assume Stephon was locked up as well. Juan and Ryan thought of the arrangement after Mr. Lawson became overly agitated about moving.

Stephon's children would move to Virginia after he bought his home. Any contact during the move could jeopardize the safety of Stephon, the Lawsons and the children. Stephon was tired and was wearing his emotions on his sleeve.

"How soon before I can call my fiancé? She's got to be going crazy."

"We'll stop there on the way to the spot."

"Moore, c'mon man if you and I are going to be working together you need to ease up on the secret squirrel shit."

Moore smiled and held the door opened for Stephon to enter Bob's Diner. Stephon wasn't hungry but decided if they ate maybe his new partner would talk.

"Table for two?" asked the young woman, who never looked up from the seating chart.

"Yes," Moore walked ahead of Stephon following the hostess to their booth in the back of the restaurant. Stephon could see the bulge from his weapon under his shirt. Craig Moore stood about six feet, and his body was well sculpted. He didn't have on anything that said he was an officer. Stephon wondered what credentials he would carry. The men took their seats and ordered two cokes as they read the menu for an early evening meal.

Stephon took off his shades and leaned back trying to relax in the uncomfortable booth. "Man, is this how it is always? I mean will I be moving from state to state like this?"

"No, you won't be that involved in other cases. You'll set them up though, but they won't have any idea you're involved in the case. We may use you to walk through the precinct when the arrest is made, but that's rare. Anyway, you'll be in the background more. It's a good gig for someone like you."

"What does that mean….someone like me?"

"Nothing man, take it down. Listen a lot of times we use cops, they can't always see what a person who has dealt with drugs or the business sees. You're that type of person."

"So what protects me? I mean I know I don't get a weapon or anything but suppose some shit breaks out?"

"You're going through some training. Investigating, processing evidence, self-defense, you'll be fine. I don't think they'll clear you for a weapon, but I've seen it done. Listen, you and I will become close. Once you get to understand the logistics of the job, and you get to know me, things will become clearer. Believe me, you'll like it."

"So the word on the street in D.C. is that I'm arrested. Do I change my name or identity?"

"No, before this is over your name will come up again, and you'll be doing time in another location."

"Won't they know that I'm not really locked up?"

"Stephon, relax man. We do this all the time. Where does the rest of your family live?"

"New York."

"Kyle's boys know about them?"

"No. Kyle and I know each other from back in the day, and drug running. They don't know my family."

"What about your fiancé?"

"He won't bother her." Stephon thought about the rape. Kyle wouldn't try to contact Brianne.

"We've taken care of the Lawsons. Mr. Lawson agreed to protection now, during the trial and periodically thereafter. If a problem arises. He agreed to move. Personally, I think he's right. They won't try to contact you that way. You'll have your boys within the next week so all bases are covered."

"Yeah I hope so. Brianne is a different story. I don't know if she's gonna like this shit at all."

Moore laughed. They ordered their dinner and talked about the cities in Virginia that were recommended for Stephon to live. When they finished their meal, Stephon felt better about the new job and his new friend.

****

Dante' dialed Angel's phone hoping she was ready to call a truce. He left a message on her voicemail for her to call him two days prior, and she hadn't called. It was close to eight o'clock. He was unable to relax. It would be a long night if he didn't get some answers. Cherese, Stephon, and Angel had been on his mind since talking to Brianne two hours earlier. He got into his car and rode past Angel's apartment. He parked and got out looking up at the second-floor windows. Angel's living room window faced the parking lot. The light from a lamp was on. Dante' followed the sidewalk which led to the front foyer. A man stood in front of him blocking the bells trying to hear the voice that was coming through the speaker in the wall.

"Hey babe, I'll buzz you in." Dante' was stunned. The man opened the door and turned to Dante', "Here man don't worry about ringing, I got the door."

Dante' heard him but the shock of Angelina's voice answering to who he thought was a stranger was raising his anger. The last encounter he had with Angelina at her apartment was with a different man. He couldn't believe it.

"No brotha, that's alright."

Dante' turned and walked out the door. When he returned to his car, he sat staring at the light in the living room window. He banged is hands on the steering wheel. He knew he was right. The baby couldn't be his.

He took the slow route home filled with red lights and traffic. Somehow, the traffic that most drivers wanted to avoid Dante' relished whenever he needed to think. Brianne was right he needed to talk to Kalliah. He dialed her number, thinking how he would start the conversation. An apology for not calling sooner, or the truth about why he didn't want to know whose baby it was.

"Hello."

"Hey Kalliah its Dante'."

"What's up? I think I still recognize your voice. Are you driving? It sounds like you're in traffic. Where are you?"

"In traffic; you got a minute, or is this a bad time to talk."

"No, as a matter of a fact, I was getting ready to change the channel on the television. There's nothing on tonight."

"That's why I'm in traffic. It tends to make me think."

"So what's on your mind so heavy?" Kalliah pretended she had no clue. Her mind was made up. If Dante' didn't mention the argument he had with Angel, that caused her to call again, she wouldn't trust a relationship with him. He could be a friend, but she didn't need a man who wasn't truthful.

"I've been trying to talk to Angelina about this baby thing since I got home. She claims she won't be able to go to the doctor until the end of the month. She's still insisting I'm the father. I got proof tonight that she's been sleeping around."

"Proof? What kind of proof?"

"I went to her apartment, and she was answering the door for another guy who rang the bell. Kalliah she knew who it was just by the sound of his voice. She answered the door telling him 'Hey Baby'. What kind of shit is that? I should have waited, and rang the bell after him just to see what the bitch would do. She's fucking and carrying my child?"

"I thought you said the baby wasn't yours?"

"You know what I mean she claims the child is mine. If it is, why is she letting other guys fuck her?"

"How do you know that's what they're doing?"

"Kalliah, what? You taking up for her?"

"No, I'm just saying you sound like you're upset 'cause you're jealous. I thought you said the relationship was over."

"It is. This is so fucked up." Dante's anger was building. He turned going onto a darkened street. He made a k-turn heading back to the corner. He turned in the direction of Angel's apartment.

"Well you just need to know if the baby is yours right?"

"I guess so, but she always does this shit getting back at me for my relationship with you."

"So now you're blaming me?"

"No our relationship just has been a problem with her from day one."

"Well you know what Dante' when you see your fiancé, the hoe, tell her there is no worry 'cause we don't have a damn relationship. I'm tired of her calling me, and you lying. It's obvious that she thinks we got something going 'cause you won't defend our friendship. I don't have time for this shit. If you do, you deal with it. I refuse to, and you got a baby coming too?"

"The baby can't be mine. Don't you get it? She's screwing some of everybody. That kid could be any one of those punks."

"Dante' stop. You told Brianne you weren't sure. You told me the kid wasn't yours. You're worried about who Angel is with, but you tell me there's nothing between you. I'm your friend Dante'. I won't be your fool. Get your life straight and call me then."

Dante' pulled into the same parking space he had before, when he first arrived at Angelina's. The light in the living room was out. Dante' doubted her guest had left. Kalliah was right it was time to get his life straight.

After ringing the bell several times Dante' was sure they were getting busy in the bedroom. There was no way to get in her home without breaking in. He dialed her cell number and left another voice message trying not to sound angry at all. He walked to his car and leaned on it, as if he knew she would cut on the light in the living room. He wanted a signal that she was at home.

A car pulled up to the front door and the same man he saw earlier got out and opened the passenger door. Angelina got out smiling. Dante' walked up to the car interrupting what he knew was leading to a farewell kiss.

"Who is this guy Angelina?"

"What the fuck Dante'?"

"Who is he?"

"I'm a friend of hers, who are you?"

"Look man did she tell you she was getting married, that she was pregnant?"

"Yeah and that you didn't want her, left her for some other chick. So why is your sorry ass here?"

"So she told you that shit, uh? Angelina you walked out my fucking door!"

"Look man, you can't walk away from your responsibility and think that someone else is not willing to handle your situation."

"Back the fuck up nigga. I didn't walk away from nothing. She's got my damn ring on her finger that says enough."

"Take your stupid ass ring." Angelina took off the engagement ring and threw it at Dante'. The ring hit the ground and Dante' bent to pick it up not paying attention. The blow to his head was enough to knock him to the ground.

"Don't walk up on me again punk."

Dante' waited until the two turned to walk toward the door. Dante' jumped on the back of Angel's new lover. The fight took no longer than five minutes before Angel screamed for Dante' to stop while putting her arms around the man she called Genairo. When Genairo stood to his feet, he pulled out a blade.

"I suggest you get in your fucking car. I ain't throwing fists no more half bred. I'll cut you from ear to ear c'mon, try me."

"Dante' get the fuck outta here."

"You better hope that baby ain't mine bitch."

"You'll never find out."

****

Stephon rang the bell to Brianne's home. He checked the address again making sure he had the right house. Brianne answered the door wondering who would be visiting after eight. "Stephon?"

Stephon turned toward her smiling. They hugged as though he was returning from war. Brianne noticed Craig waiting at the car. Stephon waved him into the house.

"Brianne this is Detective Craig Moore. He'll be my partner and friend while I'm assigned here in Virginia."

"You'll be moving again."

"No, he'll be here. But I'll be working with him in this region if he's needed in other areas, he'll be assigned to someone else."

"I see. Are you okay? I was ready to cuss your ass out."

"I told Moore that."

"Kalliah, come see who's here!" Brianne couldn't contain her happiness.

"Oh my God, Stephon, you're okay. I prayed it wasn't true. What happened?"

"Listen, it really doesn't matter. I'm here. I'll be staying close to where I'll be training until I get the home set up."

"Can't you stay with us?"

"No, he can't. We need to keep an eye on him and things in D.C. We really don't want to involve you if we don't have to. After this thing goes to trial it will be a lot easier for everyone. I won't be tagging along with him then."

"When does training start?"

Brianne changed the subject hoping she could survive being the wife of someone working under cover.

"Next week the sooner the better."

"Stephon, what about your boys?"

"They'll be here next week. I was hoping you could help me with the day-care stuff. I don't know where to start looking."

They sat talking for another hour, and Stephon was glad he was there when Miles called. Kalliah answered the kitchen phone, excusing herself thinking it may have been Dante'.

"Hey Kalliah, I finally reached Cherese."

"You sound terrible, are you alright?"

"No, I mean. I will be but right now there's problems that have to be worked out."

"Hang on Miles, Stephon is here with me and Brianne. I'll put you on speaker, so they can ask you any questions they may have."

Kalliah walked back to the living room. Stephon and Craig were laughing at Brianne's initial reaction to the news of Stephon's arrest. Now that it was behind them, she was making jokes about her comments and her attitude.

"Miles is on the phone guys. Go ahead Miles."

"Yeah, Cherese snapped. She thought I was Kyle or one of his boys at the door. She got a gun too, shit, I don't know what she got the gun for; she damn sure can't shoot. Anyway, she got a .22 Caliber and shot off two rounds warding me off, and then another when the cops showed up. I thought she shot herself, but she just collapsed. We're at the hospital now. They said she took too much shit. She probably won't remember any of this happening."

"What the hell did she take?"

"Brianne, they don't know yet. The cops went back to the house to get the medicine bottles."

"Did she try to kill herself?"

"I don't think so. I think she was trying to sleep. Maybe she just couldn't rest. Anyway, I told the cops what I knew, you know about Kyle, the bust, Stephon…..hey you said Stephon was there?"

"Yeah man I had to make the great escape. I'm good. Finish what you were saying."

"Damn, this is some ole movie shit here. Anyway I'm trying to reach her lawyer."

"Miles call Ms. Jefferson. She has that information."

"Thanks, Kalliah will you be speaking to Dante'."

"No you better call him."

New Beginnings

Two years passed before the friends were to reunite again as they had the year of McKinley High's ten-year reunion. The excitement was on the same level, but the reason was not to reacquaint with old classmates. Stephon and Brianne chose their date for the wedding and had their friends promise to be in the wedding.

It was the day of the rehearsal and the dinner. Brianne was trying to cope with new anxiety. The ceremony was small in comparison to most weddings with only a few of the old friends from D.C. being invited. Stephon did his "time" and they were constantly calling Brianne thinking the wedding would be called off. The constant ringing of the phone, getting her soon to be sons prepared, and having a house full of out of town guest made her uneasy. She kept telling Kalliah that something was bound to go wrong.

Kalliah was her maid of honor and Cherese, who now lived with them in Virginia, was a bridesmaid. Stephon chose Craig Moore, who was his partner in the D.E.A. Special Operations Group, as his best man; Miles was the groomsman escorting Cherese. Dante' hadn't answered his request to be in the wedding. He responded telling him he had death in the family and was unsure whether or not he would be able to attend. Stephon hadn't heard from him since the call which was more than a year ago. The invitations went out and when Dante's returned, he responded he would attend with one guest. Stephon was sure Dante' was bringing Angelina and was ducking the female drama.

The boys were five and a handful, but they loved Brianne, doing anything for her attention. Kevin was proud to be the Bible bearer, while his brother Keith thought, the job of the ring bearer was more important. The Lawsons were more than happy to attend the ceremony as did Stephon's parents.

Brianne's aunt and cousins promised they would be there, but needed money to stay at the hotel. That's how Brianne wound up with out of town guest. Dante's mother said she wouldn't miss the ceremony for the world, but she wouldn't get into town until Saturday, the day of the wedding.

The bride put down the list of guests with only a few who hadn't checked in for the day. She would let Stephon deal with them. They were his guests. As she looked over her banister, she noticed her Aunt going through the hutch in the living room.

"What are you looking for Auntie?"

"Oh, uh, nothing sugar. I was wondering if you had any old picture albums. The boys asked me about some of the family that may be at the wedding."

Brianne knew the lie as it fell from her mouth. **"Some things never change."** She came down the stairs to make sure nothing had been moved. Most of her belongings had been packed for weeks and were slowly being moved to the ranch home Stephon built when he relocated in Virginia. The items her Aunt was so anxious to peer in belonged to Cherese. The hutch became a place of storage. Cherese hadn't been in Virginia long enough to unpack. The trio agreed she would wait until Brianne became Mrs. Drake to claim any extra space.

"Those things there belong to Cherese. My things are packed and gone, for the most part. I don't have many old pictures of family. Sorry. Did I tell you I was glad you guys decided to come?"

"Well we almost didn't. I mean those rooms was expensive. I didn't think you would have the money, here is just as good though. This is a nice house. You selling it when you move?"

"No Cherese and Kalliah are renting it from me."

"Shame, you coulda made a pretty penny from this here. Coulda got some of your money back for what you paid to marry Stephon. Ain't nothing wrong with having money you can count on. Well, you never know how long they gonna live here. Just hope they won't tear up none. People don't think about other's property like the owner would. You know what I'm saying?"

Brianne rolled her eyes putting back the items her Aunt had rummaged through. She dared not say anything, they hadn't argued since she arrived on Wednesday. Brianne couldn't understand how the weekend was extended to mid week. Even her cousins seemed pleased with visiting that long.

"Where do Ronald and Robert work?"

"They ain't working child. Can't keep a job, won't half go to work. You know, what can I do? That's why they here with me, they can't be trusted."

Brianne looked around getting a visual of the grown men. They were older than her, still living with their mother and looking for any woman to take them in. She made a mental note to warn Kalliah and Cherese. They would be leaving Sunday morning on the train. Brianne held the tickets for their return.

****

Rehearsal was scheduled to start at five thirty. Stephon, Craig, and Miles stood outside the church talking when the coordinator and other family members pulled into the lot. They said their hellos and promised when the women arrived, they wouldn't delay the rehearsal any longer.

Dante' pulled into the parking lot and was greeted with hugs from Stephon and Miles.

"Man, it's good to see you. Let me introduce you to my partner Detective Craig Moore. This is the man whose spot you're filling, Dante' Jefferson." The men gave the common embrace and handshakes.

"Hey man, I almost didn't find the church. I was actually making sure I knew where I was going."

"Where you staying man? Dante' is from Maryland. You are still in Maryland right?"

"Yeah, I'm there. I came in from D.C. though. I went and picked up my mother. You know she had to be here for you."

"Where is she? Where you staying?"

"We're staying at the Comfort Suites off Route 95. She wanted to purchase a few things in town, so I took her to that mall. We're good though."

"Where's the ladies? Miles how have you been? How's Cherese? I feel like it's been more than two years man, damn."

"Well, the ladies I hope are on their way. I've been fine. Cherese lives here now with Kalliah and Brianne. Well, it will be just her and Kalliah after tomorrow."

Miles threw a teasing punch at Stephon, who pretended to block and then hugged him closely. Craig and Dante' laughed as though they knew each other longer than a few moments.

"So what's up with you playa? I thought you were in line for the bells? I guess you and Angel called it off, huh."

"Angel was killed man."

"What?" Miles and Stephon answered in unison. None of the men noticed the females pulling into the parking lot. Dante' saw Kalliah getting out of the car and didn't mention Angel again until after the wedding the next day.

****

The church was decorated in the colors silver and dusty rose. Everyone was sitting in the pews complimenting the beauty of the June wedding. The invitations, the flowers, the programs, all had a touch of elegance. The audience was filled with co-workers of both the bride and groom who were all waiting to meet the family members that were from D.C. No one mentioned Stephon being arrested; they all assumed shortly after meeting him, it had been a mistake.

Officers who worked with Stephon looked like they were there for security and weren't invited as guests. Stephon told them take it down for the day, but their skills were now habit, and everyone could tell they were a part of law enforcement. Keeping his work a secret was easy. Stephon simply explained he worked in evidence processing, and everyone accepted it to be true.

Stephon and Craig stepped out taking their place at the front of the church. The men wore silver tuxedos. The cummerbund set, and the boutonniere on their lapels were the color or the women's dresses, dusty rose. "The Day I Married My Angel" sung by Jamie Foxx began playing and the church fell silent. The women carried more than two dozen roses splashed with silver glitter. Cherese met Miles in the middle of the aisle, as he extended his hand offering to escort her the rest of the way.

The twins stepped proudly and were quite handsome as they proceeded without hesitation to where their father stood smiling from ear to ear. Kalliah walked the aisle alone carefully taking each step. Her beauty was followed with the release of flower petals from a basket above the aisle.

There were soft "ah's" from the audience as everyone watched in awe. The rose and white petals fell lightly on the runner that was pulled for the bride to take her last walk as a single woman. The music paused, and began louder than it had before. Everyone stood clapping understanding the song must have had a sentimental meaning to the couple.

Dante' stood in the pew with his mother who had tears falling from her eyes. "Are you okay?"

"Oh Dante' this is so beautiful."

"Are you okay?"

Dante' looked down at the toddler who was determined to stand peeking out from behind the pew. He lifted the boy so he could see as Brianne was united with Stephon.

****

The reception was held at the hall of the church. The church had a membership totaling over five hundred members and a banquet hall that could hold up to three hundred and fifty occupants. Brianne had been a member of the church for more than five years, and Stephon joined immediately after moving to Virginia. Kalliah and Cherese went to church often but hadn't become a part of the church's membership. They loved the pastor, and they loved the men who were in attendance. They teased each other every Sunday they attended as they dressed to impress the handsome Deacons. Cherese was sure Kalliah would be dating someone before the end of the year.

The hall had been decorated in the same manner as the church and the coordinator, Stephanie Watson, was accepting compliments while handing out her business cards to those who questioned her services. Dante' and his mother followed the other guests to the hall and waited for Stephanie to return to the door to check them in, give them their wedding favor, and point them to their table.

"Hey cutie what's your name?"

"Dante'"

"Dante' I don't think she's talking to you." Mrs. Jefferson smiled, hoping Dante' wasn't being sarcastic.

"I'm not, who is that handsome young fella in your arms?"

"Oh, then indirectly you are talking to me. This is my son K.C. Tell her hello man."

"He is adorable. You're at table three in the front. Thank you for coming."

Mrs. Jefferson took K.C. and walked ahead of Dante'.

"And what's your name?"

"Stephanie Watson, here's my card just in case someone sweeps you off your feet today. You might want me to coordinate your wedding."

Dante' took the card but the insinuation of him getting married caused him to tune her out. His only reason for attending was to apologize to Kalliah. He had been wrong. She was right. He owed her, as a friend.

The guest began to mix and mingle. Everyone whispered their compliments none really having an ill word to say. There was talk from the few classmates in attendance that noticed Brianne had lost a lot of weight but even that was done as a compliment.

The bridal party made their entrance and sat at the sweetheart tables in the front of the hall. It wasn't until they were on the floor dancing that

Cherese noticed Dante'. He hadn't changed much other than facial hair, a mustache and goatee. She was sure Kalliah hadn't seen him.

Kalliah was dancing with Craig, who she constantly reminded Stephon she was first in line if he ever left his wife. Stephon assured her more than once that she would be waiting forever. Craig truly loved his wife.

"Kalliah, did you speak to Mrs. Jefferson?" Cherese brought her attendance to her attention.

"No, I didn't even see her, where is she?" Kalliah's heart pumped as she looked toward the table where Mrs. Jefferson sat. Dante' was sitting next to her whispering. Kalliah didn't notice the child who sat on the opposite side of him.

"Is that Dante'?"

"Girl, you know it."

The music stopped, and the bridal party returned to their seats as directed by Stephanie. "Damn, Cherese did he see me?"

"I'm sure he did."

"If he knew he was going to be here, why isn't he in the wedding?"

Kalliah adjusted herself in her seat trying to draw his attention discreetly. "Who knows, is that a child at the table?"

"Yes, he's adorable. I wonder if that's the baby? Maybe he married her after all."

"Look Cherese, there's Stephon's other friends from the D.E.A. I think that damn Ryan Smith is sexy with that bald head."

"Girl, stop playing the game. Shit throw your cards in, you know you want Dante' one more time."

Cherese was right. Kalliah couldn't look in his direction without her body reacting. He would know it when he spoke to her. Kalliah turned her head slightly glancing in his direction. Dante's eyes met hers. He smiled as though she was caught. Kalliah was suddenly uncomfortable.

The reception was as beautiful as the wedding and after all the photographic moments were captured the music picked up its pace. The majority of the older church members left and those who knew each other joined at tables other than their own. Dante' walked between the sweetheart tables carrying his son.

"Hello Cherese and Kalliah. Congrats my brother. Brianne you look lovely. Damn to think you guys did it. I can't get over it. The ceremony was beautiful."

"Dante' we love you too, but who is the baby. He looks just like you, so I guess he's your son?"

"Can't put nothing pass you Miles."

Kalliah stood to walk away and Dante' put out his arm to stop her. "Wait babe. I can only do this once. I wanted to tell you all together. Here's my chance, I'm taking it."

Kalliah sat down hoping he would tell the truth.

"This is K.C. and yes he's my son. Tell them hi man."

The toddler buried his head into his father's shoulder, as though he was going to cry. "He's two; just turned two last week. Angelina was his mother, and it was proven that I am his father. Angel was in an automobile accident, and they took him to save him. She was on a respirator for a good while, paralyzed on one side, and for all I know she could have been brain dead. Anyway, she passed away after he turned a year old. They said she lasted as long as she could. I had test run on him shortly after his birth. Her parents consented, we all had to know. He's my son. I named him. She couldn't. Her parents barely stayed to watch her fade away so I filed for custody and was awarded immediately.

I'm sorry Stephon, when you asked me to be the best man in your wedding; I just couldn't deal with it. I was going through it then. It's been hard. I know this boy is gonna ask about his mother, so I had to get better for him. Kalliah, can I talk to you a minute?"

Dante' didn't wait for her to answer he stepped away from the table leaving his friends in deep thought. He went to the table where his mother sat passing her grandson to her. He waited on the edge of the dance floor for Kalliah to join him.

****

"Cherese come with me." Cherese followed Miles to the parking lot. He opened the passenger door and handed her a gift box.

"What's this?"

"A gift, why are you so distant to me lately?"

"Am I? Then why give me a gift."

"Listen I'm not trying to push you or anything. I saw it and your face came to my mind. I love you Cherese. I can't help that, and you can't stop me."

Miles laughed at the thought of her with the gun trying to shoot him. He promised he would never tease her about the incident, but the thought always made him laugh.

"Okay so I can't stop you. It's a proven fact. Really, Miles I do appreciate you, and I respect our friendship. I guess you can say I'm scared. Kalliah and Dante' tried to turn their friendship into love and look what happened."

"Cherese you can't be serious. Look at Stephon and Brianne. What about them?"

"They weren't great friends in school they argued all the time. They're an exception."

"We're different too. One minute you love me and the next you're pushing me away. What is it going to be?"

"Can you really put up with my insanity?"

"Cherese, shhh."

Miles kissed her gently and held her in his arms. Cherese could tell from the size of the box it was jewelry. She said a silent prayer, knowing she wasn't ready for another marriage, but she couldn't stop her love for him either.

****

"What does K.C. stand for Dante'?"

The couple reached a secluded area in the rear of the hall. Dante' pointed to the table, and Kalliah took a seat.

"You look beautiful today."

"Why did you name him with my initials?"

"I wanted to always remember you. I will always have him in my life. He will get my love and attention for a life time as you should have. Each time I utter his name I will be thinking about you. Kayson Christian Jefferson is his full name."

"Why didn't you call me Dante'? It had to be horrible to go through what you did by yourself?"

"No the horrible thing was she didn't lie. I did. She hadn't been seeing anyone. The last time we argued was over a man who was visiting her. He came up to me at the funeral to express his condolences. I wondered why none of those men showed up at the hospital. The man was her cousin Kalliah. He came to the hospital when her family did. He told me how he prayed for her, the baby and us. She didn't lie she wasn't screwing anyone but me. I found out the day she died. I loved you, and I cheated her out of a love she thought she had with me. I knew I loved you when I got with her. I made love to you, when I bedded her. That child, my child was conceived while I was thinking about you."

Dante' couldn't stop his eyes from dropping tears of sorrow. He tried to continue talking, but his emotions were taking him over. Kalliah pulled him to her breast and rocked him slowly. It was the first time he cried for Angelina.

Epilogue

The guest began to say farewell, thanking and congratulating the new Mr. and Mrs. Drake on their new beginning. They were happy to be a part of something so beautiful. Stephon and Brianne weren't leaving on a honeymoon until Monday. Brianne wanted to be sure her relatives were well on their way before she left town. She loved them and forgave them, but that had nothing to do with trust. The Lawsons took the twins with them and were on their way back to D.C.

Miles and Cherese followed a few others who were invited to Stephon and Brianne's home for the after party. Kalliah told Dante' to be sure he stopped by after taking his mother and K.C. to the hotel. As Mrs. Jefferson walked to the car, Kalliah quickened her pace to kiss her goodbye.

"Mrs. Jefferson, I don't know if I'll see you tomorrow. I wanted to say how happy I was to see you."

"Kalliah, are you and him okay now?"

"Mrs. Jefferson, I…."

"Hush child. Are you and him okay?"

"Yes. I had no…."

"I said hush. As long as you're okay, love is difficult enough without us adding our own twist to it. Don't twist it Kalliah. Embrace it, hold on in spite of all else, you'll understand it when you reflect back on it. Love like there will be no tomorrow, no chance to make up for the lost time. Love each other as friends do…always. It will be fine you'll see. You, Dante' and K.C. will be fine."

Kalliah turned watching Dante' shake hands with other guests telling them he would talk with them later. "Stephon, Miles man, you guys call me." She knew he wouldn't be stopping at the house that night.

"Dante' will I see you before you leave tomorrow?"

Dante' stopped in front of his one true friend. "I'd be lying if I said I was sure I would be back tonight. Let's do breakfast in the morning."

"Okay and what about next week when I miss you?"

Dante' gave her a questionable look. "Unless you're spoken for, I don't want to be in the middle of another relationship."

"No, you're right where I want you to be. Can we discuss this later? The longer we talk the longer it will take me to get back."

"I'll wait for you at Stephon's."

"Thank you."

Other Novels by Nanette M. Buchanan

Family Secrets Lies and Alibi's

A Different Kind of Love

Bruised Love

Skeletons Beyond The Closed Door

Gossip Line

Scattered Pieces

The Stranger Within

The Perfect Side Piece

The Hustler's Touch

Duplicity

The Corner Pew

Purchase Your Copy Today

www.NanetteMBuchanan.com

Books are available in Kindle, Nook and other ebook formats

www.ingramcontent.com/pod-product-compliance
Lightning Source LLC
Chambersburg PA
CBHW061617100726
47898CB00002B/708